MW00423179

FREE MOTION MURDER:

A LIZ MURPHY MARINERS' COMPASS QUILT SHOP MYSTERY

Mary Shepherd

ISBN 978-1-62806-370-7 (print | paperback)

Library of Congress Control Number 2023903361

Published by Salt Water Media
29 Broad Street, Suite 104
Berlin, MD 21811
www.saltwatermedia.com

Cover image by the author
Author photo by Beth Hager Photos

This is a work of fiction. Names, charcters, businesses, places, events and incidents are either the products of the author's imagination and/or used in a fictitious manner.

To Roger

ACKNOWLEDGEMENTS

So many people helped me with this book; I hope I've remembered them all.

Peter Threadgill provided me with a translation of KT's speech to her father.

Karen Mings, Valerie Heikes and Libby McClung provided information on 21st century high schools since I haven't been in a high school for a very long time.

Nancy Sakaduski, Carol Norman and Peggy Zawodny read early drafts and provided excellent suggestions. Carol observed several inconsistencies, and Peggy favorably compared my work to a famous cozy writer.

Peg Nagem edited this book and pointed out why some of my ideas were dumb before I spent a lot of time writing them. Her suggestions greatly improved this book; I can't thank her enough.

Beth Hager provided me with the professional portrait for the back cover.

The Rev. Dr. Kevin Yoho, pastor of Cold Spring Presbyterian Church, gave me a tour and brief history of his church; the Rev. Holly Shipley reviewed the funeral scene for me.

Many friends and relatives encouraged me as I wrote and tried to find a traditional publisher or agent: Kurt, Debbie, Sam and Josh Tippey, Maddie Abuyuan, Natalie and Gordon Hansen, Bill Atkins, Sandy Woody, Melinda Farnsworth, Mary Clulow, Sheila Kornegay, Ashley Tessmer, Marlena Robinson, Cindy Myers, Pam Asher-Isacoff, Karen Wick, Liz Hobbins, and friends from Delaware Modern Quilt Guild, including Pam Smith, Lorraine deMeurisse, Suzanne Worrall, Janis Nazvesky-Schertzer, Heidi Kuchta, Trish Moeller, Mary Reddington, Melissa Sopko, and Jane Stokes.

Andrew Heller and Stephanie Fowler of Salt Water Media made this book a reality and helped this nervous author make her publishing debut.

Finally, I owe a special debt of gratitude to my wonderful husband Roger. Without his encouragement, I'd have given up on writing (and golf!) many times. Thank you, hon, for all this and more.

AUTHOR'S NOTE

Lewes High School is fictional. I am aware a previous school with that name existed until the 1970s. LHS is not Cape Henlopen High School. I'd like to ask readers to think of LHS as the sort of small high school that would be here if school consolidation hadn't occurred – a small school just for teens living in Lewes and the immediately surrounding areas.

CHAPTER 1

Liz Murphy wanted to whine, complain, and roll her eyes the way her students did when they were unhappy. Instead, she maintained a neutral face as she listened to her boss, Lewes High School principal Diane Goodwin, explain what she wanted Liz to do.

"As I'm sure you know, Meg Williamson taught here at Lewes High for a few months last school year. She's still an inexperienced teacher, and I always like to ask a more savvy teacher to mentor new teachers." Diane paused, and Liz wondered if she was trying to gauge Liz's reaction to her request. She continued, "And I'd like her to work with you on your Math Bowl team, too."

No, not Math Bowl, too!

"And Meg has made a request for a special accommodation, which of course we'll do everything we can to address. She told me, in confidence, she had been diagnosed recently with bipolar disorder. I'm sharing that with you now, because as her mentor, it's something you need to be aware of. She's begun seeing a psychiatrist and taking a prescription to moderate her moods, but those medicines can take several weeks to take effect. And it may take longer to get the dosage adjusted to work for her."

Liz had heard rumors from other teachers that Meg was moody and difficult and had had issues with both students and other teachers during the previous school year. Their paths hadn't crossed before, despite both teaching math at the small high school. "Don't you think there would be benefit in having Meg continue with the same mentor she worked with last year?"

1

"I didn't see as much progress as I'd hoped for last year." Diane smiled wryly at Liz. "I know I'm asking a lot, but you're the best in your department."

"Can I think about it and let you know before classes start tomorrow?"

Diane sighed. "I already told Meg you would be her mentor this year and asked her to stop by and introduce herself during our in-service time today."

At that news, it was Liz's turn to sigh. She agreed with Diane's plan, and Diane thanked her and headed back to the front of the auditorium to begin the teachers' assembly. Liz found a seat near the rear of the room and pulled out her phone to do a little surreptitious research on bipolar disorder.

"Hi. You must be Meg. Come on in and tell me a little bit about yourself and how you got into teaching here at Lewes High." Liz surveyed the younger woman standing hesitantly at the door to her classroom. The two teachers had their profession in common, but not much else. Liz was strawberry blonde, fit, and curvy, while Meg was petite and waif-like with silky blonde hair. In short, a natural beauty. But despite her looks, she looked like she could start to cry any moment.

At last Meg entered and perched on a desk in the front row. "Hi. And you must be Liz." She paused, adjusting her position on the desk. "Let me see. . . where to start. . . I'd really wanted to get a graduate degree in math – master's degree for sure, and maybe even a PhD." She paused for a moment and sniffed. "I was in a graduate program and thought I was doing OK. Then one of the professors kept groping me and tried to get me to have what he called 'a fling' with me. I told him I wasn't interested.

Then the last time he cornered me, I pushed him away – hard. He told me I'd be sorry. Then about a week later, my advisor told me I was being dropped from the program. He said I didn't look like I was likely to get a degree, and they wanted to give the place to someone else."

"Oh, no!" Liz considered this an excess of personal information for a first meeting, then asked, "Do you think it was retaliation from the professor you rejected?"

Meg sighed. "I just don't know. Like I said, I thought I was doing ok with my classes, but the last semester I was there, I didn't do nearly as well as I'd hoped." After a pause she continued, "So I cried for a week and then I pulled out the teaching certificate I got a few years ago and applied here for a long-term substitute position. And when that sub position became an opening for a permanent position, I got hired right away." As Liz watched, Meg lost her dejected appearance. "So anyway, I'm back in the driver's seat now. My boyfriend came up with the perfect way to get back at those faculty guys, and so far, it's working out just great," she announced with a smug smile.

For the second time in the day, Liz focused on maintaining a neutral expression. She couldn't imagine what Meg could be doing to get back at them, or why she sounded so triumphant. *Time to change the subject.* "So when I talked with Diane earlier, she said she wanted you to join me coaching our Math Bowl team this year." Meg nodded. "The try-outs – it's actually just a test – will be after school this Friday. We can talk more about it now or later this week . . ." Liz's voice trailed off as she saw Meg stand and head for the door. "Nice to meet you. See you later." At Meg's departing back, she muttered, "Why, yes, it was nice to meet you, too, and thanks so much for agreeing to mentor me this year."

"Time's up."

Twelve pencils hit the desks, and twelve pairs of teenaged eyes bored into their teacher.

"Please remain seated and pass your answer sheets forward." Liz collected the answer sheets, placed them in an envelope, sealed it, and placed it in her tote bag. "Now pass your test booklets forward."

After the booklets were collected, Liz leaned against the edge of her desk and smiled at the students. "I want to thank all of you for your interest in participating on Lewes High School's Math Bowl team. As you may know, the state competition will be held locally, at Lewes College, next month."

Meg gasped, causing Liz and the students to turn and stare at her.

Liz gestured to Meg. "Ms. Williamson and I will be the team's coaches. We will select four students – three regular team members and an alternate – based on your scores today. We will not necessarily select the four students with the highest scores."

Grumbling erupted in the room, and Liz held up her hand. "Last year, we selected solely on test scores, and when we reached the semi-finals, we realized the team had a big gap in trigonometry. This year, we want LHS to be represented by a team which demonstrates mastery of *all* the topics covered in the Delaware Math Bowl. Of course, if the four highest scores cover Algebra, Geometry, Algebra II, and Trigonometry, then those will be the students selected."

The students became quiet again and Liz turned to Meg, whose face had settled back to neutrality. "Ms. Williamson, have I forgotten anything?"

"No, I don't think so. Ms. Murphy and I are both excited about coaching the team. Ms. Murphy has coached before, but this will be my first-year coaching, and I'm looking forward to it. Any questions?"

Senior Maria Benitez raised her hand. "When will we know who is on the team?"

Liz answered, "Ms. Williamson and I will score your exams this weekend, and list team members on my classroom door Monday morning. I want to add that *both* of us are scoring *all* exams and comparing our answers so that we are sure we haven't made any mistakes that might impact who is on the team."

Sophomore Ross York asked, "Is calculus included in Math Bowl?"

"No, Ross. It used to be included, but a few years ago, the Bowl committee decided to omit calculus."

Ross scowled, which surprised Liz, since she knew he wouldn't have had a chance to study it yet at LHS.

Blonde senior Ashley Stevens asked, "When you announce the team, will you say who are regular members and who is the alternate?"

"No, Ashley, we'll wait until closer to the Bowl to determine regulars and alternate. As a reminder, the team will be expected to practice each day after class until the competition. And the team will select its own captain at the first meeting Monday afternoon."

"Any more questions?" After a long pause, Liz concluded, "Then Ms. Williamson and I thank you again for your interest, wish all of you the best of luck, and we'll see four of you at practice Monday afternoon."

Despite her drama around sealing the answer sheets, Liz needed to make copies so Meg could also score the tests. With this in mind, she asked Meg to come with her to the main office.

As they walked down the hall, she turned to Meg and commented, "You seemed surprised when I said the Math Bowl would be at Lewes College. Can you tell me what that's about?"

"That's where I was going to grad school."

"I see. Their math department is hosting Math Bowl. Are you concerned about going back there? You don't have to if it would make you too uncomfortable."

"Maybe . . . No, I want to do this. I'm past my issues with their math department. And I want to do this for the kids."

Once the copies were made, Meg stowed put her copies in a small book bag and spun on her heel, once again departing without a word. Liz rolled her eyes as she repacked the originals and headed outside, savoring the fresh air on her way to the rack where she'd locked her bicycle that morning. *For the kids, my foot. I need to keep an eye on this situation.*

CHAPTER 2

Liz's pace was leisurely as she pedaled toward downtown Lewes. Seagulls whirled and cawed overhead in the mild breeze. The first week of school in September always felt long to her, and she was glad the week and the Bowl team test were done. She enjoyed her job teaching teens math, and the money – such as it was – kept the wolf away from her door. Fortunately, her expenses were low; she lived in the house she'd inherited from her parents, furnished with mid-century furniture from her grandparents. As she locked her bike in the rack in front of Mariners' Compass Quilt Shop, she smiled.

Entering the shop, Liz saw her sister and co-owner Victoria Benitez engaged with a regular customer, so she just smiled and waved. Pausing at the door, she closed her eyes and inhaled the wonderful scents of the shop – fabric and dye, mingled with a little lemon floor polish on the old pine floors – which reminded her this was her favorite place on earth. After appreciating the familiar comfort for a moment, Liz opened her eyes and scanned the quilts on the walls. A new quilt held a place of honor high on the main wall. Of course, it was of the Mariners' Compass pattern, constructed of a bold, modern palette of bright blues, greens, turquoise, and yellow. Liz smiled again. As Mariners' Compass was both the name and logo of the shop, there was always at least one such quilt hanging somewhere in view. Liz wondered who had made this one – the color choices suggested the shop's assistant manager Sheila Robbins had made this most recent shop standard.

Her entrance routine complete, Liz headed to the office at the rear of the shop. Smelling the coffee her sister had apparently just brewed knowing Liz was on her way, Liz reached for a mug, poured the fragrant blend, took a sip, and turned on the computer. She settled in to update the bookkeeping, payroll, and inventory for the week. For the several years since the shop opened, she'd been doing the business and accounting tasks. When Victoria had had her brainchild of opening a quilt shop in downtown Lewes, she knew the accounting parts of the business were not her strongest points, so she'd asked Liz to partner with her. Liz's finances hadn't allowed her to contribute anywhere near half of the start-up expenses, but with her teacher's salary to live on, she had chosen to take her pay as shares toward joint ownership. Over the years, her portion of the shop had grown to over 20%. While Liz did the back-office functions, and learned more about quilting, Victoria focused on staying on top of quilting trends, keeping the merchandise and class schedules up to date, and ensuring their customers were happy. Their partnership was working well. Mariners' Compass had become the destination for dozens of local quilters and crafters, as well as busloads of quilters from Baltimore, Philadelphia, and Richmond, all bent on buying the best current fabrics, participating in regular and specialty classes and workshops, and enjoying the camaraderie of kindred creative spirits.

Victoria joined her in the office and gave her sister a brief hug. "Hey, Liz. I'm sorry I didn't have a chance to talk earlier when you came in."

"I could see you were helping Stephanie. What's her latest project?"

"A king-size log cabin pattern for her daughter and son-in-law."

"That's a surprise," Liz commented. "That's a pretty easy pattern; she won't be challenged by it."

"Yeah, I asked her about that. She said it's what her daughter wants, so that's what she's making."

"As long as she bought lots of fabric, she can make whatever she wants," laughed Liz.

The sisters enjoyed the comfortable silence of people who have known and loved each other for years. For a while, the only sounds were the occasional clicking of keys on the computer and both sisters' coffee mugs being picked up, sipped from, and set down again. Victoria broke their silence by asking, "So how was your first week back to teaching?"

"Fine. Tiring. The first week always seems a lot longer than the others. Plus, we had the Math Bowl test after school. Twelve kids showed up, including your Maria, of course. This year I have an assistant coach, Meg Williamson. She's young; it's only her second-year teaching. She started at LHS midway through last year, so I really haven't gotten to know her yet."

"I'm glad you have an assistant, even if she is still wet behind the ears! And I'm still amazed I have a daughter who loves math. Maria must have gotten those genes from her father," laughed Victoria. They both chuckled a bit, aware math was not Victoria's favorite subject. Their smiles both got misty, and Liz knew Victoria was thinking of her beloved husband, Javier. They shared a quiet moment recalling Javier Benitez. Victoria's husband had died unexpectedly the previous year. While the renowned orthopedic surgeon had left Victoria wealthy, she was far too young to be a widow; she and their two children were still grieving. "How did Maria do?"

"I haven't graded the tests yet. I'll do that this weekend, so Meg and I can announce the team Monday morning. Our first practice is after school Monday. Maria was on the team last year, so I'll be surprised if she doesn't make the cut again this year."

"I promised Maria and Jamie I'd bring home Thai carry-out for dinner. Want to join us?"

"I'd love to. I can finish this tomorrow morning. Want me to pick anything up?"

"Nope, no need. I'll get some dishes with lots of veggies in them, so it's balanced. Jamie recently decided he doesn't need to eat vegetables anymore." Victoria rolled her eyes. "I guess that's normal for a thirteen-year-old boy. But I bet he'll wolf it down when he sees his favorite aunt eating some." Victoria checked her watch. "I'm heading home around six. Why don't you come over a little after then?"

"Sure. I'll head home on my bike and then drive over, so I won't have to ride my bike home late on a Friday night. See you in a bit."

Liz parked in driveway and smiled as she surveyed her sister's house. Even though she'd been here hundreds of times over the years, the house still amazed her. Javier had bought the waterfront lot before he and Victoria had met, and they had arranged for the house to be built soon after they were married, living in his condo while it was under construction. Like so many waterfront homes, the ground floor just held garages, casual space for the kids with a pool table and a ping-pong table, and both stairs and an elevator to reach the living areas. Up one level were four bedroom suites. Jamie's and Maria's faced the rear of the house with what the floor plans had called the "nanny's room" and guest room on the front. Up another level were the public rooms with a gourmet kitchen, a spacious area combination dining and living space, and large deck overlooking the backyard pool, basketball court, and the Delaware Bay beyond. The top floor held the spacious master suite, with a luxurious bath, separate closets and dressing rooms, a cozy balcony and a coffee bar, as well as a combination sewing room and home office. For such an enormous home, Liz still found it cozy, which spoke to Victoria's hygge decorating style. And, of course, because she loved the family living there.

Liz pushed the button on the combination doorbell, inter-com and video device. She saw her nephew Jamie's smiling face on the screen. "Hi, Aunt Liz. Come on up."

Liz used her key to open the ground floor door, then took the elevator up to the living room. As soon as the elevator door opened, she was swarmed by her loved ones. Even though she'd seen all three earlier in the day, it would be good to spend time together in a non-school and non-work setting where everyone could relax. Victoria and Maria each hugged her, while Ripper, their cocker spaniel, ran happy circles around the four, yapping as he ran. She and Jamie started their complicated handshake sequence. "Oh, no. I messed it up again." Liz exclaimed halfway through the routine.

Jamie laughed. "That's okay. You did better than last time." He showed her the rest of the routine, and they ran through it start to finish. "There, you got it!"

Liz laughed with him. "Yeah, for now I do. I'll probably forget again before the next time I'm over here."

"Ripper, hush and sit. Jamie, if you're done shaking your aunt's hand, could you set the table for us?" Victoria asked. "And Maria, can you get water for everyone, please?" She turned to Liz, "Want a beer? I picked up some Singha when I got dinner."

"Sure. It'll go great with the food. Just hand them to me and I'll open them." Liz headed into the kitchen, found the bottle opener in the first drawer she opened and pulled the caps off both bottles.

"I got a couple different stir fries, the green chicken curry with the extra Thai eggplants I know you like, and a massaman curry, too. I'll put them all out and we can share."

As Liz watched, Jamie winced as he limped between the kitchen and the dining table with placemats and napkins. "Hey, Jamie, what's up with how you're walking?"

Jamie sighed as Victoria and Maria laughed. "Coach Brown had us running a lot this week. He even sent us out with the cross-country team yesterday." He grimaced while he stretched. "I guess I didn't do as much running during the summer break as I should have."

"Wait, I'm confused. Basketball season doesn't start for a while, does it? Or are you doing a different sport now?"

"No, it's still basketball. And you're right, the official try-outs aren't for a few weeks. But Coach Brown lets anyone who's interested work out in the gym after school. We do drills and run – a lot of running! – but we don't do any scrimmages yet. I think Coach is using the running to weed guys out before try-outs."

They settled into dining chairs and began to pass the dishes around. When everyone had a plate full of their favorites, Maria turned to Liz. "Did I make the Math Bowl team, Aunt Liz?"

"I hope so, but I haven't scored the tests yet. How do you think you did?"

Maria shrugged. "Other than one of the trig problems, I think I got all of them right."

"Well, then, you probably made the team again this year."

"I hope so. Being on the team for two years will look good on my college applications." Maria continued talking about applying to colleges and mentioned some extremely expensive ones.

"I just want to remind you that, if you're still thinking about medical school, that you'll need to make sure your education trust lasts." Victoria said.

"I don't need to worry about that, Mom," Jamie interjected. "I'm going to get a basketball scholarship, so I won't have to pay for college. Then I can just get all the money when I turn twenty-eight."

Maria rolled her eyes and Victoria's and Liz's eyes met. After a long pause, Liz said, "That's a terrific plan, but it'd be good to have a backup plan, too. Just in case the basketball scholarship doesn't work out the way you want."

"I'm still growing, and Dad was tall, so I think I've got a good chance."

"Just keep your options open, Jamie." Liz advised. *Especially since you're shorter than your peers and it's not certain that you'll make the JV team this year.*

After the meal was finished and Victoria had nudged Jamie into helping her with the dishes, Liz and Maria had a few moments alone on the sofa. "Aunt Liz, you know I'm planning to go away to college next year, right?"

Liz grinned at her niece. "You might have mentioned it once or twice. Plus, none the schools you've said you're applying to are in commuting range."

Maria chuckled. "Yeah, its really on my mind a lot now." She grew more serious. "And you know I'll be living in a dorm. Do you think you could make a quilt for my dorm room bed? I'd love to have something you made, and something that isn't like everyone else's."

Liz was elated but stayed outwardly calm. "Why, yes, I'd be glad to. Have you thought any about what colors you'd like or what design you want?"

Maria paused. "No, not really." She brightened. "But I could come by the shop this weekend and we could pick out fabrics and talk about designs."

"That'd be great. I should be there all day tomorrow."

Maria reached over and hugged Liz again. "I'm so happy you said 'yes.' I was wondering if I should ask you or not, but Mom said the worst that could happen would be for you to say 'no.'"

CHAPTER 3

Saturday morning was the start of a fine late summer day – warm with light breezes and a few puffy clouds floating across a deep blue sky. As Liz walked downtown, she breathed in the salty scent of nearby Delaware Bay and reflected once again on how much she loved her hometown. Lewes was a charming resort town, even when it was crammed with tourists during warmer months.

A large bus was unloading passengers in front of Mariners' Compass as Liz arrived. Dozens of presumed quilters milled around on the sidewalk and peered into the shop's windows, despite it being at least forty-five minutes before the store's scheduled opening. As Liz approached the shop, an older woman emerged from the crowd and approached her. "Do you work here, honey?"

"Yes, I do." Liz smiled at the woman. "I expect you're with the quilting guild from Philadelphia. We're expecting you, but not for another hour or so. If you want to wait here, I'll see if the owner is okay with letting your group into the shop early."

Liz slipped through the crowd, unlocked the door, and saw her sister talking with Emma Cambridge, an internationally famous quilter and president of their local guild. Liz waved and called, "Is it okay if the quilters . . ." As Liz spoke through the open door, the crowd of people shifted on the sidewalk behind her, the door banged her shoulder, and she stumbled. As she caught her balance, the horde of quilters rushed past her into the store. *So much for checking if it's okay for them to come in early.*

The ever-poised Victoria approached the group. "Welcome to Mariners' Compass. I'm Victoria Benitez, the owner, and this is Emma Cambridge. I see you've already met my partner, Liz Murphy." Feet shuffled and a few quilters mumbled, "Sorry. We're just excited to be here and start shopping."

"We're glad you're here and we're as excited as you are. Most of our fabrics are in the room we're in now." She gestured to the adjacent area, originally part of a separate building before the shop expanded. "In the next room are notions and the rest of our fabric. Upstairs, we have a room with machines – please ask a member of the staff to help you if you wish to look at those." Victoria then gestured toward the slight young woman in an apron heading upstairs with a tray of pastries. "And finally, our classroom is also upstairs, where caterer Katya Tereschenko is setting up coffee and snacks for you." Katya smiled and nodded to the group. Victoria continued, "You can use either the stairs or the elevator to go upstairs. I'd like to ask you to keep any food or beverages within . . ."

Liz watched Emma as Victoria spoke to the Philadelphia guild members and was amused, but not surprised, to see that Emma couldn't stand someone else being in the spotlight. Emma broke into Victoria's welcome. "As Victoria said, I'm Emma Cambridge." Emma paused theatrically, expecting a reaction from the quilters. When no one spoke, she continued, "I expect you're familiar with my work. I'll be here all day if any of you want to talk with me about my quilting, my inspiration, or my techniques. This afternoon, I'll be teaching my *Basics for All* class upstairs. I'm sure you'll all agree it's essential for beginning quilters to learn the foundations of our craft the *right* way, and I know I'm the best person to teach those skills. My class is also a great refresher for those of you whose skills are a little rusty, whose skills are possibly not up to date, or those of you who aren't achieving the results in your quilting you'd like. Now that I mention it, this course is valuable for any quilter, and I'd recommend all of you take the course this afternoon. Class starts at 1:00 pm. I expect I'll see a good many of you then."

The horde dissolved into small groups of customers, moving around the shop, examining fabric, and exclaiming over the sample quilts hanging on the walls. A few brave souls ventured closer to Emma, hoping for some brief conversation with the forceful and renowned lady. Liz grinned at Victoria and headed back toward the office. Victoria joined her just before she went in. "I hope you didn't get hurt when they surged through the front door."

"No, I'm fine. A bruise on my shoulder at most."

"I hope that's all. You know, some people think quilters are just sweet little old ladies."

Liz laughed. "They're all ages, and I noticed several men in this group. But the folks in this guild from Philly sure aren't sweet – they're practically rabid. Next time, I'll make sure I lock the door behind me. Anyway, I have an hour or two of work here. Come get me if you need me to cut fabric or run the register."

Liz's morning and afternoon flew by. She finished the bookkeeping for the shop, cut fabric, rang up customer's purchases, and helped customers select fabrics for their projects. Late in the afternoon, Maria stopped by the shop. She and Maria spent a fun half-hour selecting fabrics. Maria wanted something bold for her dorm room next year, and had selected jewel tones of fuchsia, coral, and peacock blue. Liz had hoped to find time to score the exams for the LHS Math Bowl team but was having too much fun with her niece to get to them. *Maybe tomorrow.*

Liz awoke at dawn on Sunday morning to the drumbeat of heavy rain against her bedroom windows and a forecast of rain for the rest of the day. She knew from long experience the shop would have fewer customers on a rainy day, so she shouldn't be needed. Sunday had shorter hours at the shop anyway. And Victoria would call if she needed help.

As soon as her eyes opened, Abner, Liz's twenty-pound Maine Coon cat thumped down from her bed, trotted into the kitchen and sat by his bowl. Liz followed, put out a can of Abner's favorite food, freshened his water bowl, and began to consider her own breakfast. She settled on a quick breakfast of fruit and yogurt, plus her first 'must have' large mug of coffee, and then headed into the spare room she used as both office and quilting studio. The math tests could be graded without much effort, but planning the design for Maria's quilt would take a chunk of time. This rainy morning seemed perfect for the task at hand. Even though Maria's graduation was months away, Liz was eager to get started on her quilt. She'd tried to talk to Maria about what sort of pattern or style she'd like, but all Maria would say was that she wanted lots of stripes and the series of triangles known as Flying Geese. Liz took the new fabrics to her laundry room to pre-wash out excess dye and any fabric treatments remaining. She poured herself another mug of coffee and lounged on the living room sofa with her sketch pad on her lap and Abner curled up beside her. After an enjoyable hour had flown by, Liz closed the sketchbook. She had four designs sketched, each using stripes and Flying Geese in different arrangements, and was looking forward to showing her sketches to Maria to see which design her niece preferred. Only then would she start cutting fabric or sewing. She knew this would be a fun project.

But then her phone rang. The tests would have to wait.

CHAPTER 4

Monday morning dawned with fog and drizzle, so after feeding Abner, giving him fresh water, and making sure he had plenty of kibble available, Liz left her bicycle in her garage and drove the short distance to LHS, with a detour through the nearest local coffee shop's drive thru. Time had gotten away from her on Sunday when Victoria had called for an extra hand at the shop. An hour before homeroom was due to begin, Liz settled at her desk with her latte nearby and pulled out the tests. Forty-five minutes later, she reviewed the scores. She was pleased to see her niece Maria had the highest score and surprised to see sophomore Ross York had the next highest score. Senior twins Ashley and Andrew Stevens were tied for third. After the Stevenses' scores, there was a large gap to the score of the fifth-place student.

Next, she reviewed the partial scores for the four highest scorers, and saw that, except for Andrew's mediocre score in geometry, all four had scored well in all areas. This meant there wouldn't be any reason to adjust the team composition, and no reason for students to complain about unfairness. Good news – their reaction on Friday had convinced her any student dropped off the team for someone with a lower score would put up a fuss. And Andrew's geometry score wouldn't be an issue, as she and Meg could work with him on that before the competition.

Liz contemplated getting a fresh cup of coffee from the teachers' lounge as Meg burst into her classroom. "Have you scored the tests? What did you get? I think we'll need to adjust who's on the team, don't you?"

Liz looked up at Meg. "Yes, I scored them. I got Maria on top, then Ross, and Ashley and Andrew tied for third. But I didn't see any reason to changes. Is that how your scores turned out?"

"Having Ross on the team will be a disaster! He's too young, too immature, and he'll be disruptive."

"Gosh, I'm surprised. He was quiet in my geometry class last year, but I didn't have any issues with him. Can you give me some examples of what you've seen with him?"

Meg scowled. "So, you're just rejecting my input now? You think because you're the main coach you can just run rough-shod over me? Do you think you're going to get away with put-ting your niece on the team – that's nepotism, you know. You wouldn't want that to get out, would you?"

Liz stood and drew a deep breath. "Meg, I'm just trying to understand your concerns. We'll need a valid reason to keep a student who scored so well off the team. Has he been in one of your classes? Can you give me some specifics about Ross?"

Meg fumed. "No. It's clear to me you're excluding my input on this. Maybe I don't really need to be involved in this." Meg bolted out of the classroom, slamming the door behind her.

Liz sat back down at her desk, stunned at her encounter with Meg. She had ten minutes before homeroom students would come into her classroom, so she put her feet up on her desk to think. Diane had told her Meg had not-yet-controlled bi-polar disorder, but she hadn't seen this side of Meg's mood swings before now. The little reading Liz had done on bi-polar disorder hadn't prepared her for mood swings as rapid or as severe as she was seeing with Meg. However, Meg's threat to stop coaching the team wasn't really a threat at all – Liz had coached by herself last year, and the workload had been not only fine, but enjoyable. So, she didn't really want to share Math Bowl with anyone else. She wanted the team to finish higher than last year's team had, but she didn't see any reason to think Meg would make a difference in achieving that goal. Moreover, she couldn't throw a student off the team without a good reason – one that would bear the inevitable scrutiny of Principal Diane Goodwin, not to mention the student's parents. As the bell rang and students entered, she made her decision – post the four names, and deal with whatever drama Meg generated as a result. Later. Ideally, never.

For her own peace of mind, Liz was determined to keep her own behavior professional, regardless of how much or little she and Meg interacted this year. Whatever happened with Math Bowl coaching, she'd still be mentoring Meg. Shaking her head at the weirdness of it all, she posted the team composition on her classroom door and returned to her desk as her homeroom students took their seats. She turned her attention to those students; there were some she didn't already know, and she wanted to learn their names, faces, and personalities as soon as she could.

After the final bell rang, Liz went to the teachers' lounge to retrieve her lunch bag. When she returned to her classroom, she paused at the doorway. All four teens on the team were already in the room, talking to each other. As she watched, Maria Benitez nudged Ross York and said, "Hey, Squirt. What are you doing here?"

Ross shrugged and grinned up at her, "Guess I'm just good."

As Liz entered the room, Andrew Stevens called to her, "Hey, Ms. Murphy. We already picked Maria to be our captain.

21

She's the only one who was on last year's team, so we all thought she should be captain. Hope that's okay with you."

"Of course, it is. I'd said you could choose your own captain." She smiled. "And it looks like you've all introduced yourselves, so you've done the first two items on my agenda before I even got here." Liz set a stack of textbooks on her desk. "Please go ahead and take your seats. As you know, the bowl covers four topics – Algebra 1 and 2, Geometry, and Trigonometry. I'm going to pass out textbooks for the classes you aren't currently taking, so you'll have them for reference."

Liz passed out the books – all four to the three seniors and three to Ross. While she was handing out the books, Meg entered the room, looking calm and relaxed. *What's this?* Liz continued, "We have a set of workbooks to use for preparation. A typical practice session will be each of you working through a lesson, then discussion among the team. For the most part, Ms. Williamson and I will let you work independently, but we'll jump in if it looks like you need us to. And, of course, if you have questions that you as a team can't solve together, wave your hand."

As the teens settled in with the first exercise in their workbooks, a general quiz to set knowledge levels, Liz surveyed her team. First was her niece, Maria. Liz had adored her since she was born, before even. Maria was tall and slim like her mother, with dark skin, hair, and eyes, like her father. Smart, outgoing, and confident, Maria found it easy to make friends. A natural leader, as the other teens had noticed.

Next were the Stevens twins, Ashley and Andrew. They were both blond with athletic builds. Both excelled at swimming, diving, golf, and tennis, and displayed effortless ease with their peers. Liz assumed they'd either been born at the local country club or taken their first steps there. Their grandfather had been governor of Delaware a few decades ago; their parents were both attorneys and active in state politics. Liz had heard rumors their mother was considering a run for Senate next year. Liz had been surprised to see them at the try-outs; they were both good students but seemed more interested in politics and sports. As she considered, she recalled debate competitions were only held in the spring, so the twins could do both debate and Math Bowl.

Last was Ross York. Ross had been in Liz's Geometry class last year. He hadn't seemed to pay much attention in class but turned in all his homework and had high scores on all the tests. He was pleasant and personable when she interacted with him, but she didn't know as much about him as she did the three seniors. He was a bit shorter than the other students, but an attractive teenager with regular features and dark curly hair. *He's due for a big growth spurt this year. What could Meg have against him? His age, maybe?*

The teens finished their worksheet and discussed a geometry problem that had stumped two of them. Liz was pleased to see all of them contributing to the discussion. When they were finished, they turned expectantly to her.

"I think that's a good start for today. Oh, I forgot something earlier. I got an email from the bowl organizers – they won't be using alternate members this year. Instead, for individual events, the lowest score will be dropped. If a team member can't participate, then the remaining three scores will be used. And all four of you will participate in all the team events."

The teens smiled and high-fived each other.

"We also need to exchange contact information. I will give you my personal phone number, but, as you know, that's not the normal protocol for students and teachers. I expect you to keep this completely private. It's safest for all concerned that you should have it for emergencies, but it still needs to be kept private." The teens and teachers sent texts to each other for the next few minutes. "Now let's huddle and break like any other team." Ross looked a little confused, then joined the rest as they put their hands together, broke, and shouted, "Go Lewes!"

CHAPTER 5

The next morning was bright and sunny, and Liz's mood matched the weather. She bicycled to LHS, arriving just in time for the monthly before-school faculty meeting. As she entered the auditorium and took a seat, Diane Goodwin, LHS principal, began the meeting with her usual efficiency. After a welcome to all, Ms. Goodwin introduced new teachers, giving a little background for each. When she paused for a sip of water, Meg stood up, dashed to the front of the room, and began to speak. "I just want to say, I had problems last year with some people taking my food and drinks from the common refrigerator. I want everyone to know I use special imported cream cheese for my bagels, and special cream for my coffee." She glared at the faculty and continued, "I don't want anyone messing with my food this year."

Warren Johnson, long-time history teacher at LHS, turned to Liz and whispered, "Really, a brand-new teacher just interrupted her boss to tell us she only eats fancy imported cream cheese on her bagels?"

Liz shrugged and shook her head. "Looks like," she whispered.

Principal Goodwin reclaimed the floor, reminded everyone to mark their personal food and beverages, and gave Meg a death stare everyone except Meg herself saw. As Meg sat back down, Warren snickered quietly and leaned toward Liz again. "I like bagels, but there's no way in hell I'd eat one named Meg." Ms. Goodwin moved briskly on with the agenda, covering all

25

topics in thirty minutes, even with Meg's interruption. Liz reminded herself she was grateful to work for a principal who was both efficient and caring, even though she wished Diane hadn't wanted Meg to coach the Math Bowl team with her. *Is there any way I can just cut Meg loose from coaching the Math Bowl now? And just mentor her for regular classroom activities? Maybe talk with Diane about how erratic she is?* No, there wasn't a reason to discuss Meg's mood swings with Diane; she already knew about the problem. In fact, they were part of why Diane had asked Liz to mentor Meg. As she mulled it over, Liz knew their one argument wasn't enough to dump Meg, especially since Meg had seemed to be over it by yesterday afternoon. Liz renewed her resolve to try to model reasonable, professional behavior for Meg, and just move on.

Only a few of her colleagues were in the teachers' lounge when Liz entered at lunchtime. She retrieved her lunch from the refrigerator and joined Kay Ferrell, the sixty-ish girls' P. E. teacher, and Warren at a table for four. They exchanged greetings as Liz pulled out her grain and vegetable bowl and poured her homemade vinaigrette over it.

"That staff meeting was a little more interesting than normal," smirked Warren. "I'm not sure what Meg thinks she's doing." He paused and ate another bit of his pizza. After swallowing, he continued, "Hey, you're working with her on that math competition, aren't you?"

Liz looked around before sighing and adding, "Yes, I am. It's going ok, but she sure does have mood swings. Sometimes she's making a big fuss about nothing and other times she acts like nothing's happened. I'm never sure which version of Meg I'll encounter."

Just then, Tiffany Long, French and Spanish teacher, joined them. "I bet you all are talking about Meg. Have I got news for you!" Kay raised an eyebrow at Tiffany, which Tiffany either missed or ignored. "I saw Meg leaving Dr. Westborough's office yesterday when I was picking up my son."

Kay frowned at Tiffany. "Should we know who Dr. Westborough is? And is there a reason we should care?" Liz sighed to herself. If Tiffany and Kay tangled over lunch today, it wouldn't be the first time. Liz knew Warren enjoyed setting Kay and Tiffany at each other, and Tiffany had teed this one up in a way she knew he couldn't resist.

Undeterred, Tiffany announced, "He's the psychiatrist I take Jared to. He's been doing so much better since he's been seeing Dr. Westborough." Tiffany opened her lunch and took her soup to the microwave. While her soup heated, she returned to the table. "But get this, I saw Meg leaving the pharmacy next to his office." Tiffany paused, smirked, and continued, "I saw her throw away the bag, and I might have fished it out of the trash can." Tiffany gave a triumphant smile and said, "But I got the goods on Meg!"

Kay shook her head, "I'm sure not going to throw away any prescription bags in public now."

Warren snickered. Liz couldn't stand it anymore, "Surely you aren't suggesting there's something wrong with Meg taking a prescription? You know about the goose and gander thing, right?"

Tiffany laughed. "It's totally different. Jared wasn't sent to Dr. Westborough by a judge! I heard Meg was ordered to see him to get out of her DUI last summer!"

At this, Warren perked up and smiled. "It's okay, Tiffany, I want to hear more." Kay frowned at him, but he just laughed.

Tiffany was happy to oblige him. "Well, I'm sure you all

know, Meg got picked up for a DUI back in June. It was in the local papers. She told the judge she wasn't really drunk, that she'd just had one drink with a prescription medicine and had a reaction to it. I bet her seeing Dr. Westborough is related to her DUI. So now she's taking lithium tablets to get her moods leveled out." Tiffany paused and pasted a pious smile on her face, "I can only hope it does her as much good as it has Jared."

At this, Kay began talking about the curriculum changes in P.E. this year, and how the sophomores were already complaining about having to spend two weeks each on badminton and archery. Liz let her mind wander into ways she could incorporate archery, arrows, and the arc of shuttlecocks into math problems for her sophomore students. Warren sat silently, his face mirroring Tiffany's earlier smirk.

After dinner that evening, Liz sent Maria text saying she had four designs ready for her to review, and to let her know when a good time would be to talk about them. Maria's text came back immediately asking if she could come over right then. Liz chuckled and agreed.

Ten minutes later, Liz watched as Maria pulled her red convertible Beetle into Liz's driveway and bounded up her front steps. Liz opened the front door, and Maria hugged her tightly. "Hi, Aunt Liz. I can't wait to see your designs." She bent over to pet Abner. "Hey, big guy. How are you doing?" Abner purred in response and twined around her legs as Maria headed toward the kitchen.

"It's great to see you, Maria. Come on in. Would you like anything to drink?"

Maria perched on a stool at Liz's kitchen counter. "Maybe

later – after we've talked about your designs."

"I made four designs. Each of them has stripes and Flying Geese." Liz pushed her design notebook across the counter to Maria who studied them, turning the pages from one design to another.

After several minutes, Maria looked up with a hint of tears in her eyes. "I love them all, Aunt Liz. It's going to be so hard to pick one."

Liz smiled and squeezed Maria's shoulders. "And you know we can combine elements of different ones, if you'd like."

They spent a pleasant half hour comparing the design elements and sketching new ones. They eventually settled on a design with the Flying Geese triangles going up and at sixty-degree angles on the quilt, and stripes going both horizontally and vertically.

"I love it, Aunt Liz. I'm so happy you agreed to make this for me."

"I'm glad you asked me."

"And your designs are so much cooler than Mom's are. I like the fractured curves Mom's doing now, but I really love the geometric lines and angles in your designs. It must be 'cause you and I are both into math. And Mom doesn't speak that language."

The next two weeks flew by. Under Liz's mentoring, the team gained knowledge and confidence. Ross seemed more comfortable around the older teens. And Meg's moods seemed to be leveling out a little. Maybe Dr. Westborough and whatever he was prescribing was helping? With just one more practice before the competition, Liz made sure all four students had rides to the competition and knew their absences for the next two days were excused. Then she gave the team the same timed test they'd taken back at their first practice. As they began, Ashley, Andrew, and Ross all smiled – they recognized the questions from before. Maria, however, sighed and looked up to the clock at the front of the room before beginning. She repeated that twice more during the test.

After Liz collected the tests, she asked Maria if she had concerns. Before Maria could reply, Meg jumped in. "Maria, you can't keep looking around the room during a test. The proctors will think you're cheating and throw you out of the competition!"

"I wasn't cheating – I was checking the time remaining. That's not cheating," Meg retorted.

"Whether you were cheating or not, it looked like you were, and we can't have that."

Maria scowled and muttered, "I wasn't cheating. I was looking up. At the *clock*."

Ashley jumped in, "Ms. Williamson, no one is even close enough for Maria to see our papers."

Maria muttered, "I have to go to the bathroom, and I wanted to see how much time was left."

Liz held up her hands. She was reluctant to appear to favor her niece, but she was sure Maria had only checked the clock. "Everyone, let it go. Does anyone have questions about the test? I'm sure you all recognized it from our first team session." The teens all shook their heads. "If not, then I'll see everyone at Lewes College's Stalnaker Hall before 9 tomorrow morning." The teens headed out, with Maria racing ahead of the others. Liz noticed none of them said goodbye or even made eye contact. *I blew it with the kids, as well as Meg. Now what?*

Liz paused for a moment, then said, "Meg, did you really

think Maria was cheating? After you've worked with these kids for the past weeks?"

"No, I just think cheaters need to be called out. Even the appearance of cheating."

Liz shook her head. "Are you sure you want to be involved with the Math Bowl? Can you tell me why this is important to you?"

"I want to be more involved in supporting student activities, and since the Math Bowl will be in Lewes this year. . ." Her voice trailed off.

Liz gave the younger teacher a gentle smile. "It's really convenient to have the Math Bowl so close. But tomorrow you will need to proceed carefully. Proctors have specific guidance for these situations – you need to read it, understand it, and follow it."

Meg pulled a face, gave Liz a mock salute and left the classroom.

Liz sighed and shook her head over yet another of Meg's mood swings. Then she picked up her cell to call Maria but wasn't surprised when Maria didn't answer. She needed to apologize to Maria in person.

CHAPTER 6

Red and gold leaves drifted in the mild breeze and brown leaves scuttled across the road, with an occasional few getting crunched under Liz's bicycle tires. It was a rare early October day with a crisp morning temperature, blue sky, and plenty of sunshine to come as the sun rose higher in the sky. Liz had left her home just after dawn on this bright Thursday morning, almost an hour earlier than she needed to – the marvelous weather had inspired her to get outside and head for the Math Bowl on her bike. Lewes College was a few miles north of Lewes itself. The bike path between the town and the college took Liz across a large marsh by way of a wide board-walk. Halfway across the marsh, she paused for a moment to watch a blue heron stretch his neck and walk stealthily around the edge of the water, stalking any fish foolish enough to swim past the heron's legs. After a moment, the heron eyed Liz, and with a harsh cry, flapped twice and glided to the other side of the marsh. Liz inhaled the fresh, salty scent of the marsh and watched the early morning light play across the water and marsh grasses. The extra hour gave her a chance to pedal around Lewes College campus and recall her time as a student here.

Lewes College had begun as Sussex Agricultural School in the mid-1820s. Ezekiel Hammond, the founder, decreed all buildings be in a Greek Revival style, with cream-colored brick and dark gray slate roofs. In the 1880s, Sussex Ag, as it was known the locals, added what was then called a "normal school" to supply more teachers to the area. For a few decades, the school was known as Sussex Agricultural and Normal School. At the turn of the twentieth century, more curriculum was added, and it became Lewes College. While agriculture remained a strong program, Lewes College matured into a fine liberal arts college with a well-respected education department. About fifteen years ago, Liz had availed herself of both those components, receiving both degrees in both mathematics degree and education. All the campus buildings, original or newer, retained the same architecture, resulting in a consistent and serene atmosphere. Liz drank in the stately and serene environment as she cycled through campus, admiring the buildings, and recalling her time as a student here. Seeing only a few undergraduate students around this early in the morning contributed to her sense of calm.

Liz was still early when she arrived at Stalnaker Hall, home of the math department, but she noticed two other bikes already locked to the rack, plus the van for "KT Caters to You." Pausing to fluff her hair after her bike helmet had squished it, she took another long look across campus, then climbed the stone steps and entered Stalnaker Hall.

"Ms. Murphy! Come and meet my dad," Ross York called from down the hall as soon as she came inside. At same time, she was greeted by a perky undergrad sitting at a table by the door. "I'll be there in a sec, Ross," she called as she waved to him.

"Hi, I'm Kayleigh. I bet you're Ms. Murphy from Lewes High School. I've got your packet right here. I saw on your bio that you got your math degree from Lewes College. It's always so exciting to have a graduate come back to the math department." Kayleigh paused for a quick breath. "I put three schedules in your packet. One is the general schedule of events. The second shows where you'll be proctoring, and the third shows where your students will be. We learned last time that the coaches always want to know where their students are. Finally, here's a map of Stalnaker Hall – it was remodeled last year, so it's different than it was when you were here. I didn't put in a map of campus, since I knew you would already know your way around.

"Whew! Anything else? Oh yes, the caterer has already set up coffee, pastries, and snacks for faculty in Room 112, down near where Professor York and his son are." Kayleigh giggled and whispered, "He's really handsome, isn't he? I love his classes." In her normal voice she continued, "Here's your name tag, too. I'll be here both days, so let me know if there's anything you need, or I can help you with."

"Thank you so much, Kayleigh. It looks like you have everything well organized." Liz had a random thought that her grandparents would have called Kayleigh 'a vivacious co-ed.'

"Oh, I almost forgot -- the first event is the keynote address by our department chairman, Professor Ingraham. That's in the auditorium, starting at nine."

Liz thanked her again and walked down the hallway, where Ross was waving his arms at her and grinning. She joined Ross and the tall, handsome man who looked like an older version him.

"Dad, this is Ms. Murphy. She teaches my Algebra II class and coaches the math team."

"Hi, I'm Ned York. I'm in the math department here at Lewes College." He and Liz shook hands and smiled at each other. Liz couldn't help noticing Ned's classic, almost Roman good looks, as well as how his dark blue sweater set off his green eyes. And his lack of a wedding ring.

"I'm Liz Murphy. It's great to be back at LC. I haven't been back to the math department in several years. It's been spiffed up a lot since I was a student."

"Two years back, President Snyder started fund-raising efforts to restore several of the original buildings, like this one. We were in a temporary location last year, and just moved back in when this fall semester started."

Just then, the Stevens twins arrived, and Ross drifted over to talk to them. Ned and Liz agreed they could each use a cup of coffee and headed into the make-shift faculty lounge set up for the event. The only other person in the lounge was a husky young man in a brown cardigan. He stood by the coffee maker, meticulously putting cream and sugar into his cup, then tasting and adding tiny amounts again. Liz wondered if he was counting drops of cream and grains of sugar.

"Liz, this is Brian MacKenzie, one of our grad students." The younger man set down his coffee and condiments, turned toward them, and looked at a spot over Liz's shoulder. He had longish hair, neither blond nor brunette; a color Liz's mother had called 'mouse brown.' Liz couldn't help but notice he might be attractive if he got a haircut and separated his unibrow into two eyebrows.

"Hi, Brian. It's nice to meet you." Liz put out her hand. After a few long seconds, Brian gave it a tepid shake and said hello.

Ned continued, "Liz is coaching the Lewes High School team."

This seemed to be what Brian needed to make eye contact with her. He stared at her for a long moment. "I thought Meg Williamson was their coach."

"We're both coaching this year."

"I gotta go," mumbled Brian. He turned and strode to the door. When he reached the door, he turned and walked back to the coffee bar. "Forgot my coffee," he muttered. With that, he slouched away, holding his cup of coffee in both hands.

Liz turned to Ned and raised a single eyebrow. Ned sighed. "Brian's a gifted mathematician – perhaps even brilliant. I'm his advisor. I've been advising him more on interpersonal skills than math. Even as an academic, as I expect he'll be, he needs *some* interaction skills. This time last year, he probably wouldn't have shaken your hand or said hello."

They sipped their coffee and Ned smiled. "Our department's usual coffee is never very good. I'm glad they brought in a caterer for this."

Liz also smiled and nodded, trying to think of interesting small talk to make with this attractive man. Just then, a tiny brunette wearing an apron entered the lounge and waved to Liz. "Liz, it is great to see you. Are you with Math Thing?" she said with the accent of someone who learned English after Russian. As KT had. She was only five when her family left a Moscow suburb to come to Delaware.

"Hi, KT. I teach math at Lewes High School, when I'm not quilting, that is." She gestured to Ned, "Ned, this is Katya Tereshchenko. She goes by KT, probably so she doesn't have to hear the rest of us mangle her name. Her company often caters for my sister and me."

"Nice to meet you, Ned." KT was in her mid-twenties. Despite the dark circles under her eyes and her drawn, pinched face, she offered him an elfin smile.

"KT, Ned tells me the coffee here isn't very good, but since this is excellent, I'm guessing you got here early to set up. Thank you!" *KT looks tired; I wonder if everything's ok.*

Just then a gong sounded in the hallway, and Kayleigh's voice on the intercom advised everyone that the first session would begin in just five minutes. Ned turned to Liz with an eyebrow raised. "I'd recommend taking a quick rest room break before the welcome session starts."

Liz was puzzled. "The schedule says it's only ten minutes." Ned just grinned at her.

Liz entered the auditorium and admired how it had been updated since her days at the college. The old rickety wooden chairs she remembered had been replaced with sleek, modern seating. The stage and podium had been updated, too. She slid into a seat toward the back and saw Ned standing along the side wall. He met her glance and smiled. *That man sure has a nice smile. And I've always been a sucker for guys with dark curly hair.*

Chairman Lowell Ingraham strode onto the stage and raised his arms for quiet. He looked to be about sixty years old, with thinning grey hair and a soft physique. After spending a full minute attaching a small microphone to his shirt collar, he began to speak. "Welcome to the 42nd Annual Delaware Math Bowl competition. You might wonder how I know the exact number of years. As it turns out, I participated in the very first Delaware Math Bowl." He paused, allowing time for a reaction from the audience, who continued to sit quietly. "I was eighteen years old, in my senior year of high school, representing Wilmington High School. We won handily that year. That helped convince me my plan to major in math at the University of Delaware was the right path for me. Then after graduating from UD, I began graduate studies, again in math, and again at UD."

Ingraham continued to describe every step of his academic career through receiving his PhD, becoming an associate professor, assistant professor, full professor, and inexorably toward his current position as department chairman, apparently unaware that the no one in the audience had any interest in his career. After ten minutes of Ingraham's professional history,

Liz's mind began to wander. She imagined how tedious his department meetings must be and wondered if Ned dreaded them. Liz compared Ingraham's leadership 'style' to the brisk and efficient faculty meetings run by LHS principal Goodwin and reflected on how much better it was for her to be at LHS. Liz turned her attention back to Ingraham's speech as he moved on to detailing LC's math department's objectives for the academic year. She stifled a yawn and saw Ned catch her not paying attention. He grinned at her, and she blushed a little. It had been way too long since a handsome man smiled at her like that.

As Ingraham hit the twenty-five-minute mark of his 'ten-minute' welcome address, Liz saw Meg slip into the auditorium by a side door. It seemed to Liz that Ingraham noticed Meg enter as well; he paused in his speech, watched her until she sat down, ran his hand through his hair, and repeated his previous sentence. *That's odd. Ingraham's delivery had been smooth and confident up until then. Was he flustered by her appearance? And hadn't Meg mentioned problems she'd had when she was a grad student here? No, probably anyone arriving late would have distracted him.* Then Liz reminded herself Meg's tardiness wasn't her responsibility – Meg didn't report to her, and Math Bowl was their only joint activity, except for the mentoring. Liz sighed, squirmed, and wondered if Ingraham would finish before lunch, as he'd already talked through the scheduled break. Next on the schedule was the first individual timed tests, and Ingraham was already cutting into the time allotted for them.

"So let me again welcome you to the 42nd Delaware Math Bowl. I'm sure all of you have met Kayleigh. . ." He paused and gestured to Kayleigh, who smiled and waved. "If you haven't, please stop by her desk and say hello. She's here to help with any administrative questions or issues during Math Bowl. And feel free to talk with any of the faculty here in the department;

they'll be here today and tomorrow, as their class schedules permit, of course." He paused again and perused the papers on the lectern. "I see the next item on your schedule is a break, but unfortunately we're already a bit behind schedule. That seems to happen to us a lot here in the Lewes College math department, but we're good at adapting. I'll suggest everyone take a very short break if necessary, and report as soon as possible to your first timed tests."

Liz looked over at Ned, who was grinning at her. Having enjoyed a large helping of KT's coffee, she was glad to have taken Ned's advice to take a break before Ingraham got his captive audience.

CHAPTER 7

A teary Meg waited for Liz outside the ladies' room. "Liz, I need to talk to you for a little bit. I know it's lunch time on our schedules, but I just need a few minutes."

Liz sighed inwardly, wondering when she'd become Meg's Agony Aunt. "OK. Do you want to talk here?"

"No, let's go outside. It's a nice day, and I don't want any of our students to overhear us." They stepped through the main entrance and stood, alone on the front steps.

Liz tried to look more sympathetic than she felt but reminded herself that Meg's moods weren't under her control. "What's going on?"

"I just broke up with my boyfriend and I ran into one of the professors I had a problem with. I'm not having a good day and wanted to tell someone."

"I don't know what to say, and I don't know what to do, but I'm always willing to listen."

Meg sighed. "My boyfriend started accusing me of being with someone else when I really just don't want to be with him anymore. I tried to tell him, but I don't think he was listening. Plus, I was unnerved by seeing some of the professors who treated me so badly. All those bad memories came flooding back. I thought I was over it, but I guess I'm not." She wiped her eyes and took a deep breath. "Thank you for listening to me. I think that's all I really needed – someone to take a moment and care about me." With that, Meg went back into Stalnaker Hall, leaving Liz alone of the porch, her emotions ranging from sympathy for Meg's issues to a little guilty for not being more sympathetic with Meg. But she knew she *could* manage her relationship with Meg for the duration of her mentorship, and she would.

"I can't believe it, Ms. Murphy. We're in second place. We have a chance to win tomorrow!"

The LHS group had gathered in the entryway before departing for the day, the students were energized. Even Meg, off to the side, smiled. Liz beamed at them all. "Yes, I know. You're doing great. All of you scored very well on the individual events today. And you're right, Ross, you're definitely in position to win the championship tomorrow.

"Now everyone needs to head home, relax, have a good dinner and get a good night's sleep. Tomorrow has all the team events – the ones where you can work together, and the relays, where you each work independently to contribute to a single team answer. But we've practiced all of those – you're ready! It starts at 9 o'clock tomorrow morning – I'd like everyone here by 8:30. Any questions?"

The teens all shook their heads.

"OK, then. Let's huddle."

The team put their hands into the center of the huddle, and broke, shouting, "Go Lewes!"

The teens raced for the door, jostling each other, and talking with the same exuberance Liz saw every day after the final bell. Meg slipped out the door behind them.

As Liz shouldered her purse and bookbag and headed for the bike rack, Ned fell in step with her. "I saw Ross just now. He said your team had a great day."

Liz beamed at him as they walked, "Yes, they did. They're a great bunch of kids and they work well together. Last year's team did well, but this year's team is even better. I think they just might bring the trophy home to Lewes this year." She reached her bicycle and paused to place her purse and book bag into her basket and secure them with bungee cords. As she looked up to put her helmet on, she was pleased and surprised to see Ned unlocking a bicycle and donning his own helmet. "Oh, you rode here today, too?"

"Yeah, Ross and I rode here together this morning. His bike's gone, so I guess he already left." Ned smiled. "If you're heading back to town, how about we ride together?"

Liz smiled, "Sure. But I always stop on the bridge over the marsh. It's one of my favorite spots and I like to see what the birds and animals are doing."

"Sounds good. I'll stop for a gander at the marsh, too."

Liz mock-groaned at the pun, then shoved off and pedaled along the trail toward town. At the bridge, she stopped, but the only activity in the marsh she could see was a red-winged blackbird perched on a stalk of marsh grass, chirping his distinctive note. When a gentle breeze ruffled the marsh grasses, the bird teetered on his perch. He flapped several times then flew away when, as promised, Ned glided to a stop beside her.

"How about getting together for some coffee after this competition is over?"

"Sure, that sounds good." Liz was glad her voice sounded normal and didn't croak the way it sometimes did when she was nervous.

"Would Saturday morning be okay for you?"

"That works for me. I'm usually downtown on Saturday mornings. How about Java Joe's? That's right across the street from my second job."

"Sure, I like Java Joe's. Ross, my source of information on everything to do with Ms. Murphy," Ned's eyebrows wiggled a little bit as he drew air quotes around 'Ms. Murphy,' "tells me you even work on Saturdays. Can you get away from your job?"

Liz laughed. "My sister and I own Mariners' Compass Quilt Shop on Second Street. She handles the artistic side, and I do the books, payroll, and other back-office functions. It's just a few hours a week for me. I'm pretty sure the boss won't mind." Liz drew her own air quotes around 'the boss,' and grinned. They exchanged cell phone numbers and agreed to meet at 9 o'clock Saturday morning before resuming their pedaling. *Who'd have thought I'd meet someone cute, funny, and interesting at Math Bowl?*

Liz peered into her refrigerator, willing something appetizing to materialize. Not only was she out of ingredients for dinner, but she was also out of the yogurt and fruit she typically ate for breakfast. More importantly, she'd opened Abner's last can of salmon cat food this morning. And without anything for dinner, there wouldn't be any leftovers for lunch. Liz sighed, and headed back to her garage, where she had just left her bicycle. She pedaled along Savannah Road to Lloyd's Market, a gem of a grocery store near downtown Lewes. She waved to Ron, this evening's check-out clerk as she grabbed a basket. On her ride over, she'd thought it had been a long time since she'd had a Chef's Salad. She selected a bag of romaine lettuce plus a nice ripe tomato and a cucumber for her salad. While in the produce aisle, she picked up a bunch of bananas, three gala apples, and fresh blueberries. Then some yogurt for breakfast, and bacon, deli ham, a chunk of cheddar, and a bag of hard-boiled eggs. Was there room in her bicycle's basket for a box of cereal, too?

Not after she added six cans of Abner's food, so Liz left the cereal on the shelf and headed to the front.

"Hey, Liz. Haven't seen you in a while. How're you doing?"

"Hi, Ron. I'm good. I finally ran out of food, so I'm back for the basics." Ron laughed. "How are you?"

"Can't complain. Another day, another dollar. Taking things one day at a time." Ron smiled as he scanned her purchases and bagged them. "Want any more clichés?"

Liz laughed, "Nope, that's plenty." She waved as she headed out the door.

Back at home, Liz decided she was too hungry to take time frying bacon, so she assembled her salad with the rest of the ingredients. She was sorely tempted to start working on Maria's quilt while she ate, but realizing one spill of salad dressing could ruin a lot of fabric, she resisted the temptation. While she ate, she reviewed the design she and Maria had finalized, and jotted down how many three-inch strips of fabric she'd need to cut from the coral, peacock blue and cream that would form the stripes. She couldn't do the math for the fuchsia Flying Geese in her head, so she'd wait to cut those.

CHAPTER 8

Liz was pleased to see her entire team and Meg already in the main hallway of Stalnaker Hall when she arrived at 8:30 Friday morning. Today would be the team events of the Bowl, and they all needed to be present. A little disappointed Ned wasn't around, she reminded herself they would have coffee together the next day, even if he wasn't around today. She studied the group as she approached. The Stevens twins were talking with each other, Ross was gazing up at Maria with the adoring expression he'd been directing toward her over the past few weeks, and Meg talked, although no one seemed to be listening to her. Even after yesterday's energy, they still weren't responding to her. *A pity, as Meg was trying.* Liz waved to the group and ducked into the teachers' lounge for coffee. When she came back and joined the group, Meg announced she needed a pit stop and some breakfast. After Meg departed for the ladies' room, Maria leaned toward Liz and inhaled the aroma of the coffee her aunt had just brought from the lounge.

"There isn't any coffee in the student lounge, and I forgot to bring any from home today. Can I go get some from the teachers' lounge?" Maria asked Liz.

"You probably shouldn't . . . ." Maria gave her a pleading look. "Oh, all right. Just be quick about it."

As Maria headed to the lounge, Liz added, "And don't touch any of Ms. Williamson's food in the refrigerator. She's really particular about her food."

Maria nodded and dashed into the lounge, returning almost

immediately with a large cup. Ross grinned up at her, "Don't you know that's going to stunt your growth?"

Maria grinned back, "Maybe it already has, and I'd be even taller if I didn't drink it."

Liz watched as Meg emerged from the ladies' room and crossed the hall to the lounge. After a few minutes, she returned with a large cup of coffee creamed to almost white, and a bagel slathered with cream cheese and jam. The teens' banter ended when she rejoined the group, and Liz wondered if Meg had any idea of the impact she had on them. The group made awkward conversation about the recent change to cooler weather. *Really, teens talking about weather. She has no clue, and the kids aren't helping.*

Meg took long swigs from her coffee as she wolfed down her bagel. After several more minutes awkward conversation, Meg frowned and announced, "I don't feel so good."

"What's wrong, Ms. Williamson?" asked Ashley.

Meg leaned over and clutched her abdomen. "I . . ." Her face contorted and her coffee splattered across the hall as she dropped to the floor, moaning.

"Are you ok?" "What's the matter?" "Should we get a doctor?" As Meg shuddered and began to convulse, Liz grabbed her phone and hit 911.

The ambulance crew arrived in a few minutes, and emergency medical technicians surrounded Meg. Liz caught a glimpse of Meg – her face was gray, and she had lost consciousness. *Not good.* Just as the EMTs were loading Meg into the ambulance, two uniformed officers from Lewes Police Department arrived. *Why are the cops here?* Liz wondered if the EMTs had called for police, based on the severity of Meg's illness. As she mulled that over, she considered maybe Kayleigh had, given how chaotic the scene had become. *But wouldn't Kayleigh have called campus security instead? This doesn't make sense, but I'm not thinking clearly right now anyway.*

Kayleigh and one of the officers raced into the lounges, shooing everyone out and locking the doors behind them. The other officer collected samples of Meg's coffee from the floor. Just then, the gong sounded as it had yesterday. Unlike yesterday, however, Kayleigh's voice screeched as it came out of the intercom. "Everyone associated with the Math Bowl, please report immediately to the main floor auditorium. Do not report to the location on your schedules. Instead, proceed immediately to the auditorium." She repeated her announcement again and again, for the next twenty minutes.

The auditorium was in an uproar as Liz entered. Students, teachers, and college staff gestured and questioned each other about what was happening. She saw Maria sitting with Ashley and Andrew, with no empty seats near them. Ross stood near the opposite entrance to the auditorium. As Liz sat down in the back of the auditorium, she saw Ned rush into the auditorium, look around for Ross and race to him. Ross leaned into his father, and Ned put his arms around him for a moment. Liz saw Ross speak urgently to his father, but she couldn't hear any of his words. Even though she couldn't hear the words, she could see the growing horror on Ned's face.

Chairman Ingraham was on the stage again. Yesterday, Ingraham had looked smooth and unflappable, but now he was literally flapping his arms, urging everyone to take seats and be quiet. What a difference a day, and a disaster, make. When the room was finally quiet, Ingraham took a deep breath and expelled it. He beckoned to a slim man in jeans and a sport coat standing near him on the stage and handed him the microphone. Ingraham stepped off the stage and sat down in the front row.

"Hello, everyone. I'm Detective Jackson with the Lewes Police Department. As many of you are aware, Margaret – Meg – Williamson collapsed here this morning. I'm sorry to inform you that the EMTs were unable to revive her, and she was pronounced dead upon arrival at Beebe Hospital." He paused as gasps and murmurs broke out across the room. He held his hand up, and continued, "Given the circumstances, we are investigating Ms. Williamson's death as suspicious."

He gestured to a young woman standing behind him onstage. "Ms. Lucas, my associate and this year's Lewes PD intern, will be assisting me in the investigation, as will Officers Sutton and Bennett." The two uniformed officers standing by the doors raised their hands and nodded in turn.

"First, we first need to identify those of you who may have information to assist our investigation. If you were in the hallway where Ms. Williamson collapsed this morning, we need you to stay here in the auditorium. Also, if you were ever in the faculty lounge, yesterday or today, we need for you to stay here. Finally, if you had ever known or met Ms. Williamson before yesterday, we need you to stay here." While he spoke, Ms. Lucas wrote these conditions on the whiteboard, under headings of "STAY" or "CONTACT INFO ONLY."

"Those of you who are not required to stay, please form an orderly line on the left side of the auditorium and give your contact information to either Officer Sutton or Officer Bennett on your way out." Chairman Ingraham stood and whispered urgently to Jackson for a moment, and Jackson continued, "I've just been informed that high school students, even if not required to remain in the auditorium, may not leave Lewes College campus without permission of their faculty advisors, who may be required to stay. Inform the officers, and arrangements will be made for you. Finally, we request those of you who remain do not speak with each other as you wait for your interview.

"I expect complete silence in this auditorium, beginning *now.*"

Liz took deep breaths to calm herself and watched as some of her fellow teachers and most of the students from other schools lined up to give their information to the officers. After fifteen minutes, they had all departed, and Ms. Lucas began summoning those who remained to their interviews with Detective Jackson. Pleased she had brought her bookbag with tests she needed to grade, Liz settled in to work on them. After less than ten minutes, however, she found herself unable to concentrate on the exams, and gave up and let her mind wander about what might have happened to Meg.

Her cell informed her it was almost noon. Although she'd had only a scant breakfast, Liz was not interested in food. Even as she wondered about what had happened to Meg, Liz began to worry about her students. Ross was fine since Ned was with him. But Liz knew Maria and the twins would have to wait for a parent before they could be interviewed. In the early afternoon Liz felt a whoosh of relief to see Victoria arrive in the auditorium and rush to Maria. Mother and daughter clung to each other for a moment and were next to be ushered out. Victoria sent a loving look toward Liz as they left. Liz now worried about the twins – their parents often spent their days in Wilmington, more than an hour's drive away from Lewes. *Would they have to stay here possibly hours after everyone else had left?* Liz stood up to go speak to the officers about the twins' situation, but one of the officers immediately told her to be seated.

Soon afterward, Ned and Ross were summoned for their interview. Although she had met Ned only yesterday, she felt his departure as though her only friend in the group was now gone. And now she and the twins were alone in the auditorium, not counting the uniformed officers, of course.

CHAPTER 9

O ver two hours had passed before Liz was called to be interviewed. She wondered if Detective Jackson had been interviewing Ned and Ross all that time. It seemed unlikely the man would have taken a lunch break when there were still people waiting for their interviews, but she didn't really know how detectives went about doing investigations.

Liz was momentarily disoriented when she entered the interview room. The room had been a classroom just yesterday, but it now was devoid of any sense of the joy of learning. Today it seemed to exuded menace. Student desks had been pushed to the perimeter of the room and all the blinds were pulled down, darkening the room. The professor's desk was in the center of the room, with two chairs facing it. The only item on the desk was a recording device. Detective Jackson sat behind the desk, and Ms. Lucas sat behind him and to one side with a notepad and pen on her lap; she appeared eager to document their interview. Liz's only thought was to get this over with as soon as she could.

"Please sit down. I'd like to record this interview."

Liz remained standing and said, "Before we start, I'm worried about the Stevens twins. Their parents often spend their workdays at the Capitol in Wilmington. Will Andrew and Ashley be able to leave if it gets late?"

Jackson tilted his head and studied her before replying, "Their father arrived a few minutes ago. They're okay; they'll be interviewed next."

"Oh, good. I'm glad to hear that."

After Liz sat, he turned on the recorder. "Please state your name and address." Liz did so. "I'd like to start by making sure you know that we don't yet know if a crime was committed here. We'll need to get autopsy and laboratory results back before we even know what caused Ms. Williamson's death today. We're pursuing an investigation in case it turns out to have been a crime. Please explain why you are here today and your relationship to Ms. Williamson."

Liz swallowed. "We're both math teachers at Lewes High School, and we're the two coaches for the Lewes Math Bowl team. Also, Principal Goodwin asked me to mentor Ms. Williamson."

Jackson leaned forward and softened his expression a bit. "We're trying to get a picture of Ms. Williamson. Sometimes the things we learn about a victim can lead us to a clearer understanding of what happened. Could you describe Ms. Williamson for me?"

Liz wondered if he was being gentle with her or just trying to appear so. *I'm not sure; I can't quite read him.* She licked her lips and took a deep breath. "I found her challenging to work with. She got mad about minor things, and later acted like nothing had happened."

"Did you ever see her outside of school settings?"

Liz didn't need to think about that question. "No, I never did. She hadn't taught at Lewes High School very long, and this year's Math Bowl was the only thing we worked on together, other than the mentoring."

"Is there anything else you know about her that might help us understand her better? Anything you might have heard from other teachers?" As Liz hesitated, he added, "Rumors or gossip can help."

"Well, OK. When our principal asked me to mentor Meg,

she told me that Meg had uncontrolled bipolar disorder, and that she was seeing a psychiatrist and beginning to take medication. One of the other teachers told a couple of us Meg had received a DUI a while back, the judge ordered to her to see Dr. Westborough." Liz looked between the detective and Ms. Lucas for a moment. "But I want to emphasize that I don't personally know if any of that is true or not. And I never thought being sent to a psychiatrist was what happened to someone with a DUI."

The room was silent for a long moment. Liz broke the silence. "I heard the part about the DUI and Meg seeing Dr. Westborough from Tiffany Long. She teaches languages at Lewes High. She talked about how her son goes to Dr. Westborough too, and that her son's lithium prescription has done wonders for him."

Detective Jackson leaned back in his chair. "Is there anything else you can tell us about Ms. Williamson . . ." He gazed at her with his eyebrows raised. Liz felt there might be more for her to say about Meg, but she couldn't seem to think straight; Jackson's gaze unnerved her. She shook her head. "Then I'd like to ask you about the time just before Ms. Williamson collapsed." He paused for a moment. "I've heard the situation described by several others, but I'd like to hear from you about your niece," He turned to Ms. Lucas, who murmured something to him Liz couldn't hear. "Yes, your niece Maria Benitez, and her getting coffee from the teachers' lounge this morning."

Liz was flummoxed. *What did Maria's coffee have to do with anything?* "OK. I had grabbed a coffee from the teachers' lounge this morning. Maria said there wasn't any coffee in the student lounge, and she'd forgotten to bring any with her from home. So, she asked me if she could get some from the teachers' lounge. At first, I said no, then changed my mind and told her to hurry, since she wasn't supposed to be there."

Jackson's dark brown eyes bored into hers. "But there was more to the conversation, wasn't there?"

Liz mulled it over for a moment. "Yes, there was more. I told her not to touch any of Ms. Williamson's food in the lounge." Liz was pleased with herself for remembering a minor detail after everything that had happened during the day.

Detective Jackson leaned a little closer. "Was it possibly because you knew there was something in her food – something that didn't belong there? And you didn't want your niece to eat any of it?"

"No! Of course not! I had no idea if there was anything in her food." Liz was appalled and told herself it was time to stop talking any more than necessary. But she couldn't stop herself from adding, "And I still don't know if there was anything in her food." She paused for a few deep breaths, feeling Detective Jackson's eyes on her. "She complained about people eating her food at school a few times. I knew she was particular about it, and I didn't want Maria to get in hot water with her. That's all." Liz winced at how defensive she sounded. *Time to stop talking.*

Jackson stood and walked her to the door before adding, "As a routine precaution, I'd like to ask you not to leave Delaware without letting me know. Here's my card. I hope you understand."

Liz leaned against the wall of the now-deserted hallway. She closed her eyes, and tried to take slow, calming breaths to control her panic, but she struggled to fill her lungs. She knew she wouldn't be safe getting on her bicycle just yet. But all she could think was that Meg was dead, and she was a suspect. How had the day gone so wrong so fast?

CHAPTER 10

L iz hit snooze on her phone alarm five times the following morning. The fifth time her alarm rang, Abner patted a fat paw on her cheek. "All right, all right, I'm awake," she told him. After struggling to get out of bed, she took inventory – headache, dry mouth, and queasy stomach. Like a hangover, but without having had anything to drink the night before. She looked in the mirror and saw her face – pale and drawn, with dark circles under her eyes, and her normally perky strawberry blonde hair hanging limp. Working on her current quilting project the previous night had been hopeless; she couldn't keep her mind focused on it. After that failed, she'd watched a little television, but found she couldn't even follow the plot of a Hallmark movie. She had puttered around her house for hours, finally going to bed much later than usual. She hadn't slept much, but during the little sleep she got, her dreams played and replayed the images of Meg, having seizures or gray-faced and unconscious, on the floor or on the stretcher. Then there was a nightmare of being arrested and tried for Meg's murder. Detective Jackson had made it clear he was taking a hard look at her in case Meg's death turned out to be murder. All in all, not a restful night.

Liz knew she needed more sleep before facing the world. She followed Abner to the kitchen and put out fresh food and water for him. With Abner's needs attended to, she texted Victoria, telling her she would be late arriving at the shop. Victoria responded, saying to take her time. After a few minutes of deliberation, she sent Ned a text saying she hadn't slept well, and suggested they meet later than 9 am, perhaps 10 or 11. He immediately responded that he hadn't slept well, either. They agreed to meet at 11.

Liz slept soundly for the next hour and awoke feeling a little better. After a shower, a light breakfast of yogurt and blueberries, and a cup of weaker than normal coffee in deference to her queasy stomach, she felt ready to face the day. Her next issue was what to wear. She stood in her closet, contemplating her clothes for her first date with Ned. She wanted to look nice, but not like she was trying hard to impress. She checked the weather – sunny, but chilly and windy. After a couple minutes of pondering, she settled on tan slacks and dark red sweater to set off the blue of her eyes, adding a scarf to offset the solid-on-solid look of the slacks and sweater. Still feeling a bit pale from lack of sleep, she applied a smidge more make-up than usual, grabbed her favorite fall jacket, and headed out. Despite last night's sleeplessness, the thought of seeing Ned put a small spring in her step.

The fresh morning air revived her even more as she walked to Mariners' Compass, arriving around 10:30. As she entered and paused to inhale her favorite aroma of fabric, Victoria rushed over from the cash register to hug her. "How are you? I know it must have been awful. You're here earlier than I expected." Victoria took a step back and tilted her head to peer at her. "But you look great."

"Thanks. I'm OK, I think. How's Maria? And how was her interview?"

"Maria is really upset – that detective seems to think she might have killed Meg – not on purpose, but as an accident – in a prank that went wrong. I'm sure you know Maria had squabbled with her, and she *had* been in the lounge yesterday morning, even if only for less than a minute. Apparently, that detective seems to think she would have been mad enough to put something in her food. Maybe make her throw up or embarrass herself some other way. He even told us not to let Maria leave Delaware without telling him!"

"That's terrible." Liz shook her head. "He told me the same thing, so I guess he considers us both potential suspects. I kept dreaming about being arrested and tried for murder last night."

"Well, I know neither one of you could have done it. And I'll certainly tell him so if I get another chance! Are you heading into the back office?"

"Actually, no. I'm meeting someone for coffee in a little while, and I want to stay here at the window so I can see when he arrives."

"He?"

Liz felt her cheeks get a little warm; after looking away for a moment to let her blush recede, she told Victoria about meeting Ned at the Math Bowl, before things got ugly, and that Ned was a professor at Lewes College as well as the father of one of her students. Just then, she saw Ned walk up to Java Joe's and look around. Liz's face brightened, and she heard Victoria call out a cheery, "Good luck," as she headed out the door and crossed the street to greet Ned.

Java Joe's was a Lewes institution. Liz recalled having hot chocolate with her parents there before she had even started school. Her memory didn't include Victoria being there, so perhaps Victoria had already been at school. She recalled being delighted by having both her parents' attention, and how she had been careful to be a big girl who didn't spill her cocoa.

Java Joe's had been owned by several different people over the decades. All of them had kept the name and the quirk of all the employees pretending to be named Joe or Jo. Each had re-decorated the space. Gone were the fussy little window valances from the previous owner. The café now had a mid-century hipster vibe, complete with 1960's cups and plates. Liz was glad they had retained the old school curved glass pastry cases. Whatever the décor, Java Joe's always made Liz smile.

Liz and Ned greeted each other with similar warm, but tired smiles and entered the café. She was surprised at how few customers were there, at mid-day on a Saturday. Only one other table had customers. One was Liz's dear friend Caroline Dietz and the other was a woman Liz didn't recognize. Caroline had taught history and business at LHS for a few years before switching to a more lucrative career as a real estate agent. Liz and Caroline waved to each other, but Caroline continued her conversation with the other woman, gesturing to the laptop placed between them on their table.

Liz and Ned approached the counter, and the current Joe greeted Liz. "Hey, Liz, how're you doing? Would you like your usual? A skim milk latte and a scone?"

Liz smiled. "Hi, Joe. I'm good. Yes, I'd like a skim milk latte and one of your cranberry scones."

"Coming right up. And how about you, Professor – your usual Americano? And a muffin?"

Ned chuckled. "Yes, I'd like an Americano and the last blueberry muffin – that one right there," he said, pointing to a muffin in the glass case.

"Have a seat folks, and I'll have your drinks and pastries right out."

Liz and Ned settled into her favorite table by the front window. After an awkward pause, Ned broke the ice. "Wow, a lot has happened since Thursday morning," he began. "How long did you have to wait for your interview with the detective – I assume you were eventually called, right?"

"Yes. I was next after you and Ross. It was almost 3 o'clock by the time he got to me." Liz sighed. "The detective seems to think I might have murdered Meg, although he kept reminding me they're only investigating a suspicious death, at this time. He told me not to leave Delaware without his permission."

"Yeah, me, too." As Liz stared at him, Ned continued, "Meg and I had some issues a couple years ago, and he seems to think I've been angry enough to wait almost two years to kill her." A grin both wry and rueful appeared and then faded from his face.

Joe brought their drinks and pastries. "Here you go, a skim latte and scone for the lady, and Americano and muffin for the professor." Joe stood just behind Ned and wiggled his eyebrows at Liz. *Oh, jeez, grow up, will you, Joe?* She wondered if the warmth in her cheeks was visible to Ned.

Ned waited for Joe to move away before adding, "Meg made a sexual harassment claim against me when I gave her the news that she wasn't making enough progress for her to continue her graduate program. Since I was her advisor, I had to deliver the news." He sipped his Americano. "So you could say she didn't take it well. Not well at all. I was eventually exonerated, but it took months, and my reputation still took a hit." Ned sighed and continued, "And it gets even worse for me. She stalked me for months, showing up randomly at my office, and even outside my condo. So for Ross' sake, I eventually had to get a restraining order. Of course, that expired months ago. And I hadn't seen her in a long time before Math Bowl started."

Uh oh. Is Ned the groping professor Meg told me about? This sure sounds like it. But then why the restraining order? If Ned had been the groper, why wasn't

61

it Meg getting a restraining order against Ned? Whatever happened, I need to proceed carefully with him.

Liz sipped her latte and studied Ned. "So, is that why the detective thinks you might have killed her? Seems unlikely someone would wait so long." She watched as Ned took a bite of the muffin. "He's investigating *me* because I told Maria not to touch Meg's food. As if I'd poisoned it and didn't want Maria to eat any of the poison."

"That reminds me – Ross asked me to tell you he's sorry for telling the detective you'd told Maria not to touch Meg's food."

Liz gave him a half-smile and waved that away. "Please tell him its okay. I'd expect all the people who heard me say that would have told him." She looked into Ned's eyes. "But it's unusual for a teen to be concerned about one of their teachers. You've got a good kid."

Ned beamed. "He's great. And way ahead of where I was at his age."

They sipped their drinks for a few minutes until Liz broke the silence. "I guess this is where we exchange our carefully-edited histories. I'll start. I'm a fifth generation Lewes resident. Two, three, and four generations back were all farmers, and my parents were both teachers. I have one older sister, Victoria, who I think I already mentioned is the primary owner of Mariners' Compass Quilt Shop, right here on Second Street." She gestured across the street toward the quilt shop. "My parents died in a car accident the first year I was out of college. Victoria was already married, so I inherited their house and now I live in the house I grew up in. My only other relative is my grandmother, who lives in The Moorings."

"What's The Moorings?"

"It's a senior community over on Gills Neck Road. It used to be called Cadbury's."

"Oh, yes, I know where you mean." Ned took another bite of his muffin, chewed, and swallowed. "I grew up in Wilmington and moved here when I was offered a tenure track position at Lewes College. My parents still live in Wilmington. No siblings, and Ross is an only child."

Caroline and her companion stood up and headed toward the door. Caroline detoured to Liz's and Ned's table. "Hi, Liz. What's up?"

"Hi, Caroline. This is Ned York." Ned stood and they shook hands.

"Nice to meet you, Ned." Caroline smiled at him and then turned to Liz. "I can't stay – my client wants a big beach house for her extended family." She leaned over and whispered, "She doesn't seem to care about price."

Liz laughed as Caroline turned toward the door. "Excellent! Better not keep her waiting!"

Ned sat back down as Joe stopped by to see if they wanted seconds on anything. They both declined and Joe returned to reading his magazine at the counter.

As Ned took another bite of his muffin, Liz continued, "I've never been married, but I was briefly engaged a few years ago. I had dated a guy for a while, and he surprised me when he popped the question. We called it off two months later – neither of us had told anyone we were engaged nor done any wedding planning. It seemed like both of us realized it had been a mistake to get engaged." Liz paused a moment. "I'm guessing you're either widowed or divorced?"

Ned looked uncomfortable, gulped the last bite of his muffin, and looked out the window. "This is a bit awkward. Actually, I'm still married."

Liz folded her arms and snapped, "I do NOT date married men."

As she reached for her purse and stood to leave, Ned leaned in. "Please hear me out before you go." He reached his hand toward her, a nonverbal supplication, but pulled back; it was too soon.

She wasn't having any of it.

Studying his face for a moment, Liz thought he looked concerned and sad and lots of other emotions she couldn't read. "All right. I'll listen," she said as she sat back down. She leaned back in her chair and folded her arms again, prepared to hear another whiny married man story.

CHAPTER 11

As Liz watched and waited, Ned took a long look out the window and a deep breath. Liz's foot started tapping, but she stilled it as she waited. *This better be good or I'm outta here.* Ned continued gazing out the window as he began his tale. "Everything was good between Amy and me until Ross turned two. Then Amy seemed to lose her interest in a lot of things. She perked up when she met some people in a group – I can't really call it a cult; they don't do anything to keep their members tied in. Anyway, the group focused on relationships, between people and with all the elements of the world. 'How do I relate to this rock? Or that cloud?' They met a couple times a week. I went to a few meetings, but it wasn't for me. They seemed harmless, and Amy was happier than she'd been in a while. This went on for a few more years.

"Then when Ross was in first grade, the leaders of the group decided they were going to move to a ranch in the Cascade Mountains in Washington state. More than half the group moved with them, which surprised me. I hadn't realized how deep those members' commitment was. Amy stayed in Delaware, as did several other members. They kept meeting, but it wasn't the same for Amy. That summer, she decided to drive out west for a visit – two weeks she said. I expected she'd stay longer, but I didn't expect her to stay permanently.

"I took Ross out to visit for a week each of the next few summers, until he said he didn't want to go anymore. He said he hardly remembered his mom anymore, and it just seemed weird to go visit her. And Amy told me he ran up and hugged the wrong woman when he arrived on his last visit."

"Ow, that's gotta hurt."

"I'm sure it did. Then again, she was more than willing to leave Ross here with me. After that, we had the talk we'd been putting off. She told me she had no intention of returning to Delaware. I guess I'd known deep down, but I hadn't faced it. When she didn't return the first summer, we drew up a separation agreement, with me having sole custody of Ross. For the first couple years, I hoped she might come back, so I didn't pursue a divorce. As Ross got older and busier, I just focused on my work and my son. Because I didn't have a reason to file the papers, I simply let it slide." Ned took another deep breath, turned back to Liz, and looked into her eyes.

"And that's why I'm still married. First from hope, then inertia." He paused for a moment. "I like you, Liz, and I hope you'll give me a chance."

With her concerns somewhat reduced, Liz smiled. "Let's get to know each other and see how it goes."

Liz returned to Mariners' Compass but had trouble concentrating on her work. She mulled over her conversation with Ned. The issues between Meg and Ned reaching the point of a restraining order might explain why Meg hadn't wanted Ross on the team. Meg's interest in continuing to help with Math Bowl once she'd heard it was at Lewes College seemed odd, but maybe Meg just wanted a legitimate excuse to be in the same building as Ned? Or perhaps going back to LC was her way to exorcise her demons from her time there? Did the restraining order explain why the police arrived right after the EMTs? Ned seemed like a nice guy – he certainly had raised a nice son – but it looked like it was at least possible that he might have groped Meg and gotten her removed from her graduate program, and maybe even murdered her. Liz thought back to her conversations with Meg; she couldn't remember Meg's exact words about her time at Lewes College, because it hadn't seemed especially important at the time. She doubted Ned had murdered Meg. But he was definitely still married. At least legally.

Fortunately, this week's payroll was routine – everyone had worked their regular hours; there was no overtime, no vacation, no sick time for anyone. As she thought back over Ned's story of his marriage, she stood up and started to leave the office for a chat with Victoria, to get her thoughts. She stopped short and reconsidered. Victoria had been a bossy older sister during their childhoods, and this was the sort of situation that would likely bring it right back. Liz still felt unsettled, but having someone simply tell her what to do was not what she needed. She returned to her desk and computer. Besides, the shop was busy with customers and a class letting out, injecting even more shoppers into the main level of the shop. Even if she wanted to talk with Victoria, there wasn't an opportunity on a busy Saturday afternoon like this. No, this was a discussion for a patient and tolerant friend. As she finished up payroll for the week, she received a text from Caroline, suggesting a beer and an early dinner at Crooked Hammock. Liz smiled to herself. That would be just the right place and Caroline was just the right friend to chew this over with. Without hesitating, she texted Caroline back to accept, and then headed home to get her bicycle. She'd stick to just one beer and have plenty of time to ride back home before dark.

Caroline was already seated at a high-top table in Crooked Hammock's bar area when Liz arrived. Crooked Hammock was a local brew pub with a wide selection of beers and pub food. The backyard was popular in warm weather, often filled with customers, especially families letting their kids run around and play as the adults sampled the brews. Tonight, the air contained the scent of burgers and fries, and a TV above the bar promised a Ravens' football game later. Liz hugged her long-time friend, and they both settled in and ordered their beers and a Bavarian pretzel to share. After their orders arrived, Caroline said, "So tell me about the hunky guy you were at Java Joe's with. What's the deal with him?" Caroline's cheeky grin was firmly in place as she leaned to get the full scoop.

Liz laughed and sipped her beer. "Ned's a math professor at Lewes College. I met him at the Math Bowl this week. He's also the father of one of my students." She paused for another sip. "It'd be a shame if he turns out to be a murderer."

"What?"

"Oh, yeah, and there are a couple other issues. For one, he's still married."

"Yeah, not a lot of potential with married murderers, Liz." Caroline's grin disappeared. "Those are pretty big concerns. Spill it; I want details. Start with the murderer thing."

Liz gave Caroline the basics of Meg's death at Lewes College, and how she, Ned, and Maria had all been questioned and cautioned not to leave the state. "Meg caused problems for Ned a couple years ago, and he's still dealing with the fallout from that. I expect the detective picked up on how angry he is. But Meg had told me one of the professors there had groped her, and she was dropped from the graduate program after she rebuffed him. She didn't tell me it was Ned, but why would she make a harassment claim against someone else? And Ned told me he'd gotten a restraining order against her, so I'm sure there's more to the story on both sides."

"You sure can't get Meg's side of the story now, can you?"

"If only. Then none of this would matter," Liz replied.

Caroline turned thoughtful for a moment. "Anyway, if he were mad enough to kill her, would he really have waited so long? And if he knew he was going to kill her, why would he bother getting a restraining order against her?"

"It doesn't make sense to me, either, but I guess the detective is checking everyone out. You know, even hunky guys can be murderers. Wasn't Ted Bundy supposed to be really attractive, at least in a 1970s sort of way?"

"Way before our time, girl! OK, now what about the part where he's still married? I noticed he wasn't wearing a ring, but that's not a guarantee. Tell me he didn't tell you his wife doesn't understand him or is in an insane asylum."

"No, nothing quite so cliched. She joined some cult and moved to Washington state when the rest of the group moved."

Caroline laughed, "That's a new one. I've never heard that one before." Her expression got serious again. "Do you think it's the truth?"

Liz shrugged. "It's probably not the whole story, but I believe him. It seems odd he didn't get a divorce, even though he said they both agreed it was over. He said he hoped she'd come back at first, and then he just got too busy to bother with a divorce."

Their waiter stopped at their table, and they ordered dinner. Liz chose a beet salad with grilled chicken and Caroline went with her favorite Backyard Burger.

After the waiter departed, Liz continued, "I gotta tell you, though. Ned explained about not pushing for a divorce, and ended by saying, 'I like you, and I hope you'll give me a chance.'"

"Oooh. Good stuff to hear. But a little strong for a first date, especially with the possible murderer angle. Although he's a really *attractive* possible murderer."

"Well, yeah, there is that. I feel pulled both ways now. I want to give him a chance, 'cause it seems like we had a connection right off, but honestly, I want to keep things slow until we know how Meg died."

Their dinners arrived, and the conversation drifted to their respective jobs, and then updates on their other friends' lives. Liz's phone buzzed with an incoming text as they finished their dinners.

"Hey, this is from Ned. Let me see what he has to say." After a pause, Liz said, "He said he wants to talk. I'll let him know I'm with you and suggest maybe tomorrow."

"No, wait. Why not just have him join us here? We've finished eating – we can talk for a little while and I can either stay or go as you want – just give me a high sign. This way, we can both get to know him a little better. And," Caroline's trademark cheeky grin was back in place, "He's not likely to murder us when we're out in public."

Liz agreed and sent the invitation to Ned, who replied he'd be there soon.

Ned arrived just a few minutes later, hair askew and half his shirttail untucked. Liz and Caroline waved him over to their table. He rushed over and announced, "The police have a warrant and they're searching my house."

CHAPTER 12

"Oh, no! Ross isn't still there, is he?" asked Liz.

"No, he's been at a friend's house this afternoon. I called and told him to stay there until I called him again. I didn't know what else to do."

Caroline cocked her head. "Did the warrant say what they were looking for? I think they have to be specific."

Ned frowned. "I was too upset to read it carefully. I just wanted to leave as soon as I could. But the detective gave me a copy. I'll check it when I get back home."

Caroline sat with her hand over her mouth for a little while, looking from Liz to Ned, and back. "I'll admit I don't know you, Ned, but I know Liz and Maria, and I know there's no way either of them could have harmed Meg. I think the detective is barking up the wrong tree – three wrong trees, probably. Do you think the detectives will be able to figure out what really happened? If they're just focusing on you folks, I wouldn't be too sure . . ." Caroline's voice trailed off, and the three of them looked at each other in silence.

Liz broke the silence. "What do you think? Should we try to figure out what happened to Meg, instead of just waiting and trusting the detective to get it right? Being arrested and tried for murder, even if we're acquitted, would destroy our careers, and would certainly ruin Maria's life."

For a moment, Liz looked shocked such an idea had come out of her mouth, but Caroline smiled. "Although I don't know the first thing about figuring out a murder – or a suspicious death, as the detective called it. If it's really murder, it might be dangerous. But I'm in. What do you think, Ned?"

"It was hell when Meg accused me of harassment and then stalked me afterward. I spent months stressed and worried, waiting for the college to finish their investigation and clear me. I don't want to go through anything like that again if I can help it – and a murder charge would be way worse than the harassment complaint." He studied them before continuing. "We're three smart people, and we know some of the people involved better than the police do. I think we can figure out what really happened if we work together." He gazed at Liz, "Liz? Do you really think we can do this?"

"I don't have any better ideas. But first a few ground rules. First, we need to be sure we don't put ourselves in danger. If someone actually *did* kill Meg, they might be willing to hurt or even kill someone else who threatened to expose them.

"Second, we need to be sure we don't do anything illegal or get ourselves in trouble with Detective Jackson." A nervous laugh came out of her mouth before she could stop it. "Make that 'even more trouble,' since he's already looking at you, me, and Maria."

Ned assured her they'd be careful and not take any unreasonable risks. Caroline gave her trademark wry grin and admitted that, since she wasn't under suspicion, she was unlikely to be in any danger herself. Liz pulled in a deep breath, exhaled, and said, "OK. Let's investigate."

Liz was dismayed to realized it was fully dark by the time she and the other fledgling sleuths left Crooked Hammock. "Oh, no. I forgot I rode my bicycle over here. I wasn't planning to stay this long, and I really don't feel safe riding when it's this dark. Caroline, can you give me a ride home? I'll come back and get my bike tomorrow."

"I don't know," Caroline teased. "I'm not sure I want to let a murder suspect in my car with me."

Ned jumped in, "I have my bicycle rack on my car." Immediately, Caroline looked at him with narrowed eyes, a half-smile, and a raised eyebrow. "Oh, right. That murder suspect thing again. OK, Liz, how about Caroline gives you a ride and you two can talk about me. I'll follow you and I'll bring your bicycle on the back of my car?"

The three laughed, agreeing the plan made sense, and both Liz and Caroline admitted that his name would probably come up in the five-minute car ride. Ned loaded Liz's bike onto his car's rack and waited for them to lead the way. When Liz and Caroline were alone in her car, Liz leaned back in the passenger seat, closed her eyes and sighed. "I can't believe how tired I am. So much stress and almost no sleep last night."

"I bet you're ready to drop. Hey, before we get to your house, do you have names of other people who might be involved? I could search real estate records; I know it seems far-fetched, but sometimes you can learn a lot about someone from their transactions."

They pulled up to Liz's house and she replied, "I can think of a couple people from the college, but I've forgotten their names. I'll ask Ned and text their names to you later." She paused before getting out of the car. "And I'll check on Meg's DUI. I know the *Cape Gazette* publishes the arrests, but I don't remember seeing any reports on whether someone was convicted or what their sentence was."

Just then Ned drove up and lifted Liz's bike off his rack. Liz hopped out of Caroline's car and waved to Caroline as she drove away, unconcerned that Ned might be a murderer. Liz felt the same way. She turned to Ned. "Thanks for bringing my bike home. And not getting mad with my silliness about not riding in your car just yet." She was suddenly aware of his scent – guy, with a hint of cloves and pine. Without pausing to consider, she stood on her toes and kissed his cheek. Ned wrapped his arms around her and returned the kiss, but on her lips. *Yum, he tastes good, too.* Liz thought this was the first good thing to happen since Meg died. She floated into her house after they said good night.

CHAPTER 13

L iz awoke feeling relaxed and rested – so much better than the previous morning. The good feeling from her brief kiss with Ned lingered as she started a pot of coffee and put out Abner's breakfast. Before going to bed the night before, she had texted Ned asking for the names of the department head and graduate student she'd met. After receiving Ned's reply, she passed those names – Lowell Ingraham and Brian MacKenzie – as well as Katya Tereschenko, along to Caroline, like she'd promised. If Ned hadn't been Meg's groper, maybe there were other faculty members they should be looking at? She needed to ask him about other possible suspects in the math department or Lewes College more broadly.

She then texted both Caroline and Ned with the suggestion they get together for a planning session over pizza tonight. She'd see Ned tonight, again in a public place, and though she'd quit thinking about Ned as a possible murderer, meeting in a public place would keep her safe and Caroline happy. Her friend's wry humor and brains couldn't conceal her warm heart. The thought made her smile. The thought of seeing Ned again made her smile even more.

For the rest of the morning, Liz puttered around her house, watering her plants, doing laundry and the myriad chores that had accumulated in the previous week, including ten pleasant minutes relaxing in her recliner with Abner draped like a sash from her shoulder to her hip and purring. In early afternoon, she bicycled to Mariners' Compass. She entered the shop and, as usual, closed her eyes and drew a deep breath to savor the shop's scents. When she opened her eyes, she saw a long line at the only cutting table open for use. She headed to the second cutting table, found a cutter with a sharp blade, and beckoned the next customer over. As she chatted with customers and cut their fabric choices, it seemed like a normal Sunday afternoon at the shop.

By late afternoon, most customers had finished their shopping and Liz took time for herself to browse fabrics for a new improvisational wall hanging. She chose blue, green, and brown batiks for the squares and triangles, plus a bright red accent fabric and a creamy solid for the background. This was enough to get her started – she could select batting and backing after she had the top assembled. As she was carrying the fabric bolts to a cutting table, Detective Jackson entered the shop and motioned to her to join him near the door. She set down her fabrics and moved to where he waited, her heart in her throat. *Was he here to handcuff and arrest her? In front of Victoria? Or maybe this is about Maria? Oh, for heavens' sake, just go talk to the man!*

"Hello, Ms. Murphy. We were able to confirm what you told us about Ms. Williamson being fussy about her food."

Liz brightened. "Oh, that's good news. Does that mean I'm not a suspect anymore? Am I free to travel? Is my niece free to travel?"

Detective Jackson smiled and held up a hand. "Let's take those one at a time. First, you aren't a prime suspect now, and I doubt you're going to make a run for the border. So, yes, you can travel without notifying me. But, no, your niece will still need to let us know if she's leaving Delaware."

Liz mulled that over, then asked, "Was Meg's death an accident?"

Jackson sighed. "We still don't know what caused her death,

whether it was an accident on her part, a prank by someone else, or an intentional poisoning. But I'd like to thank you for mentioning she took prescription lithium. Your information changed some of the tests we're running."

"You're quite welcome. I felt bad passing on rumors about Meg, but I'm glad it helped. So, was it an overdose of lithium?"

"No, oddly. Initial tests showed lithium in her system, but at prescription level, not overdose level. It's been just a couple of days, and over a weekend, too, so we don't have all the test results back yet. We still haven't determined the cause of her death."

Detective Jackson turned to go. Liz added, "I'm glad you've verified my explanation. Are you looking at all the other people who knew Meg and were in the faculty lounge – like the math department chair and the graduate student who asked about her, Brian MacKenzie, or any of her former professors?" Liz didn't want to take that too far, since Ned had been Meg's faculty advisor. She also didn't mention KT, since, unlike Ingraham and MacKenzie, she knew and liked KT.

Jackson turned back to her, frowning. "We're looking a number of individuals. I can't really pass along any more information on our investigation. If you have additional information to provide, please let me know. If not, you need to trust the Lewes Police Department; we know what we're doing. Civilians don't need to help us do our job. Do you have any additional information, beyond what you provided Friday?"

Liz paused. "No, nothing I haven't already told you."

"All right. Let me know if that changes." With that, Jackson nodded and turned to leave.

Liz watched as the detective left the shop and strode down the street. *Does he know we decided to find the killer ourselves, or do I just have a guilty conscience about it?*

Ned was sitting in a booth in Pizza Plus when Liz arrived. Pizza Plus was Liz's favorite casual restaurant in town. It was styled as an old-fashioned trattoria with checked tablecloths and red café curtains, matching what Liz imagined a corner restaurant in Florence would look like, and what she hoped to confirm with a tour of Italy someday. It was charming, the food was excellent, and it was affordable on a teacher's salary.

As Liz approached the booth, Ned greeted her, rose, slid an arm around her shoulders and gave her with a quick kiss on her cheek. Liz smiled and slid into the opposite side of the booth. "It's good to see you. How are you doing?"

Ned shrugged. "Okay, I guess. Ross and I spent the morning putting things away – the police left a lot of mess. I can't tell if they took anything. After we got the house back in order, we went for a long bike ride, which helped relieve some of the stress for both of us."

"Detective Jackson came into Mariners' Compass this afternoon. It nearly gave me a heart attack to see him, but he just told me I can travel if I want. He told me there was lithium in Meg's system, but consistent with a prescription, not an overdose." She paused to select a breadstick from the bowl on the center of the table, and after dabbing a little olive tapenade on the breadstick, Liz continued. "I asked him about where they are with the investigation, but he wouldn't tell me anything else. He warned me not to do any amateur investigating." Liz gave a nervous laugh before she caught herself and added, "I swear, it was like he could read my mind."

"That's great." Ned laughed at Liz's startled expression. "It's great you seem to be off the hook. Not that he can read your mind." Ned started to say more but broke off as Caroline entered Pizza Plus. They waved her over and she slid into the booth next to Liz.

"Hi. Good to see you both. My 'buy-the-biggest-house-in-town' lady took a lot of time, but she finally decided on a house down the street from you sister, Liz. You know the house with the statues in front."

Liz chuckled and then groaned. "Victoria hates that house. The owners just keep putting more statues in the front yard. The first one, the big whale, was bad enough. But the mermaid and the dolphin are just too much for her."

Caroline laughed. "My client loves them, so don't expect her to take them out. If anything, she'll add more."

Liz rolled her eyes. "I'll tell Victoria. She'll be thrilled."

All three perused their menus. After a moment, Caroline continued, "Anyway, I only had a chance to look at one of the names you gave me – Lowell Ingraham – but it's interesting. He's got two mortgages *plus* a home equity loan on his house. The total debt is more than twice what the house is worth. I don't know any of his lenders, so I can't ask them what's going on. But it looks like either big debt or fraud, maybe both. And the second mortgage and home equity loan were both done in the last eighteen months."

"Whoa," exclaimed Ned. "I never would have guessed that. Other than being on his third wife, Ingraham always acts like such a straight arrow, and a wealthy one, too."

Just then, Sammy, Pizza Plus's rotund owner and waiter, came by and took their drink orders. Sammy told them about his specials for the evening, "I have chicken piccata and vege-tarian lasagna on special tonight. Both are excellent." He kissed his fingertips in a caricature of an Italian chef. "I will leave you to decide." They spent a few minutes discussing their options and settled on a large meat and veggie pizza to share, plus side salads for Liz and Caroline. Sammy returned, and when Ned gave him their order, he also asked for a large carnivore special pizza to go.

Caroline raised an eyebrow at him. "You feeling extra hungry tonight, Ned? Liz and I have salads; I can promise you'll get the lion's share of our pizza."

Ned laughed. "Yes, I am, but this pizza's for Ross. What he doesn't eat tonight he'll have for breakfast tomorrow." He shuddered a bit at the thought. "I'm glad my teenage years and cold pizza breakfast days are long past."

Sammy brought their salads, and Ned urged Liz and Caroline to go ahead. Caroline drizzled dressing on her salad and asked, "Are there any other people we should investigate beyond KT, Ingraham, and MacKenzie?"

Ned took a sip of his beer before answering. "I'm sure there are others who knew Meg and didn't like her, but I don't know for sure who they might be. How about I check on who taught her classes while she was enrolled? Can you think of anyone else, Liz?"

Liz shook her head, swallowed, and dabbed her napkin to her lips, "What about Kayleigh, the student at the reception desk for Math Bowl? Was she at Lewes College when Meg was a grad student?"

Ned nodded, "Yes, we should check whether Meg assisted with any of Kayleigh's courses or proctored any of her exams. They probably wouldn't have encountered each other otherwise." He paused for a moment to consider. "Let me see if I can check if their schedules overlapped any two years ago. Plus, I'll check this year's schedules to see who else was in the building on the days of the Math Bowl."

They all ate in silence for a few minutes, then Liz asked,

"What about Dr. Westborough? Have I told you about him yet? I don't think so." Liz gave her companions a summary of the rumors she'd heard in the teachers' lounge. "Even if the lithium didn't kill her, he prescribed it, and he's someone she knew. He might have prescribed something else we don't know about. We should look at him."

Ned frowned. "But was he anywhere near Lewes College? Could he have tampered with her food?"

"But he wouldn't have needed to be there, if he prescribed something else. Maybe Meg took another prescription with her breakfast," Caroline said.

"I also want to find out as much as we can about Meg herself. I didn't particularly like her, but I didn't think she needed killing." Liz gave a sheepish smile. "In the circumstances, that was probably insensitive, but I think you guys know what I mean. We need to know if there's something about her that would make someone *want* to kill her, or even like Det. Jackson said, play a mean prank of her. But I *know* it wasn't Maria."

Just then, Sammy brought their pizza and set in on their table with a flourish. "You like your salads?" he asked Liz and Caroline. Both nodded, their mouths too full to speak. "Enjoy," he exhorted. They each helped themselves to slices and began to nibble the just-out-of-the-oven pizza. Liz was pleased to see Ned pick up his pizza slice and eat it from his hand. She'd never liked seeing someone using a knife and fork on their pizza. Maybe that was okay for a thick, deep-dish pizza, but not the crisp, thin crust they had tonight. It was a silly thing, but this looked like yet another sign of their compatibility.

Ned broke the companionable silence, "When my parents started getting older, they wanted me to be able to check where their cars are, in case they have some emergency. I bought a couple of tracking devices and put one on each of their cars.

Now I can tell where they are just by checking an app on my phone. What do you think about getting some and tracking our suspects?"

"That's a great idea," Caroline exclaimed. "You can learn a lot about someone if you know where they drive, where they spend time, who they see . . ."

Liz leaned back from the table, eyes wide, "Is that legal?"

Caroline laughed, "Not if we don't get caught." As Liz continued to look concerned, she continued, "No, seriously, I don't know if it's legal or not. Even if we got caught doing something like that, a decent lawyer could get us off. Mostly because it's something most people wouldn't know was illegal – if it even is."

Liz wasn't convinced. "I know I've heard someone say that ignorance of the law is no excuse. I'm still a bit concerned."

Ned said, "It was certainly legal for me to use them with my parents. They knew about it, and even asked me to do it. We could argue we thought of it the same way." He continued, "I'll order some of the same brand as I bought for my parents. I'll call them replacements. And I can easily put them on sometime during the week."

"Oh, no. You don't get to have all the fun, Ned. I want me and Liz to put them on," Caroline exclaimed. Caroline and Ned bantered for a little while; the discussion ended when Ned agreed to give Liz the trackers when they arrived, conceding Liz and Caroline needed to see what the cars looked like so they could follow them later.

While her friends argued, Liz was still wondering about the legality and what the penalty might be but decided to drop it for the moment. She told herself it was more important for them to find out the truth about what happened to Meg before anyone she cared about was arrested. Or worse.

After they'd each finished another slice of pizza, Caroline

asked, "Can I see where all this happened? You guys were there when it happened, but I've never even been on campus."

Ned grinned, "You want to visit," dropping his voice, "the scene of the crime." In a normal voice, he continued, "That should be okay, if the police have finished there." He shrugged, "We could probably go over there this evening if you want." After a moment, he mused, "So Ingraham has money problems. It's hard to see how killing Meg would help him, though – she didn't have any money, at least not I know of."

Caroline jumped in, "In books, it's always the blackmailer who gets killed."

Liz rolled her eyes, but Ned said, "Hmmm... You know, I could see her finding out something ugly and demanding money to stay quiet. Maybe she was blackmailing Ingraham or someone else over something."

CHAPTER 14

Ten minutes later, Liz was apprehensive as she drove to Lewes College. Talking in Pizza Plus was one thing, but sneaking around Stalnaker Hall at night was another. She couldn't shake Jackson's warning from her head. The parking lot and the building were dark when she parked in the lot by Stalnaker Hall. She was pulling out her phone to cancel this escapade when Caroline drove up beside her and rolled her window down. "OMG, this is so cool."

No, not cool, thought Liz. "Now that I'm here, I'm not so sure this is such a great idea."

"OK. Tell you what – since we have to wait for Ned anyway – let's make him go in first and make sure no one else is around."

"I guess." Caroline continued to chatter to her as they waited, but Liz was distracted, wondering whether this would give Ned a chance to kill both her and Caroline, and leave their bodies for the students with early morning classes to find. *Stop it. Do you really think he's waiting for a chance to kill you? More like he's looking for a chance to get naked with you. And that's a much better scenario.*

Ned's CR-V arriving in the parking lot interrupted her thoughts. He closed his door without making a sound, and the three moved to the main entrance. There were scraps of police tape stuck to the framing near the door, but nothing to block their entry. Liz started as a dry leaf rasped across the sidewalk on the light breeze. Ned worked his key in the lock, and they slipped inside.

"Let's leave off the lights as much as we can," whispered

Ned. "I'm ok being here, but it'd be hard for me to explain why you two are with me. Telling someone I was showing you my office on a Sunday night isn't really plausible.

"Caroline, we mentioned Kayleigh earlier," He gestured toward the entryway. "She's an undergrad who worked the reception and admin functions for Math Bowl. It was set up right here. She gave visitors schedules, maps, directions – whatever they needed. There wasn't anything else going on here."

"Liz, Ned, did Kayleigh drink coffee? Did she go into the teachers' lounge either day?" Caroline's whisper made her seem less sure of herself in the dark hallway.

Liz shrugged, unsure. "I don't remember seeing her in the lounge, but she could have been in there."

"I have no idea," Ned said.

Ned led the way down the hall. They all tiptoed, even though it was unlikely anyone else was in the building. When they reached the point where Meg had collapsed, Liz held up her hand. "This is about where Meg first said she felt sick, and the next thing we knew, she'd hit the floor, clutching her belly, with the last bit of her coffee spilled everywhere." She gestured to the nearest door. "She had just come out of that room with her coffee and bagel." Caroline used the flashlight on her phone to look around the hallway and turned it back off.

Ned opened the door. "This room was used as the faculty lounge last week." They walked in and looked around an ordinary classroom.

"I was hoping to see it like it was last week," murmured Caroline. "Yes, I know that sounds ghoulish, but we might have learned something or seen something the detectives might not have noticed."

"I suppose Ingraham had it cleaned up as soon as the police told him he could. Whether he was involved or not, Ingraham wouldn't have wanted any reminders lingering around here. Want to see the rest?" Ned quietly closed the door behind them.

They walked down the hallway and entered the auditorium. This room was much lighter than the hallway, as the clerestory windows high above their heads let in light from nearby street-lights. Liz moved to the back of the room. "I was sitting near here on the first day." She closed her eyes for a moment. "I was listening to Ingraham drone on about every step in his fabulous career when – oh, wait – Meg came in late Thursday morn-ing. She wasn't in the hallway or the lounge with us Thursday morning."

"And she couldn't have put her food in the lounge fridge until she arrived," exclaimed Ned.

"So, the timeframe for when her food was poisoned is a bit more limited, right? And the people who could have had access might be different," added Caroline.

Liz tilted her head. "I'm not sure what this means, exactly, but we need to keep it in mind when we're working out where Ingraham and MacKenzie were at different times on Thursday and Friday. Early Thursday morning isn't an important time if the poison couldn't have been put into her food until later Thursday or on Friday."

"Do we know if Meg put food for both days in the fridge on Thursday? Before she came into the auditorium or after? Did either of you see food in the fridge marked with her name – at any time on Thursday?" They both shook their heads.

"I use the kitchenette on the third floor near my office," Ned said.

"No, I don't remember seeing anything, but then I was just focused on my own food," replied Liz.

"But we're getting clues," said Caroline. She beamed, "This is so cool. We can do this."

"Wait, I just thought of something else, and this is hard for me to say because I know KT; she caters all the Mariners' Compass events, and I like her. But she had access to all the food in the lounge, and she didn't come into the auditorium with the rest of us. Of course, she wouldn't have had any reason to go to any of the Math Bowl events. Caroline, you remember I gave you her name because she had access to Meg's food. And she had a *lot* of access, which I hate, because I really like her."

"But still, Liz, you're right," Ned chimed in. "She had more access to the food than anyone else. And she was almost certainly alone in the lounge more than anyone else was. But did she even know Meg? We need to look into her."

"They seem to be about the same age. It's possible they both went to Lewes High at the same time," said Liz. "I'll look into yearbooks from those years and see if they were both students then. And I might as well look to see if Brian went to Lewes High while I'm at it."

"I'll see if I can check Brian's transcript; they might have his high school listed."

They made their way through the still-dark hallways, out the main entrance, and back to the parking lot. Ned leaned against his car. "So, let's recap our plans. Caroline, you're checking real estate info on everyone, and any newspaper articles about them." Caroline nodded. "Liz, you're checking at school to see if you can find any connection between Meg and KT or Meg and Brian." Liz agreed, and Ned continued, "And I'll do internet searches on everyone to see what I find. Plus, internal Lewes College searches on Meg's past professors, if they're still here. And check Brian's transcripts. We'll figure this out."

At that, Caroline hopped into her car, waved, and sped out of the parking lot.

"Remind me not to ride anywhere with her," said Ned.

Liz laughed. "She has a great driving record, but it's still pretty exciting to ride with her." After a moment she said, "There's something I've been wondering about for a little while and this seems like a good time to ask you. Back when I was first starting to work with Meg, she told me about her time at Lewes College. She said one of the professors had pushed her against a wall, groped her and tried to convince her to have an affair with him. And that it was about a week after she turned him down that she got dropped from the graduate program."

"I swear it wasn't me." Liz studied Ned as he continued, "But I can see how it looks like it was."

"Yes, especially with this harassment complaint soon afterward."

Ned frowned and shook his head. "That never made any sense; I never laid a hand on her. If someone was harassing her, why didn't she make a complaint against *them*."

Liz started her car. "Well, I just thought I ought to ask you about it. See you later." She backed up, waved, and drove away. She saw Ned staring after her in her mirror.

Liz spent the rest of the evening piecing the striped parts of Maria's quilt. She had cut the cream, coral and peacock blue strips earlier, and now she was ready to begin sewing the stripe sets together. Or was she? A lot could go wrong with stripes – variations in how the strips were cut, sewn, or pressed could make the stripes curve one way or the other. She considered using starch to make the strips less flexible, or even using a fabric stabilizer. But each of those methods would require either a trip to Mariners' Compass or an online purchase she'd need to be sure not to mention to Victoria. Plus, those methods wouldn't get her sewing this evening. She decided to go ahead and just sew and press carefully and pull out her trusty seam ripper if the lines started to wobble or curve.

Her deliberations completed, Liz headed to the kitchen for a small glass of wine to relax before beginning her challenging sewing task. She knew from experience that being relaxed when she sewed made it easier to get quality results. After returning to her sewing room, she collected peacock blue and cream strips and began to sew, taking time to press carefully after each seam was sewn, gently pulling the seam to meet the stripe-width template she had cut from stiff paper, and most importantly, reversing the direction of each seam as she sewed them. By reversing the direction, any minor irregularities would even out rather than accumulate.

Despite trying to focus on her sewing, Liz kept thinking back to her conversation with Ned and trying to reconcile what he'd said with what Meg had told her. Meg hadn't told her *who* had groped and propositioned her; perhaps she'd assumed Liz would never meet any of these people. Liz recalled they'd had that conversation *before* Meg knew the Math Bowl would be held at Lewes College. Still, it seemed odd that Meg would have accused Ned if it hadn't been Ned who groped her. Then again, Ned's denial tonight had seemed sincere. Plus, he'd appeared surprised that Meg had told her someone had, in fact, harassed her and worse. His reaction seemed genuine, but perhaps he was a talented actor in addition to a mathematician. Liz sighed. She liked him and wanted to believe him, but some ugly things still seemed to point toward him. And none of those ugly things boded well for a potential relationship. Then the rest of her conversation with Meg popped back into her head – how Meg pivoted from teary to smug when she said her boyfriend had given her the perfect way to get back at them. What was that perfect idea and why was she so smug about it? Liz knew she needed to figure that out, since it could provide a reason for someone to harm Meg.

After an hour, she draped a peacock blue and cream stripe set on her fuzzy design wall and smiled at her work. She'd only had to rip out part of one seam. It looked pretty good, if she said so herself.

CHAPTER 15

"**D**ad, it's pouring rain. Can I get a ride to school today?"

Ned set down his mug of coffee and checked his watch. "Yes, but we have to leave in the next five minutes. Can you be ready by then?"

"I'm ready now. Meet you at the car." Ross pulled the hood up on his raincoat and dashed outside. Ned shrugged into his blue sweater, smiling as he remembered he'd worn it when he first met Liz, and grabbed his briefcase. He pulled on his bright orange raincoat, locked the door of their condo, and headed out to join Ross.

Lewes traffic was sluggish, as it often was with rain, and the line to drop off at the high school was longer than usual. Ned reflected he didn't need to drop Ross off in good weather, so maybe it was like this all the time. He paused to watch Ross jog along the sidewalk to the school's entrance, and only drove away when the driver behind him tooted her horn.

Even with the delays, he still managed to slide into a chair in the conference room a moment before Lowell Ingraham began his weekly math department meeting. Around the conference room were motivational posters extolling excellence, perseverance, and other virtues. Ned had always found those ridiculous in an academic setting – he'd never met anyone pursuing a doctorate or a tenured faculty position who needed to be cajoled into working hard. But soon after the posters had been installed, Ingraham had begun to reference them during his faculty meetings, so Ned was glad he'd kept his opinion to himself.

In a voice both self-important and somber, Ingraham described at length the sad events of the previous Friday morning. Ned was certain everyone in the department had already heard about the events, either the way they had happened or with gossipy embellishments. When Ingraham began to extoll Meg's excellence as a graduate student and the unfortunate events around her departure from the program, Ned felt prickles in his neck as some of his colleagues eyed him. *Damn Ingraham, anyway.* Ned knew a few of his colleagues believed his innocence regarding Meg's claims, but many were all too happy to believe the worst of a colleague. With each minute that Ingraham droned on with his revisionist history of Meg's academic performance, Ned grew more and more uncomfortable. *Why was Ingraham whitewashing Meg?* Ned started to think maybe Caroline was onto something with her theory of Meg blackmailing Ingraham.

At last, Ingraham moved on to ordinary departmental matters – how conference attendance would be determined this academic year; his perennial reminder against grade inflation, while acknowledging both parents and students had come to expect higher grades with each passing year; and a request for volunteers to assist with planning the department's annual holiday party. None of these topics captured Ned's attention this morning, and he knew Ingraham's support staff would send the details to everyone in an email later in the day. With Ingraham's voice rumbling in the background, Ned's thoughts moved to his offer to buy the GPS trackers to put on Ingraham's and MacKenzie's cars.

Recalling Liz's concern whether it was legal to place a tracker on someone's car without their knowledge or permission, Ned considered a few ways to proceed. If he wanted an answer to that question, he would need to either retain an attorney, which seemed a bit extreme at this point, or perhaps do his research at a computer that wasn't tied to him, maybe one at the Lewes Library. It would be expensive to retain an attorney, and he might need that money for a defense attorney if things got worse. Did it matter if he wasn't the one to place the trackers? Maybe he should just focus on whether *purchasing* them with that intention was illegal. Again, he would have to research that question from the library. If he bought them online, the purchase would be on his credit card and thus tied to him. *Oh, screw it.* He'd order them, and if awkward questions were asked, he'd just say they were spares for the one on his parents' car. Should he have them delivered to Liz? He'd have to ask her for her address, although he'd already been there Saturday night. If he had them sent to his condo, he'd have a great reason to get together with her again. As he mulled that possibility, he realized the room was quiet. He looked up and all eyes were on him.

"Sorry. Could you repeat that, please?"

The rest of the faculty tittered like grade school students, and Ingraham's lips pursed. "I was suggesting we contribute to flowers for Meg Williamson's funeral service once we know when it will be held. Everyone else has commented."

"Sure. That's a great idea." With that, Ingraham ended the meeting. Ned could feel Ingraham's scowl on his back as he left the conference room. He liked the idea of pinning the possible murder on Ingraham more and more.

Liz sat in her Prius in the high school parking lot, listening to the rain pound down on the roof and hood. She had named her Prius Sylvia, based on its silver color. The familiarity of her car helped comfort her on this unsettled and uncomfortable morning. Reminding herself how much she loved her job, and her students, and even some of her fellow teachers, she savored the calming sound of the rain on Sylvia's roof, and took a few steadying breaths, aware she wasn't quite ready to head into the building. Principal Diane Goodwin had called last night to check on her and offer her a few days off to "regain her equilibrium," as she had put it. Liz had declined, thinking it would be silly to stay home when she should be in her classroom, modeling a healthy, supportive demeanor for her students, and being available for the substitute teacher who would have to deal with Meg's classes. Sitting in Sylvia this morning, however, the idea of taking off a few days sounded like an excellent plan. As Liz sat, summoning strength to enter the school, a sharp knock on her driver's window made her jump. Kay Ferrell peered into the car, wearing a concerned expression on her surprisingly youthful face. Kay was one of Liz's favorite colleagues.

"Hi, Liz. I'm sorry I startled you. I heard about Meg. She wasn't my best pal, but I know it must have been awful for you to be there. Diane should have given you a few days leave. Are you okay?"

"Hi, Kay. I'm okay, I guess. Actually, Diane *did* offer. I wish now I'd taken her up on it."

"There will probably be an assembly this morning. You might want to skip it if you think it'll be difficult for you."

Liz gathered her purse and book bag, and rather than use her umbrella, simply pulled up the hood on her coat, and slipped out of the car. "That's a good idea." She and Kay hurried into the school, Kay's supportive presence giving Liz the extra strength she needed. When they reached the hallway toward the gym, Kay gave her a quick hug. "Come talk or call if you want."

Principal Goodwin was waiting for Liz as she reached her classroom. She also hugged Liz, and repeated her offer to take a few days off, but Liz demurred, saying she was already here and wanted to both see and be available for the students who were there when Meg collapsed. "I've learned a little about the investigation, too. My niece Maria Benitez is either a person of interest or a suspect, as is Ross York's father."

The principal shook her head. "Life in a small town – any tragedy hits close to lots of homes." After a moment she went on, "I've planned an assembly this morning to give students the facts, as we have them, and try to discourage wild rumors even if we can't stop them, also to let students know we have extra counselors available, especially for Meg's students. We'll have counselors in all of Meg's classes, at least for the first few days."

"I'd like to skip the assembly, if its all right with you."

"Of course, you can." The principal hugged her again. "And feel free to take time off if you need to."

Liz's day seemed to take forever. With each passing hour, she was reminded of Meg's suspicious death and wished she'd taken the day off. The attendance report showed Maria and the Stevens twins marked as out sick. She saw Ross in her Algebra II class after lunch. He had dark circles under his eyes, and he seemed completely disconnected from the class discussion. Liz thought she and Ross both could have used a 'mental health day' like Maria and the Stevens twins were taking; if you couldn't take one after the horror of last week, she couldn't imagine when.

After the final bell, Liz headed to the school's media center, what she had grown up calling the library. The previous years' yearbooks were right where she remembered. She guessed KT and Meg were both about twenty-five years old, so they would have graduated about seven years ago. Stooping to the bottom shelf and pulling out that year's yearbook, she leaned against the shelves and turned to the index. Margaret "Meg" Williamson had been a senior that year. Liz turned to the page where Meg's senior photo was and saw KT's photo on the facing page. Yes, and there was the name 'Katya (KT) Tereschenko' right below a younger version of the caterer. Both young women looked vaguely familiar to Liz, though she was certain she hadn't had either of them in any classes she'd taught back then. But the two young women had been in the same graduating class, and their last names were close enough that they could have been seated close to each other in classes where the teachers assigned seats alphabetically. Liz turned back to the index, looking for clubs or activities they might have had in common. Meg had been in a bunch of clubs, but KT had been in none. Liz re-shelved the yearbook and dashed out of the library with an apologetic smile to the scowling librarian, tapping her foot by the door. She'd stop by another time to look for Brian MacKenzie in the yearbooks.

CHAPTER 16

That afternoon, Ned had an hour free to start on his sleuthing efforts. First, he debated how many trackers he should order. Maybe there will be other suspects uncovered in their investigations? He could always use a spare tracker for his parents, and Ross would be driving in a couple of years. *Yes, I'm rationalizing. Just get on with it, Ned.* He settled on four GPS trackers and was certain to order the same ones he had bought for his parents' cars. Next, he turned to getting schedules for Ingraham and MacKenzie. Those were available on the Lewes College administrative network. He started to print them but caught himself. Printing would leave an electronic trail he wasn't sure he could explain. Better to hand copy them, which he did.

Ned then reviewed his own file on Meg from the time when he was her advisor. Pulling out her schedule for each semester she had been there, he sat down at his paper-strewn desk and began to jot down the names of all her instructors, leaving out the women professors and the man married to another man. At the end of the process, he was left with only one name – Conrad Towle. Where was Conrad? He hadn't been at the department meeting earlier today. As Ned thought about it, he realized he hadn't seen the data science professor in quite a while, perhaps not even this semester.

Ned walked down the hallway to Emily Watson's office. Emily and Conrad had been an item last year, and he thought she'd probably know where he was.

Professor Watson was in her office and Ned tapped lightly

on her doorframe to get her attention. "Hi, Emily. How're you doing?"

"Hi, Ned. What's up?"

Ned chuckled, trying to look sheepish. "I just realized I hadn't seen Conrad in a while. Do you know if he's teaching this semester?"

Professor Watson pushed her reading glasses onto the top of her head and studied Ned. "Are you looking for other people who might have had issues with Meg Williamson? Maybe looking for someone's name to give to that detective and get him to look somewhere other than you?" Professor Watson scowled at Ned. "It won't be Conrad. He's on sabbatical this semester."

Even knowing he'd antagonized her, Ned pushed on. "You wouldn't happen to know where he is and what he's doing on his sabbatical, would you?"

Professor Watson sighed. "Yes, I do. And I'm sure you're asking me based on the rumors about our relationship last year. I'd have hoped *you* of all people here wouldn't pay attention to rumors." She paused and then continued. "He's researching data science techniques at California Berkeley. On the opposite coast from here. And you'll know from the rest of the stories around here that he's such a tightwad he wasn't planning to come back to Delaware until his sabbatical was over." Another scowl. "You can't pin anything on him."

"Great, thanks. You've been a big help," Ned mumbled as he backed away, grateful for the information but wishing he hadn't been quite so transparent.

Ned returned to his office and sent a friendly email to Conrad, asking about his sabbatical and giving him some of the department news, including a mention of Meg's death during Math Bowl. He included a question about whether Conrad had had a chance to travel much while he was in California, too. *I'll probably annoy him as much as I did Emily, but I still need to ask.*

While he waited for a response from Conrad, Ned worked on getting vehicle information. That wouldn't be so easy to obtain. Ned knew he'd registered his own car with Lewes College security, but he didn't have any way to get information about other employees' cars. He'd have to think about that one, but Conrad wouldn't be a concern – the data science professor's tightwad reputation was well-known; Conrad didn't even own a car. If Conrad *had* come back to Delaware to murder Meg, would he have used a rental? Was the legality of putting a tracker on a rental car different from a privately-owned car? No matter – Conrad would be long gone by now anyway.

What about Kayleigh? He'd told Liz and Caroline he'd check her schedule to see if she had any overlap with Meg, but as he stared at his computer, he didn't see anyway to check for classes Kayleigh had been in and Meg had proctored. Proctoring exams was kind of haphazard in the LHS math department, and he couldn't find any records. Ned's brain started to hurt.

With the items he'd so blithely assumed would easy out of the way, he began to worry again about Jackson's investigation. It was now three days since Meg's death, and two days since the detective had searched his house. *Was he still a suspect?* Probably, since he hadn't heard otherwise – and he knew Liz had heard she was no longer under suspicion. What would happen to Ross if he were arrested? Or worse, convicted? Would Ross have to go live with Amy in Washington? Or be put into foster care here in Delaware? Ned wasn't sure which of those would be worse. But he was sure he would do anything to keep either of those possibilities from happening to Ross. *I'm innocent. I need to stay focused.*

As he stewed, Ned paced around his office. At the window, movement below in the parking lot caught his eye. As he watched, Brian MacKenzie walked across the parking lot, got into an old, beat-up black pickup truck, and drove away. Ned smiled at his good fortune – sometimes it's okay to just be lucky. Even though he didn't get the tag number from MacKenzie's truck, the truck itself was distinctive, and Liz wouldn't have any trouble picking it out from the rest of the cars in the lot. Now, how to get information on Ingraham's car? After a moment Ned laughed to himself – Ingraham had a reserved space.

Two days later, Ned and Liz were enjoying their first romantic date at a local Italian restaurant. As the waiter poured the last of the bottle of Chianti Classico into Liz's glass, he asked "Would you like dessert? Perhaps coffee or espresso?"

Ned raised his eyebrows at Liz. She turned to the waiter and surprised herself by saying, "Yes, I'd like a cannoli and a double espresso." *I guess I'll diet tomorrow. Maybe.* Ned smiled and asked for the same. After the waiter cleared their dinner dishes, Ned slid a small, lumpy envelope across the table. Liz reached for it, and Ned placed his hand on top of hers and looked into her eyes. "This is everything you and Caroline need." After a long moment, he pulled his hand away from hers, and Liz slid the envelope into her purse, unopened. "Brian MacKenzie drives an old black truck, and Lowell Ingraham drives a dark blue Volvo. There should only be one old black truck in the lot, and Ingraham's Volvo will be in a reserved space right by the main entrance. By the way, I ordered four, because I'd rather be prepared if we identify anyone else who needs one. But they only shipped three to me. I'm not sure when the fourth one will arrive; it's on backorder."

Liz and Ned lingered over their desserts and espressos and let the conversation drift away from murder and into more personal areas. Liz didn't want to end this evening – their first actual date. From every appearance, Ned felt the same. After two hours, they could no longer ignore the signals from their waiter that he was ready to seat others at their table, so they reluctantly left the restaurant. Ned held her coat for her, and then she slipped her hand through the crook of his arm as they walked back to her house.

At the door, their lips met in a long, lingering kiss. Liz wrapped her arms around Ned's shoulders and played with a stray curl behind his ear. She felt him pull her even closer to him. "I'd love to invite you in. But it's still too soon."

Ned nodded, gazing into her eyes. "We need to get through this business with Meg's death."

Breathless, but wanting another kiss, Liz whispered, "Yes, and fast."

Ned agreed, gave her one last kiss, and watched her until she was safely inside.

Through the screen door, Liz said good night, and watched Ned walk back toward the restaurant where he'd left his car. A small sigh escaped. She really wanted him to spend some quality time with her, just the two of them. Should she just risk it? He certainly didn't have any reason to hurt her. Of course, what she had in mind wouldn't hurt at all.

CHAPTER 17

During lunch on Wednesday, Liz's phone pinged with the sound she had set up for LHS accounts, indicating an email from Diane's office administrator, titled, "Meg Williamson Funeral Information." Liz put down her grilled vegetable wrap, opened the email, and saw the service would be the next day at one o'clock, at Cold Spring Presbyterian Church near Cape May. Teachers were encouraged to attend, if they knew Meg, and to carpool. Anyone planning to attend needed to alert the administrator as soon as possible so that substitute teachers could be arranged. Liz mulled this information over as she chewed a bite of her wrap. A funeral instead of a visitation or memorial service indicated a burial, which must mean that the police had released Meg's body to her family. So, the autopsy would have been completed. And even if all the laboratory tests weren't finished, there would be enough samples available. Liz set her wrap down; the clinical aspect of her ruminations had squelched her appetite.

Liz knew she'd want to carpool but preferred for it to be with Caroline instead of other teachers. Of course, Caroline didn't even know Meg, so it would appear odd for Caroline to be there. No matter, Liz wanted Caroline to go with her for sleuthing assistance and moral support. Meg's funeral would be an opportunity to see which of their suspects attended or not, and how they behaved. After a few more bites of her wrap, she sent a text to Caroline and Ned, passing along the basics and asking if they wanted to go with her. She got back replies almost immediately, with Ned texting, "No way," and Caroline texting, "Wouldn't miss it." She and Caroline agreed that Liz would pick up Caroline at her office in time to take the 10:30 ferry. That crossing would give them almost an hour to spare, but the next one wouldn't get them there on time.

Liz woke shortly before eight o'clock on Thursday morning. It was a rare weekday when she could sleep in and goof off. Abner seemed to realize there was no hurry this morning, so he stayed on the bed and slept longer than usual, too. Checking the weather forecast, she saw the day would be sunny, yet crisp and breezy. Liz put on her basic black dress, minimal jewelry, and low heels. She planned to take her winter coat. Though she didn't expect to be outdoors long, she still wanted to be prepared. But after a healthy breakfast of yogurt, granola and fruit, Liz was restless. Her conscience pricked at her – here she was planning to attend the funeral for someone she hadn't liked, just for the purpose of watching their suspects. Liz paced around her house for a few minutes, then decided to ponder the issue while she took a short bike ride for exercise instead of pedaling at her usual leisurely pace. She pulled off the dress, changed into cycling gear and, after giving Abner his breakfast, wheeled her bike out for a quick, head-clearing ride on the Junction Breakwater Trail toward Rehoboth Beach.

Liz returned home with pink cheeks and a clear conscience. She'd been asked to mentor Meg, and she'd worked with her in coaching the Math Bowl team. There wasn't any reason for her to feel bad about going to Meg's funeral. If anything, she knew Meg better than anyone else at LHS. After a quick shower, she changed back into her black dress, re-applied a little mascara, and headed off to meet Caroline.

Caroline was waiting in front of her office when Liz drove Sylvia up to the curb. Turning on her flashers for the moment it took Caroline to climb into the passenger seat, she then pointed Sylvia toward to the Cape May-Lewes ferry terminal. She'd reserved their place on the ferry in advance, and was glad she had, since there seemed to be a good many cars in the ferry lines for the middle of a workday. After driving on board, they climbed the stairs to the lounge and were seated by a window close to the bow when the ferry pulled away from the dock.

"I love seeing the Breakwater Lighthouse. I've been seeing it all my life, but I still love it," sighed Caroline. "The Harbor of Refuge and the Cape May Lighthouses are nice, but the Breakwater just says home to me."

"Yeah, me, too. It's one of the best parts of the ferry trip. Victoria, the kids, and I took the ferry trip to watch fireworks back in July. 'The ferry to nowhere,' as Jamie called it. But he looked like he was having a good time." Liz paused for a moment before changing the subject. "I'm worried that we're going to look pretty conspicuous at the service."

Caroline chuckled. "Yeah. From everything you've told me, Meg managed to rub everyone the wrong way. I doubt there'll be a lot of people at the service. We'll just have to act like we liked her. And that'll be easier for me since I never even met her."

"I didn't ask if others from LHS were planning to attend. I hope so since that'll make us stand out a bit less."

As the ferry neared Cape May, the captain announced that drivers should return to their cars. Along with most of the other passengers, Liz and Caroline headed back to the car deck, found Sylvia, and got in. Since they had been among the first dozen cars onto the ferry, they were able to drive away soon after docking.

Caroline found the church on her phone's GPS and gave directions to Liz. They initially drove east toward Cape May but turned north before reaching the main part of town. Glancing at the side mirror to look behind them, Caroline said, "You know, it looks like a lot of the cars from the ferry are following us. I'd thought most of them would head into Cape May or toward the Garden State Parkway."

Liz checked her mirrors and laughed. "It looks like I'm leading a parade." She frowned and glanced at Caroline. "You don't suppose all these people are heading to Meg's service, do you?"

"I don't know, but we'll know soon enough. We didn't see anyone we knew on the ferry, but we were right at the front of the lounge looking out over the water. So, if folks we knew were there, they'd have been behind us."

Sure enough, as they pulled into the church parking lot, several other cars pulled in right behind Liz's car. "This is it. We're here now. Let's head inside and see who else is here."

The organist played somber music as Liz and Caroline slid into a pew on the left side of the church about third of the way from the rear. A few minutes later, Diane, Tiffany, Kay, and Warren sat down in the pew behind them. They all murmured greetings to each other before returning to silence. Liz closed her eyes for a few moments to prepare for what might be an emotional service. Although based on her memories of attending church with her grandparents, Presbyterians were not known for drama.

As the music continued, Liz surreptitiously looked around the church. At the front was a large photograph of Meg on an easel, flanked by dozens of flower arrangements. Liz was glad they were seated toward back. The scent of the flowers was strong where she was; it would be overwhelming at the front. As they waited for the service to begin, more and more mourners entered the church. Every pew was filled, and ushers were setting up chairs in the back. Looking up, Liz saw the balcony was also filled. Many of the attendees looked to be about Meg's age. *I guess she had more friends than I would have thought.* Across the aisle was a small contingent from Lewes College with Brian MacKenzie, Lowell Ingraham and a few other people who looked like academics. She wondered if Brian or Ingraham would speak during the service. By turning her head a little further to the right, her eyes met Detective Jackson's. She started for a moment, then realized he was doing exactly what she was doing – observing the suspects. She nodded to him, then faced back to the front for a moment. Looking over her left shoulder, she spied Jackson's intern, Ms. Lucas standing in the rear of the church, on the other side from Jackson; this was probably a training exercise for her.

At last a side door opened, the minister entered the sanctuary and an older couple along with an elderly woman and a college-aged man slid into the first pew on the right. Probably her parents, brother, and either an aunt or grandmother. Liz mentally chided herself for not thinking about Meg as someone with grieving family members.

The minister cleared his throat and began the service.

From the beginning, it was clear that this had been Meg's family church and that the minister was well acquainted with her and her family. He mentioned how the Williamson family continued to attend the Cold Spring church even after moving to Lewes twenty years ago, crossing the bay on the ferry for Sunday services and other church events. He described Meg's early life and spoke of her struggles to find a career, to find love, and to find peace in her life. And how she had made so much progress on all those fronts before her life was cut short. Liz had certainly seen Meg's progress on finding peace in her life. In just the past several weeks, Meg had become easier to work with, and gone from prickly to likeable. Liz closed her eyes and thought about how Meg could have become a trusted colleague and perhaps even a friend, had she lived. Now, in this moment of calm, she felt the loss for the first time. The minister exhorted those present to seek justice, not revenge, and to strive for forgiveness when her killer was discovered. Liz knew she wanted justice, but forgiveness would be much harder for her.

After a hymn and a prayer, the minister asked if anyone wanted to speak about Meg and her role in their lives. Caroline nudged Liz, and Liz frowned back at her. No way was she speaking. After a long pause, Ingraham stood. The minister beckoned for him to come to the front of the church and he did. He cleared his throat and began to speak to the congregation.

"I only knew Ms. Williamson as a graduate student in the Lewes College Mathematics department. But even from the distance of department chairman to graduate student, I could see so much promise in her. So much as-yet-untapped potential. She was beautiful, yes, inside and out. And she was a gifted mathematician. Many of us were disappointed when she departed the college in pursuit of other goals and other adventures. She was an extraordinary young woman, and it is a tragedy that she was taken from the world so young." Ingraham paused and pulled a white handkerchief from his pocket, dabbed his eyes with it, and touched his nose with it. He folded it, returned it to his pocket, nodded to the minister, and made his way back to his seat.

Caroline nudged Liz again and they exchanged side-eye looks. Liz's suspicions of Ingraham increased. Making it sound like Meg left Lewes College to pursue other adventures, when the department had dismissed her. Or at least that was the story Meg had told her and Ned had confirmed. These people, their muddled relationships, and their contradicting stories confused her, but the whole mess just made her more determined to find the truth about Meg's death.

Ingraham was followed by a couple of teary young women who described Meg as a wonderful friend in high school and college. One alluded to her difficulties in the past year and how she was persevering and how sad it was for her to die just as she was getting her life together. Diane Goodwin was the final speaker. While her sentiments were similar to Ingraham's, Liz knew Diane's words were truthful. Ingraham's, not so much. Liz made a mental note to tell Ned what Ingraham said as soon as she could.

CHAPTER 18

At the end of the service, the minister invited everyone to join Meg's family for the graveside part of the service in the adjoining cemetery. Afterwards, Meg's family would have a receiving line and then a buffet luncheon in the church hall. Liz turned to Caroline and murmured that they could head back to car instead.

"Oh, no. We're more likely to learn something if we go talk with Meg's parents and the Lewes College crowd. And I bet that guy sitting with them is Meg's younger brother." Liz sighed, the need to get away warring with the need to learn everything they could. They joined the rest of the mourners walking toward the cemetery, then stood at the back of the crowd for the blessedly short burial rites. Mourners shifted to permit the family's return to the church first. As the crowd began heading to the church hall, Caroline nudged Liz to point out that the Lewes College contingent was returning to their cars, rather than heading into the church hall. Liz glanced in that direction and noticed a rusty black truck she assumed was MacKenzie's. *Interesting. Where's Kayleigh, the perky co-ed? Did Brian drive here by himself? Or did Brian and Ingraham drive here together? Wonder why they're all leaving now? And I wonder if Jackson and Lucas are noticing this, too?*

Liz and Caroline approached the receiving line at the entrance to the social hall. After a few minutes of awkward small talk with strangers as the line inched toward Meg's family, Liz reached the middle-aged woman she assumed was Meg's mother.

"Mrs. Williamson, I'm so sorry for your loss," Liz said. "I'm Liz Murphy. I worked with Meg at Lewes High School this fall."

At this, Meg's mother gasped, emitted a sob, and grabbed Liz into a surprisingly strong hug. Liz suppressed a squeak from the hug and a sneeze at the scent of violets.

"Oh, I'm so glad you came to Meg's service. Meg spoke of you so often." At that, Mrs. Williamson released Liz from her hug, but continued to hold both Liz's hands in hers. "I'm sure you know that Meg thought you were wonderful, you'd taken her under your wing and helped her with everything she needed to learn about teaching." Mrs. Williamson paused and gazed at Liz with tears in her eyes. "She just adored you; she said you were the big sister she'd always wished she had."

Liz took a deep breath and decided it was time for pleasant white lies. "Meg was a delightful person and a joy to work with. I'll miss her."

Though brimming with tears, Mrs. Williamson's eyes twinkled, and she gave Liz a half-smile. "Honey, I know she was a handful. But even if she didn't let on to *you*, she thought you were terrific."

"She was a beautiful young woman. I'm glad I knew her, and, again, I'm so sorry for your loss." With that, Liz moved to offer her condolences to Meg's father, and then entered the increasingly crowded church hall. As she surveyed the platters of appetizers and beverages around the room's perimeter, Caroline appeared at her elbow.

"I need a drink, and it looks like there's nothing stronger than soda here. Let's get some food and plot our approach." They filled their plates with miniature crab cakes, raw veggies, dip, and crackers, then edged away from their fellow mourners. "And *what* was that Meg's mother was saying? I couldn't hear it, but I was shocked to see her hug you and treat you like you were Meg's best friend."

"She said Meg adored me and said I was the big sister she'd always wanted."

"No, she didn't!" Caroline whispered as her eyes grew large.

"She did! Although she *did* admit Meg was a handful." Liz shook her head at the absurdity.

"So, what's next?"

"Okay, time to do a little sleuthing. Let's see. . . I can't talk to either Ingraham or MacKenzie since they both left. I don't know what I'd ask them, anyway, if they *were* here. Ingraham sure spun a pretty little tale, though, didn't he? I wonder if Jackson caught that. Who else? Wait, I know. I'll talk to her brother."

As Liz moved away, the other LHS teachers approached Caroline. Liz heard greetings and small talk. *Caroline can keep them busy while I talk to Meg's brother.* Liz meandered through the crowd of mourners toward the young man she'd seen sitting the front row with Meg's parents. He was surrounded by a gaggle of teary young women. The two on either side of him had their hands on him, one with a hand on his shoulder and one with a hand on his arm. He looked directly at Liz as she joined the group.

"Hello, I'm Liz Murphy. I taught with Meg. I'm so sorry for your loss."

At that, the young man's eyes filled, and he gave Liz a brief hug. "Let's talk outside," he whispered as he hugged her. "Excuse me for a few, everyone. I'll be back in a minute," he said as he exited the group.

When they stepped onto the porch, the young man turned, "I'm Kevin, by the way. Meg's younger brother." He fumbled in his jacket pocket and pulled out an electronic cigarette. "I'm trying to quit, but maybe this isn't the week for it." He took a long drag from it and studied Liz. "So, you taught with her at the high school . . ."

"Yes, at Lewes High School. She and I coached the Math Bowl team this year, so we worked together on that."

"She loved that." After a pause and another drag, he said,

"She thought you were terrific. She said she learned a lot working with you. Said she could talk to you about stuff." Kevin stared across the cemetery for a moment. "You treated her like you cared. She was going through a tough time, you know. She'd been fine until the past couple of years or so, when her bi-polar hit her hard. And those assholes at the college didn't help any."

Liz had a fleeting thought that she wanted to get as much information as she could without taking advantage of his grief. Even if Kevin looked like he wanted to talk.

"You mean them dropping her from the graduate program?"

"That was just the last straw. And then that guy today saying she left on her own . . ." Kevin shook his head. "Some old geezer kept pawing her and trying to get into her pants. I keep wondering if that guy had the nerve to show up here today." Kevin squinted at Liz. "I'd have thought she'd have told you about that."

"Yes, she did. But I didn't want to pass that along if she hadn't told you."

"She hated them all at the college. No, that's not right. She didn't hate that Brian guy. I never thought he was good enough for her, but she always claimed they were just friends and roommates. Yeah, right. Maybe Mom believed that, but I never did."

Liz's mind was reeling. "She and Brian were in a relationship?"

"Yep. Living together near campus." Kevin took another drag. "But they argued a lot. I always wondered if he'd gotten her booted out of the program. He's a sneaky, backstabbing sort of guy. I didn't trust him as far as I could throw him." Kevin turned off his cigarette and dropped it back into his jacket pocket. "I probably ought to get back inside. Thanks for coming today. And especially for all you did for Meg."

Liz stood on the porch for a little longer, wondering about

what she'd learned from Meg's brother. Meg seemed to have told her family the same version of events. And had been open with them about her bi-polar disorder. Liz found his speculation about a romantic relationship between Brian and Meg to be interesting, but only gave it 50-50 odds; she knew college-age men thought everything was about sex. She discarded his suspicion that Brian had been involved in getting Meg removed from her program – she was pretty sure faculty wouldn't involve other grad students in a decision like that.

As she mulled over her conversation with Kevin, the church door opened, and Caroline and Detective Jackson joined her on the porch. Caroline handed her a glass of iced tea from the buffet. Liz smiled and nodded at the detective.

"Hello, Detective."

Jackson returned her nod, "Ms. Murphy."

Liz swallowed some tea. "This is my friend Caroline Dietz. She's a real estate agent in Lewes." Caroline and Jackson shook hands. An awkward silence ensued. At last Caroline couldn't stand it any longer and said, "Well, we've paid our respects. We can easily catch the 4:30 return ferry if we leave now. Are you ready to go?"

"Before you go, Ms. Dietz, I was wondering how you knew Ms. Williamson," Jackson asked.

"Ah, well . . ." Caroline stammered for a moment. "I used to teach at Lewes High School before I got my real estate license."

"I see," replied Jackson. He looked at Liz with one eyebrow raised. Liz was sure he was working out the timeline for when Caroline would have been at LHS and whether she would have overlapped with Meg. "I don't want to delay you. I know you two have a ferry to catch." He nodded and turned to re-enter the church as Caroline and Liz fled to her car, Liz still holding the tea.

CHAPTER 19

The next day, Liz moved a large tote bag out of the passenger seat as she climbed into Caroline's car. "Can I put this in the back?"

"I guess, but that's our wigs and glasses. I was thinking we could swap our coats, just to mix up our looks a little more."

Liz sighed. "I'm still not sure we need disguises. We're just going as far the parking lot, not inside any building. We don't know anyone on campus other than Ned, and he's not going to turn us in. This all seems a bit dramatic to me."

Reaching behind to lift a bright red bob wig out of the bag, Caroline waved it and flashed a grin. "But it'll be fun and won't hurt anything."

"OK. You'll look cute. I'll look ridiculous. But since no one will see us, why not? Now let's go over our plan. We park behind the dumpster on the far side of campus, away from Stalnaker Hall, and then put on our disguises in the car. We walk separately across campus, because we'd attract too much attention in these get-ups if we walk together. You put a tracker on MacKenzie's old black truck, and I put the other one on Ingraham's Volvo. We don't act like we know each other, and we walk back here, again separately."

"Got it. What could go wrong?"

Liz could think of far too many things that could go wrong. She gave side-eye to her grinning pal, and settled back into her seat as Caroline sped toward the college. They had selected noon on Friday to place the trackers. Liz had a long gap in her schedule with her planning period right before her lunch hour, and Caroline didn't have any appointments until later in the day. Plus, the schedules from Ned indicated both Ingraham and MacKenzie would be on campus. If they could get these trackers in place today, they could start monitoring two of their suspects' locations over the weekend.

They parked and pulled the wigs out of the bag. Liz took the long brunette wig and Caroline put on the bright red bob, looking like she'd done this before. They added large glasses with clear lenses. Liz looked at herself in the visor mirror and laughed, "I'm not sure I recognize myself! OK, you go first. I'll count to a hundred, and then head out. Use your clicker to lock the car. You'll be back before me, so I can just jump in, and we can make our escape."

"That won't work, 'cause I'll be too far away by then. But I cleverly brought a spare key for exactly this situation." Caroline dug a key fob out of her purse, handed it to Liz, and climbed out of her car.

As Caroline trotted away, Liz slunk out of the car and closed the door. She looked around. There were people nearby, but no one seemed to notice her. It seemed as if all the students were either staring at their phones or in their own worlds. Liz reminded herself she was old enough for college students to consider her a dinosaur, and thus unworthy of their attention. With that thought, she walked through campus, trying to match the pace of students she followed.

Liz continued past Stalnaker Hall to the parking lot on the far side of the building. She had the parking lot to herself; Caroline had already left. Crossing the lot to Ingraham's Volvo, she stopped by the car's right rear fender, and dropped to one knee, ostentatiously tying her shoelace. Using her body to hide her hand reaching into the wheel well, she stood, trying to look like she was just steadying herself, and felt the tracker's magnet snap into place. Trying not to look guilty, she glanced around her, saw no one, and felt almost giddy with relief. Time to ske-daddle. Liz picked up her pace, strode around the corner of the building and yelped as she bounced off a toned body. Her arms windmilled as she tried to stop her fall.

Two strong hands grasped her shoulders and held on until she was steady. She opened her eyes and stared in horror into the large, dark brown eyes of Detective Jackson.

"Ms. Murphy. Such a surprise to see you here. And with your latest new hair style. I assume you're suing your hair stylist."

Liz was too mortified to speak.

Jackson continued, his voice low and smooth, "I can't imag-ine any reason you would be here in that silly get-up unless it has something to do with my investigation. And you do recall my advising you to leave the investigating to the professionals." His eyes turned darker and the skin around his mouth tightened. "If whatever you're doing interferes with the *official* investiga-tion, I'll personally arrest you for impeding an investigation."

Liz managed to mutter, "Yes, I get it." Horror and embar-rassment had her stomach in knots, and she felt immobilized by his intense, unwavering gaze. Inside, she was surprised at how sexy she found him when he was angry – dangerous, yes, but sexy, too. *How can I be attracted to him when I'm so embarrassed?*

Shaking off the intensity of the moment, and trying not to twitch with the effort, she moved past Jackson. Hoping he wasn't following her, but too nervous to turn and look over her shoulder to check, she took a long, indirect route back to the car. Caroline had long since returned; she had her disguise removed and her hair combed when Liz returned. Liz wilted into the car, pulled off her wig and glasses, and slumped in her seat with her eyes closed.

"What happened?" asked Caroline. "Did you get the tracker onto Ingraham's car? And how did I beat you back here by such a long time?"

"Yes, I got the tracker on Ingraham's car. Then I *literally* ran into Detective Jackson. He recognized me. Then he ridiculed my wig." Her eyes opened wide as she turned to Caroline. "He ended by threatening to arrest me if I impeded his official investigation."

Caroline laughed so hard she snorted. "I'm sorry. It isn't really funny, although if it were someone else, you might laugh, too."

"Maybe I'll laugh about this in ten years or so." Liz pulled her wide tooth comb out of her purse and used the visor mirror to remove the effects of the snug fitting wig. "I need to get back to school. I don't want to get fired *or* arrested."

"Cheer up. We got the trackers on. And I think I'll have time to work on MacKenzie's real estate history soon."

Liz was getting ready for bed when her phone chimed with an incoming text from Caroline. Picking it up and seeing it was to both her and Ned, she read Caroline's text saying she had big news and suggesting they meet at eight tomorrow morning, at the cannons by the canal. Liz shrugged and sent a text saying she'd be there. Then Ned's reply said he'd be there, too. Abner jumped up on the bed and curled into a large circle at the foot of her bed. Liz smiled as she snuggled under her quilt and reached down to pet Abner one last time for the day; she was looking forward to seeing Ned again.

CHAPTER 20

T he next morning's damp mist made driving Sylvia downtown a wise choice. The line at Java Joe's was already out
the door when Liz arrived at a few minutes before eight. She saw
Ned near the cash register and waved when he turned toward
the door. He handed her a latte, then put his arm around her
shoulders and kissed her cheek. "Any idea what news Caroline
has?" he whispered into her ear.

Liz shook her head, the nearness of Ned making her face
warm. "No clue. But I'm eager to hear it." They sipped their
drinks as they walked toward the 1812 Memorial Park together.
The park commemorated Lewes' survival of a battle against the
British in the War of 1812. Five cannons from that war sat in
the tiny park, pointing away from downtown Lewes and toward
the canal that ran between Lewes and Rehoboth Beach. As the
wind whipped up whitecaps on the dark gray water of the canal,
Liz turned up the collar of her jacket and pulled her scarf a little tighter. Charter fishing boats were moored along the canal,
but all were idle on this chilly morning. Weather like this sent
tourists scurrying for warmer activities.

When Liz and Ned reached the park, Caroline was already
sitting on one of the cannons, wearing a heavy-duty raincoat,
with her feet extended in front of her, looking pleased with
herself. The morning drizzle meant they had the park to themselves. "I'm so excited," she exclaimed. "I didn't think I'd find
out anything, but I did!"

"And good morning to you, too, Caroline," Ned injected.

Caroline laughed and looked up at the gray sky. "You'll be excited, too, when you hear this." She paused and looked at each of them in turn. "Get this. You've got graduate students. They aren't making any money, probably eating ramen every night. They wouldn't want to live anywhere they could afford to buy. So, I had to look at leases."

Caroline paused for another sip of coffee, and Liz said, "Any chance you could pick up the pace here, Mata Hari? It's pretty cold out here."

"Hey, don't rush me, this is too good." Caroline made another dramatic pause and Ned rolled his eyes. "I saw that, Ned. Anyway, I don't work leases – sales are much more lucrative – so I don't have access to those files. I've been watching the two agents who work leases and figured out which file cabinets they use. It took a lot longer to see where they keep the keys to those cabinets, but last night I finally saw one of them put the keys away. I waited until everyone had left – I wore gloves, just in case someone might find my fingerprints, but I didn't think I needed a disguise since no one else was around. Besides, it's my office, too. Anyway, I opened the file cabinet, and eventually found the MacKenzie-Williamson file."

"What?" exclaimed Liz and Ned together.

Caroline laughed, her eyes bright with triumph. "Oh, yeah. A *single* file for the house they rented *together* a couple years ago."

"This is huge," said Liz.

"Damn straight," agreed Caroline. She grinned like a cat with feathers sticking out of its mouth.

The three pondered the ramification of this development in silence for a few minutes, sipping their coffees in the rain, and watching the waves on the canal. After a while, Liz broke the silence. "We need to know whether they were in a relationship, friends, or just roommates. Ned, you were around them at the college – what do you think?"

Ned turned back to Liz and frowned as he spoke. "They knew each other, of course. It's a small department, so any of the graduate students would know each other. I never thought Brian had the social skills to be in a relationship, with Meg or anyone else. Frankly, I'm surprised they were either friends or roommates."

"Well, Meg's brother said they weren't just roommates, but friends with benefits. And they argued all the time. Should we tell Jackson about this? Seems like maybe we should – Jackson told me to tell him if I had any new information. Of course, it might get you in hot water, Caroline. I guess I could figure something out . . ." Liz's voice trailed off.

"*I'm* not going to tell Jackson anything," Ned asserted. "He's already got me as one of his suspects. I don't want to attract any more of his attention."

Caroline raised an eyebrow at Ned. "Even if it got him to look more closely at MacKenzie? And less at you?" Ned shook his head.

All three sipped their coffee in silence for another long moment. The drizzle increased to a light rain, and all three pulled up the hoods on their coats. Liz broke the silence. "You know his first question is going to be 'How do you know this?' I don't plan to tell him we investigated real estate records – he's already threatened to arrest me once. I *really* don't want to lie to him, and I can't see how I would tell him this and then refuse to tell him how I found out. And besides, Jackson probably already knows all this."

Ned agreed, "I only see trouble for us telling Jackson about this. It confirms we're snooping in his case. And suppose they weren't living together any longer – he'd think we're inventing stuff to distract him. And besides, they would have looked at

Meg's home situation, so they *should* already know this."

"OK, so the answer is 'no'," said Caroline. They all mulled over other possibilities for using this gold nugget of information.

"I want to ask him about it," announced Liz. The others stared at her. "No, not *Jackson* – I want to ask *Brian* about living with Meg. I met him the first day of Math Bowl. And Meg's brother thought Brian was a nasty backstabber who got Meg thrown out of the program. I'll figure out some time to accidently run into him." Liz used air quotes around 'accidently.' She continued, "I'll offer my condolences to him and watch his reaction. And play it by ear from there."

The three were silent for a moment. Liz began slowly, "Everyone was saying how much better Meg had been recently, and since I knew – as her mentor – that she'd started taking lithium, I did some research on it. Lithium is lethal if someone takes too much, but Jackson said Meg didn't overdose. I also found saw an article that said it *could* be fatal if taken with St. John's Wort, which is a common herbal remedy, but it has a lot of potential side effects. I wonder if she also used St. John's Wort and her death was just a horrible accident."

Ned looked stunned. "So that's what they took." When he saw Caroline's and Liz's puzzled expressions, he explained, "After the police searched my house, the medicine cabinet was empty. They took all my over-the-counter medicines, but I couldn't figure out what else they took. I don't take any prescription medicines, so I didn't have to deal with those being gone. It must have been the stuff Amy left behind, and they're probably all expired anyway. I don't even remember all the vitamins and herbals she took." Ned grimaced. "This just keeps getting worse."

"I know. I'm sorry. However, my work here is done, at least

for today," Caroline announced. She stood up, bowed deeply, cupped her hand around her ear, and said, "I hear commissions calling my name." She waved and bounced down the street toward her office.

After Caroline left, Ned turned to Liz. "Brian should be around all day on Monday. Do you have a gap in your schedule where you could get away from school?"

Liz nodded, "Yes, my planning period is right before lunch."

"Maybe you could come over for an early lunch on Monday? You can grill Brian, and we could have lunch together. Maybe you could bring some sandwiches or something for us? That would make it look more natural for you to be in Stalnaker. And, no, I'm not really just trying to get you to spring for lunch." Ned grinned.

Liz agreed. Lunch with Ned would be even better than getting Brian to spill his secrets.

CHAPTER 21

As Liz started to say good-bye and head to the shop, Ned caught her hand. "Do you have time to show me your shop? We could do it another time if now isn't convenient."

"Of course. It's still too early for the big Saturday rush." He continued to hold her hand as they walked to the shop and through the door.

Liz watched Ned as they entered the shop. In her experience, non-quilters showed only polite interest in the shop and its contents. Liz knew the racks of fabrics were gorgeous, and the wall hangings were artistic and intricate at the same time. Ned looked impressed, maybe even entranced, by the shop. Eyes wide with delight, he turned to Liz. "It's marvelous!" He pointed to three wall hangings. "Tell me about those. They're the same, but different."

Liz smiled. "Those three quilts are all made with the Mariners' Compass pattern. That's our shop's name and logo, so we always have a few on the wall here." She pointed to the rightmost one of the trio. "This one is made in a traditional set of fabrics, similar to our logo." She moved to the center quilt. "This one is made with a modern palette of colors – it makes the pattern even more striking, doesn't it?" She gestured to the final quilt. "And this one is actually made out of felted wool instead of the woven cotton the others are made of."

"Ross recently had a history unit on Mariners' Compasses. Did you know they were originally used to show wind direction, instead of cardinal directions?"

Liz's eyes widened. "No, I never heard that before. I probably should have done some research beyond Mariners' Compass as a quilt pattern."

Ned repeated his praise of the shop's vibrancy, thanked her, and turned to leave, saying he didn't want to keep her from her work.

"Wait a minute, mister. You haven't seen even half the shop yet." Liz grabbed his hand and tugged him through a doorway into what had been a separate building before Victoria convinced Javier to double the shop's size. Liz saw his attention was captured by the area full of tools. "Most of those are for cutting – rotary cutters, cutting mats, rulers for straight cuts, and templates for other shapes. They let you get more accurate cuts than with scissors."

"And what's all the fluffy stuff?" he asked, pointing to the far wall.

"That's batting. We sell twenty-five different types of batting. It's the inside layer of the quilt." Ned looked puzzled so Liz continued, "A quilt is three layers. The layer you saw on the wall hangings is the top. There's another fabric layer on the back. And in between is the batting. Batting makes it warm and gives it body."

Liz was enjoying showing off the shop to him, and smiled with pleasure when he asked, "Is there more?"

Liz again tugged his hand. "We have a couple rooms upstairs, too." They took the elevator to the second floor, where Liz pulled a keyring out of her purse and unlocked the door to their right. "This is our machine room," she said as she opened the door.

Inside were two types of machines. One type was easily recognized as sewing machines; the others were several feet long. "What are those?" he asked, pointing to the large machines.

"Those are long arm quilting machines. When you sew with a regular machine, the machine stays put, and you move the fabric – kind of like drawing by holding a pen steady and moving the paper under the pen. With these, the fabric stays in one place and the needle moves across the fabric – more like writing. And they handle large quilts easier. We occasionally sell one – and celebrate when we do – but mostly either we use them to quilt for customers or rent time on them to customers for them to use."

"Wow. I never knew such machines existed."

"Would you like to give it a try?" Liz flipped some switches, and the machine came to life. "Put your hands here. . . Push this button to start stitching . . . You can move it at any speed, but mostly just move it like you're writing. Go ahead, just nothing naughty, 'cause we get kids in here sometimes."

Ned laughed, pushed the button, and wrote

"Nice work. You're a natural." Liz smiled, turned the machine off and headed to the door. As they exited the machine room, Ned came face to face with a large block of a woman.

"Young man, are you a quilter?" the block asked in an imperious tone.

Ned smiled at being called a young man. "No, ma'am, not yet. But I'm so impressed with Mariners' Compass it could happen."

Liz spoke up, "Emma, this is Ned York. Ned's a math professor at Lewes College. His son is one of my students." She gestured toward Emma, "Ned, this is Emma Cambridge. She's president of our local quilt guild and teaches a lot of classes for us here. If you were a quilter, you'd know how famous she is."

Ned and Emma shook hands. "I was showing Ned around the shop this morning."

Ned looked impressed, perhaps with Emma, but more likely with the shop. "The shop is great. I had no idea it was as large as it is, and the atmosphere here feels so creative."

"It's nice to meet you, Ned. If you decide to start quilting, be sure to take my beginners' class. It's the best way to get started. And now I must go make sure everything is ready for my class this morning." With that Emma disappeared into the other room on the same floor.

Liz grinned at him. "Emma really is an internationally famous quilter. I wasn't just throwing her a bone. She's won best-of-show awards on four continents, as she frequently reminds us. Her reputation and classes bring in a lot of customers. She creates amazing designs, and her craftsmanship is outstanding. She's been around forever. She doesn't just stay on top of the trends, she sets them. An influencer before we'd heard the term. I'm sure she was on the ark, teaching the animals to quilt." Liz dropped her voice to a whisper, "She's not just an old bat, she's an *essential* old bat."

Ned laughed. They headed back downstairs, taking the stairs this time.

They ran into Victoria as soon as they reached the bottom of the stairs. "Oh, Liz, I didn't see you come in," she said.

Liz introduced Ned to her sister and added, "Ned's son Ross is on the Math Bowl team with Maria." Turning to Ned, she said, "Maria is Victoria's daughter, my niece."

"Oh, yes, I've met your daughter. My son is quite taken with her, too."

Victoria gazed at Ned with sympathy. "That was such an awful thing to happen at the Math Bowl." She shook her head, "And that detective still thinks Maria might have killed that woman. At least he doesn't suspect Liz anymore." Victoria's eyes widened. "Were you there? Did you know her?"

"I was in a different room when she collapsed, but I knew her from her time at Lewes College." Ned paused for a long moment, "And I can commiserate with your daughter – the detective still considers me a possible suspect, too. It's been a difficult time for me and my son. I hope they can find out what happened soon."

Victoria surprised Liz by reaching out and giving Ned a hug. "I'm sorry you and Ross are going through this. I know how hard it is."

Just then, Detective Jackson entered the shop. Victoria strode toward him.

"I hope you're here to tell me you've cleared my daughter. My daughter that you never should have suspected in the first place."

"Yes, Ms. Benitez, we've cleared your daughter. We found a witness who told us exactly what your daughter did – that she was only in the teachers' lounge for a minute or less, and that she didn't go near Ms. Williamson's food."

Victoria appeared only slightly mollified. "Well, good. And about time, too."

Ned smiled at Victoria, "It was good to meet you." To Liz, he said, "See you later, Liz." He nodded at Detective Jackson and started to walk past him.

Jackson put out a hand to stop him, "Edward Alan York, you are under arrest for the murder of Margaret Williamson."

"But I didn't!" Ned exclaimed. He stood still as Jackson placed handcuffs around his wrists. "Liz, take care of Ross. I need a lawyer, see if you can find one for me, will you?"

Liz held her breath as she watched Detective Jackson put Ned into the backseat of his unmarked car and drive away. She turned to Victoria. "I don't know any lawyers. Do you?"

"The only lawyer I know is LaShawn Williams. He did our wills and trusts, but he's definitely not a criminal lawyer."

"Do you think he could recommend someone for Ned?" Liz was trying not to panic.

"I'll call him and see what he says." Victoria pulled her phone out of a pocket and looked around. "I'll call him from the office. No need to make an even bigger spectacle than we've already had."

Liz stayed on Victoria's heels as she speed-walked to the office and listened to her side of the conversation. Victoria finished with, "That's great that you can keep it in the family. . . Thanks again, LaShawn." She hit End on her phone and turned to Liz. "LaShawn's brother LaVon is a criminal defense lawyer. LaShawn said he'd call his brother and let me know if there was any reason LaVon couldn't help Ned. And that we should know Ned is in good hands unless we hear back from him."

Liz pulled Victoria into a tight hug. "Thank you. I wouldn't have known where to start." After releasing Victoria, she added, "Now we need to figure out a plan for Ross. This is Saturday, so I doubt any lawyer is going to get Ned released before Monday morning. He'd probably okay staying at home by himself if this were a normal situation, but I think we need to make sure he's with other people."

"He knows Maria and Jamie, so he could stay with us for the weekend."

Liz considered that idea for a moment. "Let's hold that as an option, but I think it'd be better if he were with a friend's family. He's got such a crush on Maria . . ." Liz's voice trailed off as Victoria laughed.

"Yeah, I'd forgotten that. Probably not the best idea. I have to get *some* sleep this weekend, so I can't be watching them all the time."

"I'll call Ross and let him know what's going on. And see what he wants to do."

Liz was glad she had Ross' phone number; she rarely kept student's numbers in her phone, but she'd made sure the team all had contact information for each other. Pacing back and forth in the small business office, she called Ross and broke the news to him as gently as she could. She was pleased that he stayed calm, and that he readily named a friend with whom he occasionally stayed overnight. Once the plans for Ross to go his friend's home were set in place, Liz emphasized that she would be available to help him any way she could, and that he should call if anything came up. With the most urgent matters taken care of, she closed her eyes, took deep breaths, and tried to relax.

When Liz left Mariners' Compass that afternoon, she was dismayed to see Ned's car parked on Second Street near the shop, with the parking meter flashing red. *He'll get a ticket for sure, and probably get towed if it stays there all weekend.* She pulled out her phone and called Ross again. She knew, if he was anything like other teens, he'd hate to talk on the phone, especially in front of his friend, and would much prefer to text. Even so, he answered on the first ring.

"Hi, Ms. Murphy. Has something else happened? Have you heard anything?"

"No, I haven't heard anything, Ross. But I just noticed your dad's car is parked downtown, at an expired meter, and I don't want it to get towed. Do you have a spare key for the car? Or know where it is?"

"Yeah, I know where Dad keeps the spare. It's hanging on a hook by the front door at home."

"That's great. How about I get Maria, so I'll have someone to drive my car when I'm driving your dad's car? Then we'll pick you up and we'll go over to your home and get the key. Then I can move the car back to your condo parking lot. Maria can be the extra driver, so I have a ride after we move your dad's car. That's confusing, but is it okay with you?"

Ross agreed, and then told her whose house he was at, and how to get there. Twenty minutes later, when Liz pulled up with Maria, he was waiting outside. Liz saw he had his backpack with him; it looked like he didn't plan to return to the Coopers.

"Thanks for thinking about this, Ms. Murphy. I know Dad would hate it if something happened to his car," Ross said as he climbed into the back seat.

They arrived at the Yorks' condo and Ross headed into the condo with his backpack. He returned in a moment without it and handed Liz the key through the driver's window. "I've been thinking about it, and I really don't want to stay with the Coopers all weekend. I'll be fine here. I've got your number, and I promise to call if anything happens."

Liz had seen this coming when she saw Ross return without his backpack. "No, I'm sorry, Ross, but that can't happen. It's just not safe. Your dad specifically asked me to take care of you, and I know that leaving you alone all weekend wouldn't meet his definition of taking care of you."

"I'll be fine. Really." Ross started for the condo.

Maria stepped out of the car and said, "Come on, Ross. I know this isn't what you want, but Aunt Liz is trying to look out for you, like she told your dad she would."

Ross turned and sighed. "Okay. Let me get my backpack. I'll be right back."

In a moment Ross trudged back to the car. Maria put her arm around Ross' shoulders and squeezed for a moment as she took his backpack and got onto the backseat. Ross climbed in the passenger seat. He sighed again. "Chris and his mom kept asking me lots of questions, and I just didn't want to talk to anybody."

"Let's talk about some alternatives. Do you have another friend you'd be happier staying with?" Liz asked.

Ross shook his head, not making eye contact. "I'm tired and overwhelmed, I just want to be alone and sleep."

Maria chimed in. "Do you know my brother, Jamie? You could hang out with him this weekend. Jamie's really low-key – I'm pretty sure he'd leave you alone if that's what you wanted."

Liz didn't look directly at Ross; having dealt with teenagers for years, she knew that touchy subjects were best dealt with by gentle conversations and minimal eye contact. Starting the car, she said, "You could stay with me if you want. I promise to leave you alone and let you sleep. I might even feed you, too."

Ross met her eyes in the mirror, his eyes wide. "Could I? But you wouldn't tell anyone, would you? I don't want it getting around school. Gym class would be hell if the guys knew I stayed at a teacher's house!"

Maria snorted, "I promise not to tell a soul. I've got your back, and that goes for school, too."

"And I promise not to tell anyone except your dad."

At that, they drove back downtown. When Liz got out of her car, Maria took her place in the driver's seat. "I'll follow you back to the condo, Aunt Liz. And then you can take *me* home."

While in Ned's car, Liz took advantage of the opportunity to surreptitiously check out his car. Nothing out of the ordinary, just a standard, well-kept car, lacking anything interesting.

Maria arrived as soon as Liz had parked in Ned's assigned space. Liz carefully locked Ned's CR-V, then gave Ross the keys which he immediately took inside the condo. Ross returned to the car with math textbooks. "Just a little light reading for later."

Liz dropped Maria at her home, and then pointed Sylvia toward her own home. On the way, she asked, "You've told the Coopers you aren't coming back, haven't you?"

"I'd hoped they'd just figure it out, but I guess I should."

As Ross texted, Liz wondered just what she'd gotten herself into by inviting Ross to spend the weekend with her.

CHAPTER 22

Yesterday had been a long, stressful day. Fortunately, Liz had no outside obligations on Sunday. The shop was fully staffed, and she'd finished payroll and bookkeeping Friday after school. After the shock of Ned's arrest Saturday morning, she knew she'd need a little time at home to de-compress and de-stress. It was a good thing that Ross wanted to sleep. Still, she wanted to be available if he needed anything. Quilting was the perfect solution.

After a light lunch of leftover pasta and salad for Liz and a few treats for Abner, both woman and cat returned to the sewing room. Abner jumped onto the windowsill to survey the front yard and Liz went back to piecing Maria's quilt. She'd finished the peacock blue and cream stripe sets before, so she turned her attention to the coral and cream stripe sets. Slipping into a creative groove, she found she was able to construct them with a little less attention, leaving her brain free to wander. When making a quilt as a gift, Liz thought about the person who would receive it. Today, as she pieced the stripes, images of Maria came to mind – a happy, chubby baby, a boisterous toddler, a first grader missing her front teeth for her school photo, and finally, the smart beautiful young woman she was now.

After finishing the coral and cream stripe sets, Liz took a break and headed to her kitchen for a snack. Somehow, staring into her refrigerator made her wonder how Ned was doing in police custody. She finally selected a Granny Smith apple and a can of lime seltzer water. What would Ned be given to eat in his cell? And was Ross okay? The last time she'd passed by her guest room, she heard deep breathing, almost a snore. Ross was sleeping soundly. *Let sleeping teens lie.* Should she call the police station and ask to visit Ned? See if Ross wanted to visit him? Not right now, for sure. But trying to visit Ned herself was a possibility. She considered it as she crunched her apple. By the time she discarded the core, she knew she wanted to try.

Liz started with a phone call to the non-emergency number. Before the first ring ended, an eager-sounding man answered.

"Lewes Police Department. How may I help you?"

"Um, yes." Liz was suddenly tongue-tied and wondered if this was as good an idea as it had seemed two minutes ago. "A friend of mine was arrested yesterday, and I was hoping I could visit him."

"What's your friend's name, ma'am?"

"Ned York. You probably have him as Edward York, but he goes by Ned." Why am I rambling?

"Yes, ma'am, he's here. Right now, on Sunday, he's only being allowed visits by relatives. Or his attorney, of course. Since you called him your friend, I'm guessing you aren't either of those."

"No . . . I'm just a friend."

"Is there anything else, ma'am?"

"Actually, yes. Can you tell me when he'll be arraigned or have a bail hearing or whatever is next for him?"

"His bail hearing is scheduled for tomorrow morning. Thank you for calling."

"Wait. Can you tell me if his lawyer has been to visit him?"

There was a pause on the line. Liz heard the rustle of papers and another man's voice in the background. "No, ma'am. I can't release the names of visitors to you."

Liz sighed. "All right. Thank you."

Liz returned to her quilting studio, and spent a little while pressing the stripe sets she'd made earlier. Her earlier concentration was broken. With her mind no longer on Maria, she could only wonder about Ned's situation. And especially, what evidence had been found that convinced Detective Jackson of Ned's guilt. Meg's symptoms had been both sudden and overwhelming, Liz could only think she'd been poisoned somehow and by someone. Since no one else was even ill, it looked to Liz like it must have been something in the food Meg – and only Meg – ate. Was it just chance that no one else had been poisoned? No, she thought, someone must have known what food Meg would eat and had been willing to risk others eating the same food. Whoever had done that had risked the health of a lot of people in order to harm Meg. There was a recklessness there that made Liz shudder.

Liz moved on from her stripe sets to the Flying Geese blocks. Since she hadn't made these in a while, so she checked internet references for specific instructions on how to make them. Realizing she would need a few dozen of the blocks, she opted for the technique that would create four at a time. The first one took her some time to complete, as she was checking back to the article to make sure she was lining up the fabric pieces and then sewing correctly. She double checked before cutting the blocks apart and was pleased to see the Flying Geese were the right size and would have sharp points on the triangles when she sewed them into the long strips needed for Maria's design. But even as she sewed with increasing confidence, her worries about Ned remained. She wanted to believe he was as nice as he was attractive, but she'd seen him arrested yesterday. Could he be guilty? She'd do everything she could to discover to the truth about Meg's murder, hoping against hope that Ned wasn't responsible.

Ross emerged from her guest room mid-afternoon, yawn-
ing and stretching. "I can't believe I slept so long, Ms. Murphy.
Thank you for letting me sleep, but am I in trouble?"

"It's not a problem for me. Are you hungry?" Ross mulled
that over for a while and admitted he could eat, if it wasn't any
bother.

"Would you like a grilled cheese sandwich and tomato
soup?"

Ross perked up. "That'd be great, Ms. Murphy." As Liz
heated soup and rustled up the quick sandwich, Abner thud-
ded his way into the kitchen and stopped a few feet from where
Ross sat at Liz's kitchen table. "I didn't know you had a cat, Ms.
Murphy. I didn't see him last night."

"He was probably napping somewhere when we got home
and came out for his dinner later."

"He's huge. Is he a normal cat?" Ross asked.

Liz laughed. "Yes, Abner's a Maine Coon. They were bred
to be large, with thick coats and big furry paws to thrive in
Maine winters."

"Abner's a funny name for a cat."

"I wanted to give him a name that sounded like he was from
Maine." At that, Abner walked over to Ross and rubbed against
his legs.

"Can I pet him?"

"Sure. He's asking you to."

Ross petted Abner until Liz brought his lunch over to the
table. As soon as the food was in front of him, he began to wolf
it down. He paused, as if he just realized he could be a tad more
polite, and he set down his spoon for a moment. "Have you

heard anything about Dad today?"

"I called the police station to see if I could visit, but they told me only his lawyer or relatives could visit. I'd just called myself a friend, so I couldn't fib and say I was his sister." Ross chuckled. "They told me his bail hearing would be tomorrow, Monday morning. Do you want to visit him?'

Ross shook his head. "No, I don't want to see him in jail. Unless you think it'd make him feel better. . . No, it'd probably make him feel worse for me to see him through bars. If he stays there a long time, I'll visit, but I definitely want to go to his hearing tomorrow."

"Of course. I'll drop you off on my way to school in the morning."

"I'll bring my books, so I'll have something to do if I have to wait a long time."

CHAPTER 23

Although Liz had sporadically been keeping an eye on the tracking app she had set up on her phone, there had been little activity with either suspect. That changed Sunday evening, when she saw Ingraham on the move, noting his location change as his car traveled from his home toward downtown Lewes. She told Ross she needed to run an errand, then jumped in Sylvia and headed downtown after Ingraham. Sylvia would allow her to go anywhere Ingraham went and would also be a large and comfortable disguise in the unlikely event Ingraham could recognize her from the Math Bowl or the funeral. Plus, if Detective Jackson were anywhere nearby, she was sure she could come up with a believable half-truth.

Liz spotted Ingraham's Volvo pulling into a rare empty space in one of the downtown lots. There was an empty space nearby in the same lot. Unbelievable luck! She watched as he and a much younger woman – perhaps his current wife? – exited the car and headed toward Second Street on foot. Liz counted to sixty, giving them a minute head start, and then strolled in the same direction. Turning the corner onto Second Street, she saw them enter a restaurant. Slowing to glance ever-so-casually into the restaurant window, she saw the host leading them past the bar and into the dining area. Liz smiled to herself – a week ago she'd never considered tailing someone, and she'd just now had her first success. Nothing criminal observed, nothing that would hint at a motive for murder, but it still gave her a thrill to have 'tailed' someone without getting caught. Or arrested.

Or worse.

Liz had seen even less movement from Brian. Brian's truck had gone to a small shopping center on Saturday afternoon, probably a trip to the grocery store there. Other than that, his tracker showed him either at the address on his lease or at Stalnaker Hall. Liz assumed his six-hour stretch at the math building on Sunday was his way of taking advantage of quiet in the building to study and work on his research. Or was he getting away from a house that now felt too empty? Regardless, Liz was vaguely disappointed in the seemingly dull lives these two suspects were leading. On Sunday evening, she made a mental note to ask Ned if either Ingraham or MacKenzie might be moving around Lewes on a bicycle, which could make the trackers pointless. While she drove back home from downtown, she thought through all the information they had gleaned so far. As she did, she remembered sending payments to KT for her catering jobs at Mariners' Compass. She didn't recall the address she'd sent those payment to, but it would be easy to check the next time she was in the shop.

A little after ten o'clock on Monday morning, Liz got a text from Ned, saying he was out on bail, and thanking her for arranging a lawyer for him. She replied during the next class change, asking him to call her during her lunch break if he could.

And so Liz wasn't surprised when her phone rang along with the lunch bell. "Hi Ned. How are you?"

"I'm so glad to be out of that jail cell. It was the longest weekend of my life." Ned drew a ragged breath. "I can't thank you enough for sending LaVon Williams to help me. He got my bail hearing scheduled for first thing today, persuaded the judge I'm not a flight risk, and got the police to turn over the evidence they based the arrest on. He was terrific."

"I'm so glad. Victoria was the one who found him. His brother, LaShawn, is also a lawyer, but he does wills and trusts and real estate. He'd done Victoria's will and trusts, so she asked him if he knew any criminal attorney he could recommend. And it turned out he did."

"And I'm so grateful you let Ross stay you over the weekend. I know he was happier with people he knew rather than a random foster family if Child Protective Services had placed him somewhere. Plus dropping him off at the courthouse for my hearing."

"I was glad to do it. He'd stayed at the Coopers part of Saturday but wanted to stay at the condo alone when we moved your car. I offered to drop him at other friends, but he didn't want to."

"I hope he wasn't any trouble."

Liz laughed, "He wasn't any trouble at all. He slept most of the time I was awake, so I just fed him a couple times. He met my cat, and the two of them are pals already."

"I'm so glad he was here for the hearing this morning, too. It made me feel better, and I think having him there helped nudge the judge to releasing me on bail. LaVon emphasized that I've never been in any legal trouble before, that I'm a college professor, and that I'm a single dad to Ross."

"I'm guess it's going as well as it can right now." Liz paused. "You said LaVon got the evidence the police have. Can you share that?"

"Of course, I don't see why not. It was the jar of St. John's Wort that Amy'd left behind. Apparently, Meg died from too much serotonin in her system. That can be produced by too much lithium – which we know wasn't the case – or by taking St. John's Wort with lithium."

"So how were you supposed to have gotten her to take St. John's Wort?" Liz asked.

"It was found in her food, so the detective claims I put it there sometime when none of the Math Bowl people were in the lounge. He pointed out that I have keys to the building, and I could have put it in her food after hours or early in the day before anyone else was around.

"So, according to the detective, I have motive from the harassment claim, means from having Amy's herbs, and opportunity by having keys to the building." Ned paused and sighed. "LaVon pointed out that there are plenty of other people who had motives, St. John's Wort is commonly available, and lots of people could have gotten to her cream cheese. He also pointed out that the St. John's Wort they confiscated from my house was well past its expiration date and shouldn't have been potent enough to harm her."

Liz mulled that over. "But whoever tampered with her food would have had to know she was taking lithium, right? Otherwise putting an herbal supplement in her food wouldn't harm her."

"Yeah, LaVon was all over that. He asked if the police knew how long she'd been taking the lithium, and they admitted it was more recent than the last time I'd seen Meg. They seem to believe I've had an on-again-off-again affair with her and would have learned about the lithium from her."

"Wow, we've got a lot to research. Who knew about Meg's lithium? Who wanted to harm her? And who could get to her food? And speaking of food, do you still want to get together for lunch? I know we'd planned to have lunch today, but life intervened."

Ned laughed weakly, "I really wanted to have lunch with you today, but, yeah, life sure did intervene. Can we reschedule for tomorrow?"

"Sure. We could do what we'd planned to do today, just tomorrow. I'll bring sandwiches, and maybe find a way to question Brian, while I'm there."

"That's great, and if you want to question Brian, go ahead. But I'd really just like to see you."

The crisp sunny weather continued into Tuesday morning. Liz was disappointed her plan to question Brian MacKenzie prevented her from riding her bicycle to work. Taking Sylvia meant less exercise, but greater speed; she wasn't sure she would have time to pick up lunch, pedal at a furious pace to Lewes College, talk with Brian, have lunch with Ned, and then race back to LHS during her preparation and lunch periods. And returning late wouldn't be something she'd want to explain to Diane Goodwin.

Liz taught on autopilot through her morning classes. Most days, she had limited empathy for students who didn't pay attention in class, but she gained a bit more today. By the end of her Algebra I class, she was glad she had mastered teaching the material years ago and could both explain it and answer questions while her mind was spinning in completely different directions. Like how to question MacKenzie.

At last, she was free. She dashed to her car, stopped by her favorite deli to pick up the sandwiches she had ordered right after homeroom, and drove to Lewes College. Now, what order to do things? Carry the food to Ned's office? Carry the food with her while she talked to Brian? She decided to take the food to Ned's office, question Brian, and then eat with Ned. That way she wouldn't be holding food while she talked with Brian, and Brian wouldn't ask her why she was there with food. Now she just needed a reason to be there in case Brian asked. Considering possible answers to that question in her mind, she realized she was wasting valuable time, so decided to just wing it.

Liz pulled in and parked in the now-familiar Stalnaker Hall lot. She couldn't resist looking around for Detective Jackson and was glad she saw neither him nor his intern. Breathing a sigh of relief, she grabbed the food and trotted up the stairs to Ned's office on the third floor. As she appeared on the threshold, Ned turned from his computer. "Hi, Liz. It's good to see you, and with food!"

"Hi, Ned. It's not haute cuisine or even hot cuisine, but the sandwiches from Patty's are really good."

In a much quieter voice, Ned said, "I saw Brian earlier today, so I know he's around today." Ned cleared a space on his desk for their lunch, and added, "I know Brian is socially awkward, but I don't really think he's dangerous. Still, I'm not entirely comfortable with you talking to Brian alone. If you aren't back in ten minutes, I'll just happen to drop in on Brian to make sure everything is ok." Liz thought it was an excess of caution, but she agreed and headed up to the fourth floor, where graduate students had offices.

Liz passed Brian's office, then doubled back, pretending to be surprised to see him. "Brian, I'm so glad I ran into you," she exclaimed as she entered his office. If you could call it an office. The blinds were closed to exclude as much natural light as possible and the lights in the room were off, so the closet-sized room was more like a cave than an office. She had only recognized him from the light cast by his computer. Moving a small stack of books off a tiny stool, Liz sat and took her jacket off. Continuing in a more somber tone, she said, "I'm so sorry for your loss." Brian looked up from his computer and stared at her. "I'm Liz Murphy. We met the first day of the Math Bowl. You know, before Meg . . ." Her voice trailed off, and she willed Brian to say something, anything. When he didn't, she continued, "It's tragic, really, for you to lose someone close to you, and so young. I saw you at her funeral, so I know you cared about her." She knew she was babbling, but she needed some sort of conversation to happen.

Brian stared at her for a long moment, then turned back to his computer. "I really didn't know her all that well."

Liz pressed on. "Oh, I thought you were closer, and you two lived together."

Brian gave her a fast, sharp glance, then looked somewhere past her left shoulder. "Who told you that?"

"Oh, I just heard it around somewhere. I don't remember who told me that."

At that, Brian sighed and turned to look out the window. "She shouldn't have died so young. And she got such a raw deal here. She was smart. . . and good at math. They shouldn't have made her leave here."

"Do you know what happened?"

Brian turned back toward Liz, still not making eye contact. "I heard a few different versions, and I never knew which one to believe. And even her version changed some over time. But I think it was Ingraham who made her leave." Brian paused for a moment. "And that shrink she saw was bad news. Another guy just trying to get her into bed." With that, his face darkened, and he stood, drawing himself up to his full height. "I'm working. I'm busy. You need to leave."

"Well, all right." Liz fumbled with her purse and jacket,

stalling for time as she put the books back on the stool. "Let me just get my stuff. . ."

Brian loomed over her, his voice low and emphatic. "Leave. Now."

Liz jumped up and grabbed her things. She took one last look at Brian as she turned to leave. Did he have tears in his eyes?

CHAPTER 24

Liz forced herself to appear calm as she walked from Brian's office to the staircase and down to Ned's office. Her heart was still pounding as she entered his office, closing the door behind her. She tried not to gasp when she got a closer look at Ned's face, pinched, with dark shadows under his eyes. She wanted to rush over and hug him, but his office door was glass, and this was his workplace, after all.

"How did it go? Did you learn anything?" Ned had put water bottles beside the sandwiches on his desk.

Liz laughed weakly as she sat down. "I learned Brian is not a nice guy. Not just awkward, like I'd thought before." She sighed and sat down on one of Ned's extra chairs. "I started by offering my condolences, and he claimed he barely knew Meg. Of course, I'd seen him at Meg's funeral, so that was fishy." She described the rest of the conversation. "He kind of scared me when he told me to leave. I'd forgotten how large he is."

"Let's eat and think this through." Ned unwrapped the sandwiches and they agreed he would take the ham and Swiss cheese on rye with dark mustard and Liz would take the turkey with pepper jack cheese on whole grain bread. After he'd swallowed his first bite, Ned said, "So he said he barely knew her, but seemed angry when you let him know you knew they were living together. It sounds like he's minimizing his connection to her."

Liz nodded and twisted open her water bottle. "But there were some things Brian *didn't* say. He didn't deny living with her.

And he didn't say they were just roommates – you know, poor starving grad students sharing a house to save money. Of course, he didn't say much of anything at all." They both chewed as they mulled over the situation. "But really, can you see the two of them together as a couple? Meg was so volatile. And so focused on having everything just exactly the way she wanted. Plus, don't you think she'd be out of his league?"

"Yes, I do." Ned paused for a moment to sip his water. "OK. Let's look at this another way. We don't know they lived together. They signed a lease together. Can we think of why anyone would do that if they weren't going to live together? It's not like a parent co-signing a car loan."

They mulled this over for a couple minutes before Liz broke the silence, "I can't think of any situation where that would make sense. I think we should assume they lived together, at least for a while. They must have been either roommates or in a relationship." Liz took another bite of her sandwich. "Neither makes sense to me. If they were roommates, why didn't he just say so? But I still think it's unlikely they were in a relationship; they're just too different. And not different in a way where they'd be attracted to each other, but different in a way where they probably wouldn't like each other." Liz's face felt warm. Discussing what might make a relationship work or not work suddenly made her uncomfortable.

Ned looked out the window for a moment, then turned back to Liz. She noticed his cheeks were a little darker now, too. "I think you're right, Liz. I just can't see those two in a relationship, either. I bet they were just roommates, and he doesn't want that fact getting to the police – if they don't already know."

Liz smiled. "You know, if I were Brian, I wouldn't want everyone here in the math department to know I was even rooming with her, especially since she was dropped from the program. I can see why he'd be embarrassed if their living situation were common knowledge in the department. I could see Brian being attracted to Meg, but not the other way around." Liz ate more of her sandwich. "There were a couple more thing in the conversation. First, he claimed not to know the circumstances of her getting dropped from the program here, said he'd heard different stories, even from Meg. But then said he thought Ingraham had done it. And he said she was smart and good at math. Oh, yeah, and the other thing was that he threw shade on Dr. Westborough, which means he knew Meg had been a patient of his. Then he seemed to switch from angry to sad – I thought I saw tears in his eyes as I was leaving. Still, I think we ought to focus on Ingraham for now. Yes, watch where Brian goes, but my money is on Ingraham."

Ned finished his sandwich. "We talked about Dr. Westborough before, so I did the research on him we'd talked about. He's had some problems with some of his women patients. He was warned by the state licensing board *twice* in the past ten years for being sexually involved with patients, but he managed to keep his license."

Liz jumped in, "Wow. Good info. Do you suppose he got involved with Meg? She was young and pretty. What if they had an affair, and then she blackmailed him about it?"

Ned stared at the ceiling for a minute. "You think Meg was blackmailing both Ingraham and Westborough? That seems like a stretch. But, yeah, it would be consistent with how she acted around here – she always wanted to press any advantage she thought she had."

"We don't know if she was blackmailing either of them, but I think Dr. Westborough's history means we should take a closer look at him, too. He might have just as good a motive as Ingraham does. He didn't have an opportunity to mess with her food, but he definitely knew about lithium, since he prescribed it! And he could have recommended that she take St. John's Wort, too, knowing it and the lithium could kill her. Although that seems pretty haphazard – it might just make her sick, and she could tell someone about him recommending it. Wouldn't her pharmacist give her a warning if she bought St. John's Wort at the same place she got the lithium?"

Liz finished her sandwich, balled up the paper wrappings and tossed them in Ned's wastebasket. "This is a lot to think about and a lot we have to consider." She stood and picked up her jacket. "I'd love to talk it through with you, but I have to get back to school. Ned, I'm just so glad you're out of jail. And back home with Ross."

"Me, too. Ned sighed. "Now I have to figure out the money side of this mess. I borrowed against my retirement for the bail and emptied my savings for LaVon's retainer. LaVon's good, and a good lawyer doesn't come cheap. I'll be broke if this goes to trial."

Even though the glass door would make her action visible to anyone in the hallway, Liz reached over and placed her hand on his. "You're strong. And you're innocent. You'll get through this."

CHAPTER 25

At the end of the school day Wednesday afternoon, Liz checked the tracking app on her phone. Neither of the suspects had traveled anywhere other than between their homes and Lewes College campus for the past few days, so it almost seemed like a formality to check again. Collecting homework and tests to grade, and stowing them in her book bag, she headed to the parking lot. Her plan was to head to Mariners' Compass for a few hours. The shop stayed open late on Wednesday evenings, with one-day sale items and, often, an evening class. This would mean additional customers buying fabric, and she could assist by cutting fabric or working the cash register. And she could check on the address where she'd sent KT's payments. Even it was just a business address, it might help her get a tracker on KT's vehicle.

As Liz climbed into her car, her phone buzzed with a notification that one of the suspects was on the move. She sat in her car and checked. Sure enough, Lowell Ingraham was driving north on DE Route 1. She sent a group text to Caroline and Ned, but neither were available to follow Ingraham; Ned was leading a late afternoon seminar, and Caroline was with a client. Liz decided to follow Ingraham on her own and get information on KT's address later. With Sylvia at a stoplight, she sent Victoria a text, letting her sister know she wouldn't be at the shop this afternoon, and then pointed Sylvia north on Route 1, some twenty minutes behind Ingraham. The tracker showed he was still headed north.

After driving forty-five minutes, Liz pulled off at an exit, and checked Ingraham's location again. He had stopped. Studying the location, it seemed as if he were at a casino. *Hmmm, that might explain the financial issues, with gambling losses rather than blackmail.* After a few more minutes on the road, Liz pulled into the casino's parking lot and spotted Ingraham's Volvo. Now, where to park? Backing into a spot where she could see his car, but where her own car wouldn't be in his line of sight if he left the casino, she gave a little huff of satisfaction. A huge pickup truck beside Sylvia gave her nice cover. Of course, it might not be there when she came out, but for now it was good.

Before entering the casino, Liz used her phone to check the amenities at the casino and to see what she could do without actually having to gamble at games she didn't know much about. It seemed she could play slots, or at least pretend to play slots, with quarters. The bag of quarters she kept in Sylvia for downtown parking meters would keep her in business a while. Viewing the casino's layout on her phone, she selected a group of slot machines where she could observe most of the gambling area. Of course, Ingraham could be in the casino's restaurant, bar, or hotel instead. She doubted he had driven all the way up here for a spa treatment, although it was possible. If he were in the spa, she'd just have to accept she'd lost him. She couldn't stalk him while he got a massage. *Ick. Now if it were Ned. . . Okay, Liz, back to business.*

After tucking the bag of quarters into her purse, Liz put on her strong, confident, "I know what I'm doing face," and entered the casino. The exterior of the casino was reminiscent of the Acropolis in Athens. As she walked through the sliding glass doors into the atrium lobby, Liz wondered if the employees would be wearing togas to continue the ancient Greece theme. Instead, the décor evoked a tropic lagoon. To her right was a waterfall, where the water slid down three stories into a koi pond. The walls held many aquariums, and there was an aquarium under the glass floor. She tried not to jump as a manta ray slid under her feet. Next to the waterfall was an enormous statue of Neptune with his trident, with a bunch of people taking photos of themselves with the statue. *Enough gawking. Time to gamble.* She headed to her left, where the flashing lights and sounds of the slot machines beckoned.

Liz had never gambled – she worked too hard for her money to give it away – but she wanted to avoid the attention an obvious newbie would attract. Strolling further into the casino, she chose one of the machines and sat down. She was pleased to see it would take her quarters. She had a fleeting thought she ought to be able to expense her gambling expenses to her PI firm, and then stifled the smile that came with the idea of her running an investigation company.

Liz pulled out a quarter and put it in the machine. Just then a middle-aged waitress approached, "Want anything to drink, hon?" From the sound of it, the waitress had begun her life in Baltimore. Liz gaped at the waitress' costume – a long, snug-fitting blue and green sequined dress, with a mermaid tail trailing behind her feet. The waitress chuckled, "I can always tell first timers from the way they look at our uniforms."

Liz pulled herself together enough to say, "I'd like a glass of club soda and lime, please." After the waitress brought her drink, Liz took the opportunity to look for Ingraham. She spotted him playing blackjack at a table near the middle of the room. This was great – she could keep an eye on him while she dropped just enough quarters into the slot machine to look like she was playing.

After an hour the waitress returned. "Want a refill, hon?" she asked. The waitress looked over at Ingraham's table. "Is that your boyfriend over there? I noticed you've been keeping an eye on him."

Liz figured the idea of snooping on a boyfriend sounded better, and less memorable, than snooping on a possible murderer. "Yeah, you got me. Is he in here often?"

The waitress leaned down and lowered her voice. "He's here every Wednesday, and after he gambles, he goes upstairs with a lady every week. You might want to find yourself a better guy, girlfriend. He's a stinker." The waitress glided off to deliver other drink orders. Liz settled in to wait for her club soda while dropping an occasional quarter into the slot machine, and trying to be more subtle as she watched Ingraham out of the corner of her eye.

Liz mulled over the waitress' information. Ingraham's wife could be jealous, and if she suspected Ingraham had been involved with Meg – true or not – that might be a motive for her to want to get rid of Meg.

After another hour, Ingraham checked his phone, finished his hand, and strode out of the gaming area. Once in the atrium, he greeted a young blonde woman wearing a short, skin-tight knit dress. Her four-inch red heels and little red purse matched her skimpy dress. Liz wasn't devoted to fashion, but she knew better than to make an outfit matchy-matchy like the blonde had. As Liz watched, his greeting extended from a hug to a long kiss and then to an embrace with a long grope on the woman's behind. *Probably not his daughter, although she's young enough to be.* As Liz watched, Ingraham detached from the blonde just long enough to get a key from the reception desk, and entered the elevator, once again entwined with the obviously willing blonde. Liz noted the elevator paused on the eighth floor before returning to the reception area. Liz was sure Ingraham wasn't put off by the blonde's shoes, purse, and dress matching.

Gambling and an expensive, much-younger girlfriend could explain financial problems. *Was it possible that Meg had somehow known and blackmailed him about it?* Liz decided to wait ten minutes before heading up to the eighth floor. She wanted to confirm the floor only held hotel rooms but didn't want to run into them while doing so. Looking for a place to let the ten minutes pass without wasting any more money, she spotted the ladies' room near the rear of the lobby. As she entered the ladies' room, she heard a familiar voice, but couldn't quite place it. "I tell you, I saw her here. She's been here about two hours. She was watching Ingraham . . . Looked like she'd never been in a casino before . . ." Liz froze by the door, debating whether to stay and listen or flee. After a long pause, the familiar voice continued, "Well, okay, Detective. Do you want me to bring her in for more questioning or not? Hang on, I'm in the ladies' room for some privacy, and I think someone else just came in."

That settled it for Liz. She raced for her car, her heart pounding. She drove across the street and parked behind a fast-food restaurant. She needed to get her thoughts together and her heartrate back to normal before doing anything else. Some sleuth she was – Detective Jackson's intern had watched her for over an hour and she'd never noticed. After she'd almost been caught placing the tracker on Ingraham's car, she should have realized she needed to be more careful. And with the conversation she'd just overheard, she knew Detective Jackson would not be happy. Did her future include handcuffs?

CHAPTER 26

After her heartrate returned to normal, Liz texted Ned and Caroline to ask them to join her at Crooked Hammock if they were available. They both were. Unlike their last visit, they settled into a table in a quiet corner, away from the families playing outside and the football game on the televisions in the bar area. When they each had a pint of craft beer in front of them, Liz described her visit to the casino, emphasizing Ingraham's behavior with the young and friendly blonde, and minimizing her narrow escape from Detective Jackson's intern. Even so, Caroline and Ned roared with laughter at the image of her running out the casino to evade young Ms. Lucas.

Once Ned got his amusement under control, he adopted a serious demeanor as he told them more about Lowell Ingraham. "Ingraham is married to his third wife now. His first wife died of cancer almost 30 years ago. His second wife was a lot younger than him. About ten years ago, she divorced him and moved back to Des Moines, where she grew up. He married his current wife right after the divorce was final, which I always thought said more than a little about why wife number two left. Wife number three is probably about our age, more than twenty years younger than he is."

Liz mused, "I wonder if wife number three knows about his trips to casino with the lady who might be in the running to be wife number four? I think I saw wife number three when I tailed Ingraham to the restaurant last week. Is it possible wife number three thought Meg was in the running to be wife number four? That might make an excellent motive to kill off her competition."

The three contemplated these possibilities as the waiter delivered their food to their table. After a few bites, Caroline swallowed and said, "So, for the money angle, we have at least three possible reasons for Ingraham to have money problems. One would be gambling debts; another would be losing a lot of money in his divorce settlements, and the third might be blackmail from Meg about his gambling or his fooling around. It sounds like he isn't going to win any 'Husband of the Year' contests . . ." Caroline paused while Liz and Ned hooted with laughter, "so Meg might have threatened to tell the current Mrs. Ingraham about the even younger women looking to succeed her." They agreed to continue to keep an eye on Ingraham, but there was no need to follow him to his Wednesday afternoon rendezvous again. They knew Jackson and his intern were watching that angle, and Liz was happy to avoid any further embarrassment.

After they finished their dinners, Liz told the others she had discovered a connection between Meg and KT, from their time at Lewes High School, and possibly before. "I've been looking into KT, too. I hate to think it, because I like her, but still. . . I've sent catering payments to her for Mariners' Compass events, so I'll check the address of her business the next time I'm in the shop. I was planning to do that before I followed Ingraham this afternoon." Liz gave a weak smile and her cheeks flushed at the memory. "And I'll check with some other teachers to see if I can find out if Meg and KT were friends, enemies, or whatever in high school. I started teaching at Lewes High shortly before they were both there as students, but I don't remember either of them. I'll ask teachers who were there before me and try to find someone who remembers one or both of them." After a moment, she added, "I was annoying the librarian by being there after the last bell, so I didn't have a chance to look for Brian in any of the yearbooks. Not that it matters much, since they certainly knew each other in grad school."

Ned caught Caroline up to date on Westborough's licensing issues and added, "We've learned a lot about these people in a short time," mused Ned. "I wonder how much more Jackson has learned." He grinned at Liz, "I don't suppose you'd want to ask him about the investigation again, would you?"

"I'm pretty sure I don't want to." Liz proclaimed as the others laughed. "He warned me once and threatened to arrest me another time. You're welcome to go chat him up if you want."

"Oh, heck, no. I've seen more of Jackson that I ever want to. I've seen him through the bars of a jail cell!"

"And another thing." Ned continued. "I went through Meg's class schedules and looked at all her instructors and professors. I ruled out everyone except one guy, Conrad Towle. He's on sabbatical in California, so he's a long shot. I sent him an email. He'd already heard about Meg's death and told me he hadn't left California. He's got a reputation as extremely frugal, so I really doubt he bought an airplane ticket and flew back here to kill Meg."

Their waiter stopped at their table and collected the dishes from their meals. Caroline asked him for the check. She opened her wallet and pulled out several bills. "I need to get going pretty soon. Are you guys ok with me just leaving my share here?"

Ned and Liz agreed and waved as Caroline left.

After Caroline's departure, Liz hoped for something more intimate with Ned for the remainder of the evening. Instead, Ned was looking all around the restaurant, anywhere except at Liz. Something was different. She waited for him to speak but didn't have to wait long.

"I've had my lawyer draft divorce papers."

"Okay. . . and?"

"And Ross saw them on my desk. I knew he and I needed to talk about it, but our conversation happened sooner than I'd planned." Ned took a sip from his almost-empty beer glass. "Anyway, he's pretty upset. He's still hoping Amy will come back to Lewes and we'll be together like we were."

"Do you think that's likely?"

"No, I don't. And deep down, Ross doesn't expect her to, either." Ned toyed with his fork for a moment. "I guess he's been holding onto hope even though she'd told him she wasn't coming back. I told him I should have filed the papers years ago, once I knew she wasn't coming back. He kept telling me he likes you, and this isn't anything against you."

Liz laughed weakly, "That's good to know."

"Anyway, I told Ross we weren't getting serious, just hanging out together occasionally. I hope you understand. I like you, Liz, but with the arrest, my life is completely upside-down right now. I'm just trying to hold it all together – still be a good dad to Ross and do the basics I need to do at the college." He sighed and looked at her for the first time since Caroline left. "I'm sorry, but I just can't handle romance now. It wouldn't be fair to you. I know I won't be at my best until this is resolved."

Liz mulled this over for a moment. "That makes sense. I know this is a tough time for you. Do you still want to work with us to find out who really did kill Meg?"

"Oh, yes! That's my second priority behind Ross." He paused for a moment, "Now that I think about it, I wouldn't be surprised if Ross is more upset about the arrest and just putting out his anger about the divorce instead of admitting how scared he is about my arrest."

It was Liz's turn to look around the restaurant instead of

meeting Ned's eyes. After an awkward silence, Ned added, "I probably just need to give Ross – and myself – a bit more time to get a handle on our new situation."

The waiter brought their check and they each counted out enough cash to cover the tab and a generous tip. Ned gestured to the waiter, who immediately returned. "We don't need any change." They headed to their cars, saying 'good night' without the kiss Liz had grown accustomed to.

CHAPTER 27

Liz was hurt but did try to understand. As she started Sylvia and headed for home, her thoughts bounced like a ping-pong ball. Her thought that Ned should own his feelings and not put his decision on Ross soon shifted a bit to how she'd never want to come between him and his son. Wondering if she'd ever see Ned again on a romantic level moved to impatience with her own internal drama, because of course she'd see him even if only while they hunted for Meg's killer. Her annoyance at having been moved into the friend zone morphed into being pleased to have made a friend, always a good thing.

As Liz drove home, her phone buzzed, but she didn't recognize the number. Debating whether to answer, her curiosity got the better of her. "Hello."

"Hello, Ms. Murphy. This is Detective Jackson. I'd like to ask you a few more questions. Are you at home?"

Liz wanted to say she'd been expecting his call but hoping to avoid it. Instead, she replied, "No, but I should be there in just a few minutes."

"Alright. I'll see you there soon."

Jackson hadn't arrived yet when Liz got home. Coming in from the garage, she heard her landline ringing. She rarely used it but had left it in place from when her parents lived there, as her parents' old friends used it to call her. Expecting the caller to be someone she had known all her life, she grabbed the phone without checking caller-ID. When she answered, however, she knew it wasn't one of her parents' friends. Instead, she heard a voice say, "Stop snooping or you're going to get hurt."

"Who is this?" Liz exclaimed.

The caller barked a laugh. "Nice try. Just stop snooping." A dial tone buzzed in her ear. She left the receiver off the hook in case Jackson could trace the call, even though she doubted it was possible. Belatedly, she checked Caller-ID, but it only said, 'UNAVAILABLE.'

Just then, the doorbell rang. Liz raced to the door and checked the fisheye to be sure it was the detective. She yanked the door open and exclaimed, "I'm so glad to see you."

Detective Jackson's eyes narrowed. "That's not the greeting I usually get. Is something wrong?"

"Yes, I just got a threatening phone call. Not on my cell, but on my parents' old landline. Someone told me to stop snooping or I was going to get hurt."

Jackson sighed. "I was planning to tell you to stop snooping, too, but without the threat." He pulled out his notebook. "What can you tell me about the caller? Man, woman? Young, old? Any background sounds?"

Liz paused, "The voice sounded like it came out of a computer. I couldn't tell anything about the speaker." She thought back to the call. "No background noises, either."

"Your caller probably used an electronic device to disguise his or her voice."

"Yeah, that sounds right. Oh, wait, I didn't hang up. Can you trace it?"

Jackson shook his head. "No, tracing a call doesn't work like that. Could I come inside and sit down?"

Liz thought for a moment. "You said I'm not a suspect anymore, right? If that's true, then, yes, please come in. Can I get you something to drink? Coffee, tea, and flavored seltzer are about all I have. Although I have a half bottle of wine, too. . ."

"Seltzer sounds good."

Liz opened her refrigerator, "Let's see, I've got grapefruit, lemon, lime, lemon-lime. . ."

Jackson chuckled, "Just surprise me."

Liz returned with a couple of glasses and handed one to Jackson. "Have a seat." Jackson settled on her sofa; Liz sat in the armchair facing him. As she watched him, she saw his eyes flit over the entire room. She guessed those gorgeous dark brown eyes didn't miss a single detail.

Just then, Abner trotted into the room, took a long, appraising look at Jackson, and hopped onto Liz's lap.

"That's some cat you've got there."

Liz laughed. "That's what everyone says. This is Abner. Abner, say hello to Detective Jackson." Abner gave the detective another unblinking look, then settled on Liz's lap and most of the armchair, as well.

"And hello to you, too, Abner." Detective Jackson cleared his throat. "You've got a nice place here, Ms. Murphy."

Liz replied, "Most of the furniture was my grandparents, original from the 1950's and 60's. I've added a few pieces, but mostly I'm glad that mid-century is having a comeback. It makes me look more stylish than someone who's just using her grandparents' furnishings."

"My grandparents weren't so cool, I'm afraid, so I've bought a few pieces online." He cleared his throat a second time, pulled a mint out of his pocket and popped it in his mouth. "I'm not really here to ask you more questions, other than 'What were you thinking following Ingraham to the casino this afternoon?'"

Liz felt herself blush as she tried to find a reasonable explanation. She fiddled with her drink for a little while. As the moments passed, she felt her cheeks keep getting hotter. At last, she admitted defeat. "I don't have a good explanation, not even a plausible lie." She gave a rueful smile and then got serious again. "But since you arrested Ned, you must believe he murdered Meg. I'm sure he didn't, and I'd like to find something that clears him. I think you can admit that my anonymous caller probably wasn't Ned."

Detective Jackson sighed. "You're right, it probably wasn't Professor York. But chasing after Ingraham does nothing to clear other suspects. We're pursuing a few more suspects as it is. And since Ms. Lucas was at the casino today, you know we're keeping an eye on Ingraham."

Liz leaned forward, "Who else do you suspect?"

"As I've told you before, I can't give you that information. But this is a dangerous business, as you see from your anonymous caller just now." Jackson's eyes bored into hers. He closed his notebook and stood. "It's not a game, Ms. Murphy. Please don't do anything else that might put you or your friends in danger. And if anything else threatening happens to you, I want you to call me immediately. Do you still have my card? If not, I'll give you another one."

Liz smiled at him. "Yes, I still have your card. And if you'll wait a second, you can watch me put your number into my phone." She pulled Jackson's card out of her purse and waved it at him, smiling, and tried to juggle both the phone and the card.

Jackson laughed. "Just work your phone and I'll tell you my number." He spoke the numbers and Liz entered them. His dark brown eyes turned serious. "And I mean that about calling me if anything else happens to you."

It was Liz's turn to sigh. "I will, and I'll be careful so nothing else happens. But I wish you'd figure this out really soon." With that, she walked Jackson to the door.

Jackson turned to face her, and Liz was again struck by his

gorgeous eyes and slim, muscular physique that was sure to give her some interesting dreams that night. "I'll have a patrol car drive by your house several times tonight and future nights until we have a resolution. Please be careful. I don't want anything bad to happen to you."

Even though it was getting late, Liz was too keyed up from the evening's events to sleep. As she did so often in such times, she headed to her sewing room. She found Abner napping on a pile of fabric. At least he wasn't on the Flying Geese strips or the stripe sets she'd assembled for Maria's quilt. He raised his head to look at her, yawned, stretched and closed his eyes again to continue his nap.

Liz placed the Flying Geese strips on her design wall, and placed the stripe sets around them. She tried a few different placements, changing how close the Flying Geese sets were to each other and the angles between the Flying Geese sets and the stripe sets. Within a few minutes she was satisfied with her arrangement and took a picture on her phone to make sure she could re-create it if she needed to. She also pulled out the sketches she'd worked on with Maria to confirm her arrangement matched what Maria had said she wanted. Liz paused and pulled out the protractor she kept in her sewing room. *Yep, sixty-degree angles between the Flying Geese strips.* Somehow, her designs always seemed to have sixty- or ninety-degree angles in them, and this one was no different.

Liz mulled over the events of the day as she trimmed the components and sewed them together. Following Ingraham to the casino and being spotted by Jackson's intern, getting put into the friend zone by Ned, the scare of the threatening phone call, and finally her conversation with Jackson. By the time she placed the completed quilt top on her design wall, she was at peace with the idea of friendship with Ned and wondering whether she and Jackson – what was his first name, anyway? – might have a connection other than this case. She was not, however, at peace with the knowledge that a murderer was out there somewhere. Maybe one who had her phone number. Did they also know where she lived?

CHAPTER 28

The next morning was chilly, with intermittent rain showers, so Liz drove Sylvia to school again. As she pulled into the teachers' parking lot, a vague thought tickled her subconscious. She paused, sitting in her car, listening to the rain, hoping the thought would surface. Within a few moments it did – she had sat here, also in the rain, on the first day back to school after Meg's death. Her friend Kay had first startled her, then comforted her. Kay had also offered to talk if Liz needed it. Liz realized Kay was just the person she needed. Even students who don't take higher level math classes take P.E.

Liz checked her watch and saw she still had about twenty minutes before homeroom began. She pulled up her jacket hood, grabbed her purse and book bag, and hurried toward Kay's office next to the basketball court.

"Hi, Liz." Concern shown in Kay's gray eyes as she studied Liz. "I heard you were trying to figure out what happened to Meg."

Liz wanted to deny it, but Kay's obvious concern swayed her to admit it. "Yes, I guess I am. Caroline Dietz is helping me and so is Ross York's dad, Ned. Ned York appears to be the prime suspect, if it is murder, and my own niece is also a suspect if whatever happened was a prank gone wrong. And you know Caroline is always up for a great adventure."

Kay's eyes twinkled. "And you're helping Ross' dad just for the kindness of it?"

A corner of Liz's mouth went up. "Sounds like you've heard

I'd started dating Ned, too. But he wants to just be friends." Liz wasn't surprised – Lewes High School was a small school in a small town, and any news, good or bad, traveled quickly. "I'd like your help. I was teaching here when Meg was a student, but I don't think I ever had her in any of my classes. I was hoping you remembered her, and possibly Katya Tereshchenko, too."

Kay looked away for a long moment. "I suppose you're trying to see if KT might be involved in Meg's death. When I heard you were trying to find out what happened, I thought you'd come by to ask about them." Kay gestured toward the bleachers across the basketball court. "Let's sit there for a few minutes before homeroom. I want to be sure we can see if anyone else is in the area while we talk."

After they were settled on the first row of the bleachers, Kay sighed. "I can't discuss discipline specifics with you, but I hope talking in generalities will help." Kay paused again and turned toward Liz. "It's only been seven or eight years ago, but schools have become much more aware of how much bullying goes on it schools, how much damage it can cause, and how to take steps to deal with it before it gets out of hand. We aren't great at it now, but we're a lot better than we were when Meg and KT were students."

Liz was stunned. She'd wondered about personality conflicts or competition between the girls, but the pieces were starting to fall into place. KT had been, and was still, much smaller than her peers. And she spoke with an accent. Either one of those could have painted a target on her back, but both might have been too tempting for someone like Meg.

Kay continued, "I can't tell you about a fight in the locker room, for example, or any resulting suspension, of course."

"No, of course, not. Even years afterward, confidentiality rules still hold." Liz agreed, her mind whirling.

"But I will say I expect Diane would find a way to help you learn what you need to. I know she's worried about Ross and how his father's legal problems are affecting him."

Liz spent her homeroom period mulling over how she could access LHS' disciplinary files, also wondering whether files for years-ago events would even still be around. In the years she'd been teaching, she hadn't been involved in any situations requiring more than scolding a student during class or in the hallways. She pulled out her handbook from her desk and re-read the discipline section. Should she just ask Diane for access to Meg's and KT's files? Or try to sneak her way into them? She settled on asking, and then snooping if she didn't get anywhere by asking. Liz used the intercom to buzz the office administrator and set up a meeting with Diane during her preparation period.

Diane Goodwin pursed her lips, "It's not that I'm unwilling to help, but Detective Jackson took all of Meg's files away right after her death. Both her current employment records and her student records."

Liz paused to think. "OK. Can I look at Katya Tereshchenko's file? She had access to Meg's food during the Math Bowl, and I'm trying to understand if there's anything in their past relationship that might shine some light on the recent events."

Diane stared at Liz. "You know those files are confidential, even after all these years." She turned and gazed out her office window to the school's front yard, seeming to hold a debate with herself. After a long moment, she turned back to Liz, her face resolute. Even though her office door was closed, Diane lowered her voice. "I need a trip to the ladies room. Please don't touch the keys to the filing cabinets that I'm carelessly leaving behind. I'll be back in fifteen minutes." With that, Diane strode into the storage room adjacent to her office, pulled a large key ring from her purse, sorted through the keys, found the one she was looking for, stuck it into the lock of one of the file cabinets, and walked out of her office, closing the door behind her.

Liz was delighted in her good fortune. Checking that Diane's administrative assistant couldn't see her through the window in the office door, she walked into the storage room, unlocked the file cabinet, and found KT's folder. It was too thick for Liz to read it and absorb its contents in just a few minutes. It was also too thick for Liz to copy everything with the ancient, lumbering copier in the storage room. Liz looked around again, saw she was unobserved, and wished she'd brought her bookbag. With luck she could read it during her free period and get it back into the file cabinet before anyone missed it. She closed the file cabinet as quietly as she could, wincing as the metal drawer slides screeched.

As she turned to leave the storage room, Liz remembered wanting to check on Brian MacKenzie, too. She found the right cabinet and tried three keys before one opened the cabinet. A quick glance at her watch showed her she still had time before Diane's return, so she flipped through the M folders. She was disappointed to find one with MacKenzie as the last name, but with "LeeAnn" as the first name. Sighing to herself, Liz left the storage room. Not even looking up from her computer, Diane's assistant asked if she needed another appointment with Ms. Goodwin since the principal had not yet returned. "Maybe later. I'll let you know," replied Liz.

Liz clutched the folder as she speed-walked back to her

classroom. She locked the door behind her, opened the folder on her desk and began to read. After twenty minutes, she closed it. Even though she hadn't read everything, she'd read enough to know KT and Meg had been involved in multiple disputes, ranging from shouting matches during class to a fist fight in the girls' locker room. In each case, KT had been determined to be the instigator and Meg had been portrayed as the victim, which didn't make sense to Liz. After coaching the Math Bowl team with Meg, Liz doubted that was the correct interpretation. In the document on the fight, KT had insisted Meg had mistreated her for years and she just couldn't stand it anymore. But the document stated KT had no evidence to support her assertions, and so KT had received a three-day suspension.

During her lunch period, Liz returned the folder to Diane. She gave Diane a half-smile as she handed her the file. Diane nodded once. "Thank you." She paused. "As I'm sure you know, this never happened. But I wish you the best in your endeavors."

As she returned to her classroom, Liz decided to attend the Lewes Quilt Guild meeting on Sunday. She didn't always attend, but KT would be catering the meeting and Liz could ask her some questions about Meg and the food at the Math Bowl. It would be a full weekend; Saturday was the Lewes Sidewalk Sale, so she, Victoria, and the assistant manager Sheila were meeting Friday evening to prepare their displays for the sale.

CHAPTER 29

It was sunny when Liz left her home Friday morning, but after checking the forecast, she drove Sylvia instead of riding her bicycle. And she was glad she had, because it was pouring rain when she left Lewes High School that afternoon. She snagged a parking space right in front of Mariners' Compass and darted into the shop. As she shook her umbrella and raincoat, she saw Victoria and Sheila waiting for her near one of the cutting stations. Sheila Robbins had been a friend of Victoria's since they had been in first grade together. Even then, Sheila had been tall and slim. In high school, her flawless chocolate skin, perfect natural hair and six-foot tall model-slim figure had turned heads. And after high school, she'd headed to New York City to model professionally while studying fabric styling at the Fashion Institute of Technology. She'd told Victoria that her professors had been so into fashion that they'd always made allowances for her absences to model at fashion week in Paris or Milan. Liz had always a tiny bit intimidated by her glamorous looks but whenever she was with Sheila, she was disarmed by her friendliness. Sheila was marvelous at assembling fabric groupings and their regular customers asked for her to help them select fabrics when shop wasn't busy.

"Hey, Liz. Think it might rain?" asked Sheila as Liz squelched across the room toward her and Victoria.

"Oh, yeah. I think it might. I sure hope it's nice tomorrow. We won't see anyone at the Sidewalk Sale if it's raining like this." Liz gave Victoria a quick hug and looked at the fabrics Victoria and Sheila had pulled from the racks for the Sidewalk Sale. "You two have put some nice collections together already. Have you thought about what sizes you want to do for them? I mean which ones would be packaged as charm packs, fat quarters, or full-yard bundles?"

"Not yet. We were just getting to that when you got here," replied Victoria.

Liz took in the fabrics again. "You've got a nice selection of cute kid-oriented fabrics, batiks, solids, and autumn and holiday groupings. The kid fabrics are especially appealing. Just look at those bunnies and puppies! I hadn't seen those before." she exclaimed.

"Yes, the children's fabrics will appeal to new aunts and grandmothers, even if they haven't sewn anything in years. With some luck, they'll buy a lot and sign up for classes to brush up on their skills," Victoria replied.

Sheila picked up the ribbon that would eventually go around charm packs. "I'd suggest some charm packs and fat quarters of each group of fabrics," she said. "From previous years, the fabrics on our tables entice new sewists to become customers, and draw our regular customers into the store. I'd leave the full-yard bundles inside the shop. If shoppers see fabrics they want a yard of, they're probably familiar enough with the shop to just come in to select those."

"You're right as usual, Sheila," Liz smiled at both her sister and friend. "How about I start cutting the autumn and holiday fabrics?"

"And I'll start on the batiks and kid fabrics, if you can take the solids, Sheila," said Victoria.

"Do you think we have time to put some Jelly Rolls packages together?" Liz asked.

Both Sheila and Victoria laughed. "We put a dozen of those

together earlier today, and it was about the only thing we got done all day." Victoria reached behind her, picked up a roll and waved one in the air at Liz. "And besides, you know you can't call it a Jelly Roll unless its from Moda."

"Of course, cutting a dozen strips of a dozen coordinating fabrics takes a while. And that just makes one *Jelly Roll*. I'm glad you guys did that. Okay, time to cut." Their plan complete, each headed to a cutting station and began to cut either the five-inch squares known as charm squares or the eighteen- by twenty-two-inch rectangles called fat quarters.

"Hey, Liz. So, tell me about the rest of your evening with Ned after I left you two lovebirds at the Hammock the other night. I want all the details."

Liz laughed at Caroline's lascivious grin and wiggling eyebrows. As she expected, Caroline had been the first person to stop by her tables at the Sidewalk Sale Saturday morning. She'd arrived early to set up the tables and place the fabrics and class pamphlets in attractive arcs on the tables. Fortunately, the previous day's rain had gone, leaving warm sunshine in its wake.

"Hi, Caroline. There's not much to tell." Liz grinned, hoping Caroline would assume a night of romance and leave it at that.

"Your place or his? I'm gonna guess yours, 'cause of his kid."

"Nope to both." The smile fled Liz's face, replaced by sadness. "Actually, he put me in the friend zone as soon as you left."

"No! I don't believe it. I tell you, that man is crazy about you. Dish!"

"I kind of understand. These aren't his exact words, but

I think he's feeling overwhelmed by being arrested for Meg's murder, and what might happen to him and Ross if he's convicted. Plus, he had his lawyer do the papers for divorcing his wife, Ross saw them, and got upset. He said he'd wanted to talk to Ross about the divorce, but Ross saw the papers before he had a chance to."

Caroline mulled that over for a little while and toyed with a few of the packs of charm squares. "I still say he's crazy about you, but he does have a lot going on right now. And sometimes men see a relationship as work instead of a source of support."

Liz laughed. "You're right about that. Hey, you mess up those fabrics and you're going to have to take a class and make a quilt with them!"

"Not a chance, girl. You know I flunked all forms of home ec. I love to sell houses with great kitchens, but *I'm* not going to cook in one." Caroline awkwardly put the charm packs back where they were. "Hey, I gotta go." Caroline stepped around the table to give Liz a quick hug. "We usually get a few potential buyers during the Sidewalk Sale, and I don't want to miss getting a rich client 'cause I'm not in the office." With that Caroline smiled, waved, and strode off down Second Street toward her real estate office. Of course, she hadn't gone more than a few yards before stopping to greet someone else.

As Caroline left, a couple of regular customers and members of the local quilt guild stopped by. Liz greeted them, and they agreed they would do more shopping before or after the guild meeting on the following day. Just as they wandered on down the street, Liz was surprised to see Diane Goodwin and Kay Ferrell approach her tables.

"Hi, Diane. Hi, Kay. Are you two looking to become quilters?"

Kay laughed. "I did try quilting years ago, and liked what I made, but it seemed to take forever to make templates, cut out the pieces and sew them together."

Diane jumped in, "We were talking about it the other day in the teachers' lounge, and I told her that I was sure the tools and techniques made it faster and easier now. So, we agreed we'd give it a try. And where better than your shop?"

Liz beamed at them. "I'd love for you two to join the ranks of the local quilters. We have beginner classes and a guild that's very welcoming to new quilters. In fact, we have a Basics for All class this afternoon at one o'clock, if you want to start right away. Or you could take one of our pamphlets on the classes we teach and think about it. For this afternoon's class, we provide all the equipment and materials, so you don't need to buy anything to use in the class."

Diane and Kay looked at each other and checked their phones for the schedules. "There's no time like the present!" Kay said and Diane nodded her agreement.

"Great." Liz lowered her voice, "Emma Cambridge is the instructor. She has pretty strong opinions about how to quilt, but she's won quilting competitions all over the world. Don't be put off by her style – she really knows her stuff."

Diane and Kay laughed. "We'll be back at one, then. You won't still be working the Sidewalk Sale by then, will you?" asked Kay.

"No, my sister Victoria and other shop employees are taking other shifts during the day. Even though I stand all day to teach, it seems harder on my feet out here. But I might still see you in the shop when you come back."

CHAPTER 30

Liz spent the rest of her shift selling fabrics and signing up other students for various classes. She was checking her watch just as Victoria came out of the shop and joined her. "How's it going?" she asked.

Liz smiled, "Pretty good. I've sent my boss and another teacher into the lion's den with Emma this afternoon. And . . ." Liz paused to pull up her portable credit card reader and show the total to Victoria, "Our take for the morning looks good."

"You're a natural at this." Victoria scowled, and Liz turned to see Detective Jackson walking up to their table. Still scowling, and arms folded to hide the fists she had clenched, Victoria continued, "I hope you're here to apologize for suspecting my daughter."

Jackson gave Victoria a winning smile, "I know you've been upset about that, but you *do* know we've arrested our prime suspect. And, as I mentioned before, we've found a witness who confirmed Maria's version of her time in the teachers' lounge, that she was only in the room for a moment and that she didn't go anywhere near Ms. Williamson's food."

Victoria was only partially mollified, "Well, I could have told you Maria didn't hurt anyone. And I believe I *did* tell you that."

"Yes, ma'am. But I trust you understand that we have to verify what people tell us." He lowered his voice and leaned toward her slightly, "Once in a while, someone involved in a crime lies to us."

Jackson's charm broke through Victoria's grumpiness, her

fists unclenched and she grinned. "I'm sure that happens a lot. So, Detective, are you a quilter by chance? We have several men in our local guild. It's not just for women, you know."

Jackson smiled, "Actually, no, I'm not a quilter. I stopped by to see if Liz wanted to join me for lunch." He turned toward Liz, "How about it? Can you get away from your booth? If we go now, we could probably get a table at Agave when they open."

Ack! He's gorgeous, but he did arrest Ned. . . who just wants to be friends. "Sure, that sounds good. Victoria was just taking over for me here."

"Great. Let's hurry. Agave will be full as soon as they open." Jackson took her hand and drew her away. Liz waved over her shoulder at Victoria, who gave a slow wink.

"My luck must be holding," said Jackson as they slid into one of the handful of tables in a bay window at the front of the restaurant. "I wasn't sure we'd get a table, much less a prime one in the window." He grinned at Liz. "I've always thought they put the best-looking customers in the windows to help bring in more."

Liz laughed. "I don't know about that, but it's definitely a coup to get any table here on Saturday, much less the day of the Sidewalk Sale."

Their waiter brought glasses and a carafe of water and promised to return after they'd had a chance to look over the menu. Liz studied the menu longer than she needed to – it provided some cover to the nervousness she suddenly felt on what might be called a date with the attractive detective with the smoldering eyes. . . who had threatened to arrest her last week. *Water under the bridge, Liz, that was then and he's gorgeous NOW.*

Jackson broke the silence. "What do you think about chips and guacamole? Or maybe queso?" He waggled his eyebrows at her. "Maybe we could split a pitcher of sangria, too?"

Liz laughed. "Guac or queso sound good, but their pitchers of sangria are more than I'm up for today. A *lot* more, actually."

Jackson grinned. "Can't blame me for trying, though, can you?"

The waiter returned and they ordered chips and queso to share. Liz ordered iced tea and Jackson ordered a Dos Equis.

"No, I'm not on duty today, in case you were wondering," Jackson said.

"Actually, Detective Jackson, I wasn't wondering about you ordering a beer, but I *was* wondering what your first name is. I noticed your business cards just say 'Detective Jackson.' I doubt your parents named you Detective, or did they?"

Jackson laughed. "Why don't you guess?"

Liz laughed, "Sure, I'll guess. Will you spot me the first letter?"

"R."

"Okay. Let me think of men's names that start with R. . . Rufus?" Jackson laughed and shook his head. "Reginald?" More laughing and head shaking. "I've got it – Robespierre!"

"Wrong again."

"Okay, I give up."

Jackson was still laughing. "It's Robert. My friends call me Rob."

"Hmmm. Rob, you say. And you're sure that isn't short for Robespierre?"

"I'm positive!"

The waiter brought their chips and queso, and they ordered the rest of their meal – mole enchilada for him and chicken tortilla soup for her. Liz was amazed at herself; she was being witty and flirty with this attractive guy and not feeling nervous or awkward at all. Although she *was* being careful not to drip the queso on the table, or worse, her shirt. "I love the queso here. Well, actually, I love everything here. This has got to be the best Mexican restaurant on the East Coast."

He grinned at her. "I haven't sampled them all, but it's the best one I've ever eaten at. I've loved everything I've ever eaten here."

The waiter brought their food and they settled in to enjoy it. Liz squeezed lime juice into her soup. As she looked up, she saw Ned and Ross walking by on the sidewalk. Ross waved enthusiastically at her, and she waved back. Ross nudged his father and pointed to Liz. Ned frowned at them through the window, and then strode off down the street, leaving Ross behind, looking confused. Ross waved to Liz again and trotted after his dad.

Liz smiled and turned back to her food as the gorgeous man across from her raised his eyebrows. "Looks like someone's got a jealous boyfriend."

"Probably someone does, but not me. Ned and I are just friends."

Now he raised a single eyebrow at her. "Really? 'Just friends' look happy to see each other, smile, and wave. My keen detecting skills tell me he's not happy to see you. . . or perhaps not happy to see you here with me."

Liz sighed. "We aren't dating. The last time I saw him, he was really clear about wanting to be just friends." She shook her head. "But you're right, he didn't look happy. To be fair, he's got a lot going on right now."

He deadpanned, "Oh, yeah, that murder charge. That makes a lot of people grumpy. But, hey, at least he convinced the judge to grant him bail. He could still be cooling his heels in jail."

After lunch, Liz and Rob stepped out onto the crowded sidewalk in front of Agave. There were now dozens of people in line for tables. He gave her a quick peck on her cheek, and said he hoped he'd see her again soon. Even after lunch and that almost kiss, Liz still struggled to think of him as 'Rob' instead of 'Detective Jackson,' or even *hot* 'Detective Jackson.' He might have arrested Ned, but she'd enjoyed her lunch with him, and realized she *did* want to see him again. And that made it easier for her to start thinking of him as 'Rob.'

As she headed back toward Mariners' Compass, Liz spotted a stall for KT Caters to You, and headed over to talk with KT. Fortunately for Liz, there weren't any potential customers at KT's stall.

"Hi, KT. How're you doing?"

"I'm good. How about you, Liz? Interested in some cookies? I've got peanut butter, snickerdoodles, and chocolate chip. I know how much Americans love chocolate chip."

"Sure, I'll take a dozen back to the shop. We have extra staff working today for the Sidewalk Sale. I just have to be sure I put them where no one will get crumbs or smears on the fabrics."

"Do you want all one kind or a mix?"

"A mix would be good." As KT selected cookies and slid them into a bag with her tongs, Liz looked around all the promotional materials KT had in her stall. She still needed to find KT's address. But the only items she saw had just a phone number, web address, and email address. So, she still needed to look at her records in Mariners' Compass. "I want to thank you for helping clear my niece. The detective said a witness confirmed her version of events and I'm guessing that witness was you."

"Yes, it was me. But you don't need to thank me – I just told him what I saw. Your niece never went anywhere near Meg's food. She was just in the room for a moment."

"Still, I'm glad you did. It was really worrying her to be a suspect. And my sister was really upset. So that's all good now."

KT grinned at her. "And the detective kissing you – is that all good now, too?"

Liz felt her cheeks start to warm. "I ran into him at our stall today and he wanted to have lunch together. It surprised me when he kissed my cheek."

KT laughed. "Sure."

Liz paid for her cookies and said good-bye to KT. Heading back to Mariners' Compass, she could feel the warmth in her cheeks, lingering long after her lunch date had ended. Getting to know Rob better felt good to her. And since Ned had taken himself out any possible romance, at least for now, why not?

CHAPTER 31

Liz was up, dressed, and out of her house early the next morning. She was on a mission. When Java Joe's opened at 7:00, she was the only customer waiting, since it was too early for even the devout church crowd. After sidestepping Joe's questions about her relationship with Ned, whom Joe called "The Professor," she stepped out the door and crossed Second Street to Mariners' Compass. Juggling coffee, keys, and her bookbag, she set her coffee down on the sidewalk to unlock the shop's front door, being careful to lock it again behind her. The last thing she needed this morning was some early-bird customer coming in the shop two hours before they opened. Grateful she'd completed the payroll and inventory earlier in the week, she'd decided this morning early hours could be devoted to sleuthing. She went straight into the office and turned on the computer, spending a moment inhaling the cozy scents of the shop. When the shop's bill payment system appeared on the screen, she tapped the keys for a moment and found what she sought – KT's address. *Darn, it's just a post office box.*

Liz leaned back in the desk chair and closed her eyes. She rubbed the tracker between her thumb and fingers. Her plan had been to find KT's address and put the tracker on her personal car while KT was busy the shop catering this morning's guild meeting. After a few minutes she decided to place the tracker on KT's catering van and use the van's location to determine where KT lived. She'd prefer to track both of KT's vehicles, but she only had one tracker left; Ned had ordered four, but only three had arrived. But now they needed a couple more for KT's second vehicle and for Dr. Westborough's car. Should she track KT's car or van? Ask Ned to order a few more trackers? Following their 'be discrete' approach to traceable communications, she sent Ned a text asking if he had 'another thing.'

Liz stared at her phone, perplexed. Ned's reply text stated he thought he had the right number of 'things' and they were fine. While she contemplated a response for a few minutes, another text from Ned arrived. "OMG Sorry Please disregard previous message. Yes, I have a spare and I can bring it to you if you need it now." Liz snorted and then blushed as she realized what he might have meant earlier. Good to know he has the right number of things – she would like to confirm that for herself. And it was good to know his thoughts ran in the same direction as hers. Sort of. Even if they were just friends, and he'd looked so grim when he saw her at Agave with the detective who had arrested him. Liz sighed over the conflicting messages she got from Ned. Plus, she still didn't know for sure about Meg's groping accusation.

Liz texted back that she'd use the remaining one for KT's business vehicle but would need another for KT's personal vehicle. Ned responded that they could use his parents' spare on the personal vehicle, when they found it. And in the meantime, he would order another in case he needed it for his parents.

An hour later, Victoria arrived and greeted Liz with a hug. Soon afterwards, KT rang the doorbell at the shop's back door. Liz stayed at her computer and listened to KT and Victoria chatting as they entered the elevator and their voices disappearing as the doors closed. Liz would need to find a window of time when she could be sure KT wouldn't return to the van parked in the alley behind the shop. After a few minutes, Liz heard KT come back downstairs and leave through the rear door. Biding her time, she continued to rub the tracker between her fingers. After another long pause, Liz heard the distinctive sound of a wheeled rack of trays being wheeled into the shop and then into the elevator. One of the wheels rattled like the wonky grocery store carts Liz always seemed to select.

Liz eased out of the office, tracker in hand. She scanned the first floor and knew this was her best chance. She slipped out the door, scanned the alley for possible witnesses, and seeing no one else in the alley, placed the tracker on the rear fender of KT's van. She was back at her desk at least two minutes before KT came back downstairs. *Yay! For once this went off without a hitch!*

The guild meeting featured a special guest speaker, discussing free motion quilting. As Tina, the speaker, had written an early book on the subject, the guild had been excited to hear her. She began with the basics – free motion quilting can be done on either a long-arm machine, or a domestic machine. Her talk put the focus on using domestic machines, where the quilter lowered the feed dogs to allow the fabric to move under the needle. She emphasized that the resulting stitches would be shorter or longer, based on how fast the fabric was moved, and described it as drawing where the pen was held in place and the artist moved the paper under the pen. And that keeping constant pressure on the foot pedal was essential to achieving even stitches. That way, the quilter would only need to focus on how fast they were moving the fabric. She discussed ways to ensure the constant speed – on most machines it meant dialing down the speed range and then flooring the pedal when stitching. Trying to maintain constant pressure on the foot pedal at an intermediate speed was much harder.

Tina spent a little while demonstrating how to set up the machine, and then showing different patterns. She passed around several samples, showing both what to do and what not to do. Liz was pleased to see the guild members engaged in Tina's talk. Victoria had overruled Emma by bringing in this speaker, knowing full well Emma would gladly be the only speaker at every guild meeting. Victoria knew more variety was needed in speakers' personalities as well as techniques if members were going to stay active and interested. The guild members did appear engrossed as Tina addressed the apparent contradiction between planning and spontaneity, and then illustrated the concepts with an example where the free motion quilting moved across colors, patterns and complemented the design features of the quilt. Tina concluded by showing stippling – one of the easier ways to use free motion quilting. By making gentle curves with the machines, the quilter could add interest and texture to large areas. The only guidelines were to avoid any abrupt changes of direction and to avoid crossing previous stitching lines. Liz was interested in this presentation since she considered using free motion quilting on Maria's quilt, but she found her mind kept returning to how she could best approach KT after the meeting ended. As Tina addressed the ways to include whimsy and even humor in free motion quilting, Liz's gaze shifted to Emma. Emma was many things, but neither whimsy nor humor came to mind.

Liz shifted in her chair and her eyes widened. *My life is like free motion quilting right now.* Like stippling, especially: she knew where she wanted to end up but had no firm plan on exactly what path she would take to get there. She knew she wanted to find out who killed Meg, and she really wanted the killer to be someone other than Ned. She also knew she'd enjoyed her lunch with Rob and hoped she'd see him again. Who knew where this path would take her?

As the guild gave Tina a rousing round of applause, Liz wondered if it really was steam coming out of Emma's ears. The question-and-answer session took another twenty minutes, and, after more applause and more Emma-generated steam, the guild moved into the regular Show and Tell part of their meetings. Liz had intended to bring the quilt top she had made for Maria but had forgotten it in her zeal to start sleuthing early in the morning. She resolved to bring it next month when the entire quilt would likely be finished. The guild meeting ended with Emma reminding everyone about the topics for the upcoming meetings in November and their plans for a holiday luncheon in December. Most of the guild members headed downstairs to shop for fabric and other supplies.

Liz approached KT. "Here, I'll help you clean up. And that will give us a chance to talk." KT shrugged but didn't object. As they collected dishes and silverware into one of KT's boxes, Liz began, "I understand you and Meg knew each other in high school."

KT's dark eyes blazed, "Yes, we knew each other in high school. From first grade through two years of college in the same dorm."

"But you weren't ever friends, were you?" Liz pressed, even though she knew the answer.

"Friends!" KT scoffed. "Meg was nasty to me from the first time she saw me."

"I can believe that. I'd heard about her getting you in trouble in school."

"That was the worst. None of the teachers cared if she

bullied me, and they had to notice. Meg was not . . . shy . . . about it? I don't know the right word. But when I respond, I was suspended. Three days away from school and Meg was not punishment for me."

Liz and KT wiped down the tables in the meeting room. After a bit, Liz said, "My friend Ned has been arrested for Meg's murder. I want to help him clear his name. Can you tell me anything about your interactions with Meg at the Math Bowl? You might have seen something the rest of us missed." Liz's conscience pricked her a little; she knew she was trying to substitute KT for Ned as a suspect but didn't want KT to catch on and shut down too soon.

"Oh, my God, Liz. Yes, I will help you." KT closed her eyes and exhaled. "Meg was late the first day. Everyone else had left the lounges when she came in. It was just the two of us, but she didn't say anything at first. She put some things in the refrigerator, took a pill out of a bottle in her purse, and swallowed it with some water. I don't know what it was. It looked like medicine, not illegal drugs. But I don't know." KT paused for a moment and eyed Liz. "She started to talk about how bad my food is, but then she stopped. She looked at me and told me she was sorry for being a bitch to me for so long. She said she wanted to be a better person. I couldn't think of anything to say. I just stared at her and then she left." KT finished loading her rolling cart and started pushing it toward the door.

Liz tilted her head, "That's surprising."

"I was shocked. I never expected it from her." KT shook her head and pushed the cart out to the elevator. "I will save you from asking. I hated her, but I did not kill her. I wanted to kill her when we were in high school, but not now."

Liz cut fabric and rang up customers' purchases for the next hour. When most of the customers had departed, Victoria walked over to the cutting station where Liz was working. "I think the rush is over for today. Sheila and I can handle any customers that come in between now and closing, if you want to head home."

Liz checked her watch. "Yes, I'd like to go. I can get in some time on Maria's quilt if I go now. I'm meeting Ned and Caroline for dinner later."

Victoria hugged her. "Thanks for coming in today. We had a much bigger turnout for the guild meeting than normal. I guess we had a lot of members who wanted to learn more about free motion quilting. Plus, several of our members brought guests, who I hope will end up joining."

Liz returned her hug. "I'll see you later this week, then."

At home in her sewing room, Liz studied the quilt top, or flimsy, as some quilters called a quilt top that had not yet been quilted to batting and backing. A guild meeting always increased her enthusiasm, and, she believed, boosted her creativity. After Tina's demonstration, she was eager to try free motion quilting. But first, she'd need to practice – she didn't want her first efforts to be on Maria's quilt.

Liz reviewed her notes from the demonstration. After changing the presser foot on her machine and sandwiching together two layers of scrap fabric with batting in between, she gave it a try. An hour later, she'd improved, but she still was getting wildly varying stitch lengths, and the lines that should be smooth curves still had angles and sharp jogs in them. Tina had recommended practicing a little every day to develop smooth stitching lines. *I'm going to have to get a lot better before I'll want to do this on a real quilt, especially one that's a gift for my beloved niece.*

Liz checked her watch and realized she had about twenty minutes before she needed to leave to meet Caroline and Ned. That was enough time prepare the quilt sandwich for Maria's quilt. Her first task was to pick up Abner from where he was lying on Maria's quilt. She measured the quilt top and then cut backing and batting several inches larger than the top. Liz then taped the backing onto her worktable and smoothed the batting on top of the backing. Working in sections, she pulled back the batting and sprayed the backing with fabric adhesive. After the batting was smoothed and secured to the backing, she repeated the process with the batting and the quilt top. She pressed the quilt sandwich smooth, double-checked that she'd turned off her machine and unplugged her iron, and headed out the meet her friends.

CHAPTER 32

Pig and Publican was hopping when the sleuths arrived. Of course it was, even though it was a Sunday night. They snagged the last three bar stools, near the oyster shucking station. The pub was known for imported and local brews, good food, and vintage Belgian travel posters on the walls. Friendly, efficient staff and a great location between downtown and the beach made it a thriving local hangout.

They ordered beers and hot pretzel bites with mustard and cheese as they reviewed the day's specials. While they waited for their pretzel bites to cool enough to touch, much less eat, Liz updated Ned and Caroline on the threatening phone call she'd received, how the ensuing conversation with Jackson had gone, and how happy she was to have gotten off with just a scolding and warning. Liz waved off their exclamations of concern, saying she was being cautious.

Liz looked everywhere but at Ned when she added, "Detective Jackson has officers periodically keeping an eye on my house at night."

Caroline raised an eyebrow when she saw Ned giving Liz a little side-eye at that. "Patrol officers or Jackson himself?"

In the charged silence that followed Caroline's question, Liz decided that sometime later she'd tell Caroline about having lunch with Rob, as she now thought of him. But there was no reason to rub Ned's nose in the situation. Especially since he hadn't seemed particularly thrilled to see her having lunch with the detective who had arrested him a week before.

Eager to change the subject, Liz said, "I learned a lot about KT and Meg in the last couple days, too. Meg had bullied KT from first grade on, they had a big fight in the locker room, and Meg convinced everyone KT had started it. No one believed KT when she told them about Meg's relentless bullying." Liz took a sip of beer then continued. "I also spoke with her earlier today at Mariners' Compass as she was catering the guild meeting. She admitted hating Meg but claimed she didn't kill her. Even though she'd wanted to in high school. Oh, I almost forgot, I got the tracker on her van without getting caught!" Liz lifted her glass and the others clinked theirs against hers in celebration.

Caroline waved a pretzel as she spoke, "I'm glad something went right for once." She then added on a more serious note, "It's kind of like you, Ned. KT hated Meg but hadn't seen her for a few years. I just don't think people wait years to kill someone. We need to be looking at events – and people – in Meg's more recent life."

"I'm not ready to rule out KT," Ned objected. "She'd suffered years of abuse from Meg. In my case, it was just one event. Pain when you're young is harder to shrug off than when you're older and more resilient."

Liz was mulling this over when the waiter returned to take their dinner orders. Ned ordered the bratwurst platter, Caroline went for the fish and chips, and Liz chose the Thai drunken noodles. Liz ate another pretzel dipped in mustard. After she swallowed, she focused on Ned, "I don't think you can have it both ways, Ned. KT was upset none of her teachers spoke up on her behalf, and that was years ago, too. Either years-ago anger is a motive or not." Ned opened his mouth to object but closed it without speaking.

"Now, now, kids, let's not squabble. We're all in this together," Caroline smiled at both Liz and Ned, trying to lighten the mood. "Let's review *our* suspects – not Jackson's suspects. First up, Ingraham. Money problems, and willing to commit fraud. Killing Meg would solve his problems if she was blackmailing him. And," she nodded at Liz, "Your visit to the casino showed he hasn't bothered to be discreet in his affairs."

Liz shook her head, "All true. I'm just glad I got out of the casino without getting arrested." She paused for a moment as Ned grimaced. "Oops, lots of landmines here. Now let's look at MacKenzie. He tried to mislead me about his relationship with Meg and their living arrangement, which is suspicious just by itself. And even if he didn't out and out lie, he certainly avoided the question and got a bit scary in the process. He looked really sad at one point – a bit too sad for someone he said he barely knew. Plus, he said he thought Ingraham was responsible for getting Meg removed from the math department. And he did show up at Meg's funeral. . . *with* Ingraham."

"Brian was right, Ingraham *was* responsible for Meg's removal," said Ned.

"I didn't know that!" Liz exclaimed.

"Of course, it was Ingraham's decision. And his idea. But he made *me* give her the news. He's the sort of guy who insists on making every decision in his little fiefdom, but always wants someone else to be the bad guy."

There was a long pause while Liz and Caroline considered this latest information. At last Caroline spoke. "So, Meg was more likely to blame you for getting thrown out of the department and not Ingraham. But if MacKenzie thought it was Ingraham's decision. . . Does that change anything? Or do you think MacKenzie was just trying to throw some suspicion on Ingraham?" She sighed. "I'm confused."

"Me, too," agreed Liz. "But we still don't have a motive for MacKenzie, do we? Unless Kevin was right about their relationship. Still not plausible, though." She paused again. "Oh, I almost forgot, I couldn't find any record he attended LHS, so I couldn't get any information about him from his high school years."

Ned said, "Let's take a look at KT now. From the way you described her, Liz, KT was volatile and still despises Meg. I know you like her, or at least sympathize with her. But we do need to be sure." He smiled at Liz, "With your good work getting the tracker on her van, we can keep an eye on where she goes, figure out where she lives and put another tracker on her personal vehicle if we think it will help. Look at it this way, Liz. We're looking for evidence to prove her innocence, too. Will that ease the awkwardness a bit?"

Liz looked thoughtful and then nodded. "OK. I do like KT, but I can live with that."

Ned looked at Caroline, "I did some research on Westborough. He's got a history of questionable relations with young pretty patients. He's been warned by his licensing board, but he still has his license."

Caroline leaned forward, "So maybe he had an affair with Meg? Do you suppose she was blackmailing him?"

"Possible," Ned responded. "That's a lot of possible blackmail, though."

"No, if we think Meg was capable of blackmailing Ingraham, then she'd be capable of blackmailing Westborough, too. And he could have tampered with her prescription somehow, though I'm not sure how, if she got them filled at a pharmacy. I wonder if Westborough gives samples, the same way my regular doctor does. . ."

"I forgot to tell you – KT said Meg took a pill when they were talking in the teachers' lounge. If Westborough messed with her prescriptions, or suggested she add St. John's Wort to her lithium, that might have been the pill she took."

Caroline jumped in, "Wait a sec. Why are you guys talking about St. John's Wort? Did I miss something?"

Ned gave Caroline an abbreviated version of what he'd learned from his bail hearing, where he had learned that there had been St. John's Wort in Meg's food, and that St. John's Wort with lithium can cause death from an excess of serotonin.

Caroline shook her head. "If Westborough wanted Meg dead, he would have had to do it some way that didn't involve the food at Math Bowl. Of course, he could have urged her to take the St. John's Wort, knowing it could kill her."

"Are we looking at two people who might have tried to kill Meg? That seems like a stretch, but it's possible, I guess." Liz said.

Ned nodded and continued, "It's possible. Unlikely, but possible. But let's consider this – even if Westborough wanted to tamper with Meg's pills, she'd still get her prescription filled at a pharmacy. Westborough wouldn't have had direct access to those pills. He'd have had to change her prescription, and Jackson would be all over that. But Jackson might not know if he'd given her samples."

The tilt of Caroline's head and the squint of her eyes showed wheels turning. "The timing might be right for the pill, same as the coffee and food Meg ate. It's a shame we can't see the all the toxicology reports Jackson has – those would give us a better idea of whether it was in her coffee or the pill she took, in addition to her food."

"At my bail hearing, the detective said it was in her food, but he didn't specify which food it was in or how it was put into her food."

The waiter brought their dinners and the three sleuths focused on their food for a few minutes. Ned broke the silence,

"So we agree Westborough is a suspect, and his motive might have been being blackmail about a possible affair with a patient." The others nodded and he continued, "But are we likely to learn anything more about him if we watch where he drives? I don't see what we would learn, and I'm not sure the reward is worth the risk. What do you two think?"

Caroline shook her head, "I think we need to question him instead of tracking his movements." She smiled at her friend, "Liz, don't you think you need a session with a psychiatrist?"

Liz laughed. "I'm not sure if I need a session, but I think I'll book one. Diane Goodwin is still worried about me, so I think she'd agree to me taking some time off to see Dr. Westborough."

As they finished their dinners, Ned said, "So we just need one more tracker – for KT's car, right?" Liz and Caroline nodded. "I'll let you know when it arrives." With that, they split the check, and each headed to their own car, waving, and saying "Good night." Liz made the short drive home with her mind reviewing all they discussed and considering how to open a conversation with Dr. Westborough.

CHAPTER 33

Monday afternoon was a slow time at Mariners' Compass. As usual, Victoria had left one of her employees in charge so she could take Mondays and the occasional Tuesday off. Today's clerk in charge was Susan, an older lady whom Liz believed could run a small country; running a quilt shop for an afternoon would be easy for her. Liz took advantage of the dearth of customers to change the displays in the shop's front windows. The shop had just received more kits for Thanksgiving table runners, so she displayed those in the front windows to entice quilters who wanted fun and easy projects for the fall. Liz stepped outside the door for a moment to admire her arrangement. As she stood on the sidewalk, viewing the displays from multiple angles, she saw Lowell Ingraham walking along the sidewalk on the other side of the street. *I need to ask him questions about Meg. How can I do this and make it seem natural? My luck is improving!*

Liz dashed back into the shop, calling, "I'll be right back," to Susan as she passed the startled manager. Racing out the shop's back door, she turned and trotted down the alley between buildings, emerging about a block away from Ingraham, just as if she were walking toward the store. This way, she would appear to be accidently meeting him on the sidewalk, instead of chasing after him from behind.

"It's great to see you again, Professor Ingraham," she gushed, smiling brightly, even as he looked a bit confused.

"Um, yes . . . Have we met?"

"Oh, well, no, actually, we haven't met formally. I'm Liz

Murphy. I was at the Math Bowl you hosted last month, so I learned who you are, but I didn't actually have the opportunity to meet you." Liz reset from bubbly to solemn. "Ms. Williamson's death was so tragic, don't you agree? She and I were colleagues at Lewes High School and the coaches of their math bowl team."

"Terribly tragic. I'm so sorry for your loss," Ingraham intoned, having rearranged his facial expression from puzzled to mournful.

"As I am for yours." Liz paused as Ingraham broke eye contact and gazed down the street. "I guess you knew her when she was studying in your department."

Ingraham continued to gaze down the street, "Yes, of course. Not well, but somewhat. She was a gifted mathematician, but, unfortunately, she was not especially well-suited for the higher-level academic environment. It's still a tragedy to lose someone so young, and under such questionable circumstances."

Apparently, he hadn't seen me at Meg's funeral, because that's not what he said there. "I'd heard there were some issues while she was at Lewes College – maybe mixing her personal and academic life too closely." Even as she spoke, Liz wondered if she had pushed Ingraham too hard with that comment. Would he just end the conversation?

Ingraham looked back at Liz, with his eyebrows raised and his mouth tightened. Liz was struck by the way Ingraham's chameleon-like demeanor changed so smoothly and quickly into the exact socially correct expression. "I'm not at liberty to discuss personnel issues in the math department. All issues were successfully resolved. As of this time, I am personally still uncertain whether any accusations were unfounded or just without sufficient evidence." Ingraham paused to frown at Liz. "But Ms. Williamson left lingering suspicions in her wake – suspicions that are even more unsettling after her death."

Liz's mind raced. *Is he trying to throw Ned under the bus? I am so glad he didn't see me at the funeral. I wonder if Detective Jackson — I mean Rob — knows about this?* "Was there anyone in the department she seemed close to? Other students or faculty, perhaps?"

"I was only aware of her relationship to a fellow graduate student, a Brian MacKenzie. And rumors of an on-again-off-again relationship with her advisor, Professor York." A momentary smirk played across Ingraham's face. *Why, yes, he is trying to throw Ned under the bus.*

Mind still racing, Liz considered Ingraham's words. For a man who wasn't at liberty to discuss personnel issues, he'd said plenty. She wanted to keep him talking, so she went for broke.

"I'd heard a rumor Ms. Williamson actually stooped to blackmail. Did you include that in the accusations you mentioned?"

Ingraham drew a full breath and pulled himself to his full height. His face now registered offended indignation, "That's beyond the pale, young lady. I will not discuss such scurrilous rumors about any members of my department."

Just then, a slight woman younger than Liz slid to Ingraham's side and slipped her arm through his. She seemed oblivious to his indignation and smiled brightly at Liz, "Hi, I'm Bitsy. Do you work with Lowie?"

Liz introduced herself to the woman who was probably wife number three and explained how she had met 'Lowie' at the Math Bowl. She shook hands with Bitsy. Ingraham harrumphed, "Ms. Murphy, we have dinner reservations in a few minutes, and I don't want to be late for them. Good day to you."

Liz smiled at being called "young lady," and wondered if he called Bitsy that when they argued. She watched them walk down the street and heard Bitsy say she didn't know they had reservations. As she walked back to the shop, she mulled over the conversation. Ingraham had been eager to throw suspicion on both Brian and Ned. She realized she hadn't learned anything earth-shattering, but his reactions convinced her he'd known Meg much better than he let on. He'd gotten huffy when she mentioned blackmail, but he hadn't denied it. Had she touched a nerve?

CHAPTER 34

L iz's cell phone rang later that evening. She was surprised to see the caller was Ned, as she hadn't expected to hear from him again so soon. She took a deep breath, let it out, and answered before the call went to voicemail.

"Hi, Ned. What's up?" *That sounded friendly, not overjoyed. I can handle this.*

"Hi Liz. The tracker for KT arrived today. Do you want to go put it on her car tonight? I'd suggest we go around midnight. By then it should be fully dark with the clouds over the moon."

"Sure. I have her address from tracking her van."

"Great. I'll pick you up around midnight."

"OK. See you then." They chatted for a few minutes more before Liz added, "and be sure to wear dark clothes." *What do I have that's black and sexy, and appropriate for sneaking around? Oh, no, don't go there. This isn't a date; this is sleuthing.*

Ned drove slowly down the street where the tracker had shown KT's van to be. There it was – in a driveway with five other cars. "How are we going to figure out which one is hers?" Liz asked.

The light from the dashboard was just enough to see Ned smile at her. "Let's look for things that say, 'twenty-something.' Like decals and catering stuff in the car." He touched her arm for an instant. "I've set the dome light to stay off when the doors are open. I think we should leave the doors open just a hair in case we need to get back in fast."

Liz nodded. They eased out of his car and walked to the driveway. The night was dark, and Lewes was quiet this evening. She started as an owl hooted from a tree behind KT's house. Ned put his arm around her shoulders and squeezed. "It's fine. No one will see us."

When they reached KT's house, Liz paused by an elderly Toyota compact covered with beach, surfing, and food decals. She pointed at it and whispered, "Do you think this is the one?" Ned nodded. As she crouched by the car's right rear fender, the yard was lit with several bright security lights. Ned tugged her behind the car. His tug made her lose her balance and she landed on her behind, releasing a small "oof" when she landed.

A long moment passed, and Liz got her feet back underneath her. After a couple minutes she lost patience and peeked around the back of the car to see KT standing on the front porch. Their eyes met, and Liz's heart sank. Was this the day Detective Jackson would arrest her? Was she going to spend the rest of the night in a holding cell?

As she watched, KT turned and stuck her head back through the doorway and spoke in rapid-fire Russian. "Не беспокойся, Папа, это всего лишь опоссум что здесь был неделю тому назадю." KT returned to the porch and barked, "Get out of here. Scat!" She went back into the house and closed the door with a bang.

Ned pulled her arm and whispered, "Let's get out of here. I know KT saw us. I don't know what she said – she could have been telling someone to call the police."

"But she said 'Scat,' like she was talking to an animal. I think she was giving us an out." Nevertheless, as they hurried back to Ned's car, Liz's heart was pounding. The sound of the engine starting and both doors closing wasn't loud, but Liz felt they echoed down the street, ricocheting off the houses on both sides. She wished they'd used her almost silent Prius, but it was too late now. While Ned drove back to her house, she opened the tracker app on her phone, but didn't see any of the suspects' vehicles on the move. She hoped the information they would get from this latest tracker placement would be worth the risks they had taken. She also hoped she hadn't damaged her relationship with KT. She'd have to wait and see.

Liz's conscience prodded her as she left Lewes High School. She'd approached Diane Goodwin about seeing a therapist about Meg's death, and Diane had approved her time away from the classroom, arranged a substitute for two class periods, and encouraged her to make as many appointments as she felt she needed. While Liz hadn't *exactly* lied to her principal, she hadn't mentioned she planned to see the same psychiatrist Meg had seen. Nor had she mentioned she wanted to learn more about Meg's relationship with Dr. Westborough, the prescriptions he had prescribed for her, and if he gave samples to his patients. She knew Diane had approved this time off to help her cope with Meg's death, not to search for Meg's killer. Diane knew she was looking for Meg's killer, but Liz hoped the principal wouldn't see this visit to Dr. Westborough for what it really was.

Despite her conscience's complaints, Liz was happy to be leaving school before the school day ended – kind of an adult version of playing hooky, which she had never done as a student. Depending on whether claiming to be sicker than she was that time in fourth grade counted. Liz rolled down Sylvia's windows, took deep breaths of the crisp October air, and drove out the

LHS parking lot toward Dr. Westborough's office.

Arriving a few minutes early, Liz steeled her nerves for this current deception in the name of sleuthing, and stepped into Dr. Westborough' waiting room. It was a sparsely furnished room, pleasant yet bland. A moment of panic ensued when her conscience reminded her that she didn't intend to be honest with Dr. Westborough, any more than she had with Diane. Could she sneak out and mail him a check for the wasting an hour of his time? While she debated with her unruly conscience, a portly man with a wispy mustache opened the inner office door, introduced himself, and ushered her into his office.

The inner office had the same décor as the waiting room, but with the addition of bookshelves bearing titles she couldn't quite read from the chair Dr. Westborough pointed her toward. A sickly plant in a macrame basket hung near the window, adding an odd 1970s note to the office. And there were boxes of tissues on all flat surfaces. After a moment, she realized Dr. Westborough was waiting for her to speak.

Liz introduced herself and explained to him a teacher she had worked with had died suddenly and she was having trouble dealing with the situation.

"I was there when she collapsed, and I just can't get the image of her lying on the floor out of my mind. I was trying to be strong and brave for the students who were there, too, but I feel like I'm stuck in that place and time." Liz paused for a moment, surprised that she was more affected emotionally than she'd expected to be. "Is this the sort of thing you could help me deal with, and eventually get over?"

"Yes, I expect so. Grief is one of the areas I work in frequently. Its common for all of us to struggle with death, both of others and as it affects our own sense of mortality. Can you tell me more about what happened and your feelings?"

Liz focused on the plant. "I don't know if you heard about the death – it was in a few articles in the *Cape Gazette*. Meg Williamson and I were coaches for our high school's math team, and she collapsed at the competition. It was before the second day of the competition started. She and I and the students were standing around in the hallway talking when she collapsed. The police came and questioned a lot of us. I was a suspect for a while, and a friend of mine is still a suspect.

"Anyway, one of the reasons I'm here is another teacher told me Meg had seen you professionally and you'd given her a prescription that helped her enormously. I thought maybe it would help to talk to someone who knew her, too."

Liz paused and looked at Dr. Westborough, who continued to look at her without any overt expression. "One reason I feel so sad about this is I didn't really like Meg. She was hard to work with. It doesn't make sense, but I keep thinking if I'd liked her, she'd still be alive." Liz looked back at the hanging plant and continued, "I know that's crazy. I know I didn't do anything to hurt her, and I have nothing I to feel guilty about, but it's still in my head. And actually, I don't even know what killed her. She died suddenly while eating, so it was probably poison of some sort, but it's frustrating not to know, and the police won't tell me anything.

"Is there something you can give me to make me feel better? Maybe something like what you gave Meg? If it helped her, maybe it would help me, too?"

Liz raised her eyes to the psychiatrist, wondering if she'd overdone it a little. After a long moment, he spoke, "I'm sure you understand my professional ethics prevent me from discussing another patient with you, or even confirming or denying whether someone is a patient. Even if the person is deceased." Dr. Westborough's expression changed a little, but

Liz had trouble reading it. "And I'd also need to understand your issues in much greater depth before prescribing anything."

"Well, I guess I don't really know how this works? Should I talk more about my interactions with Meg?" Liz paused and Dr. Westborough nodded.

Liz thought it was now or never, so she asked, "Or maybe we should talk about your relationship with Meg?"

Dr. Westborough leaned back in his chair, showing a reaction for the first time since Liz had arrived. "I've already told you I can't discuss whether Ms. Williamson was a patient or not."

"No, I'm talking about whether you had a non-professional relationship with her. Like the one that got you warned by your licensing board."

Dr. Westborough's face darkened, and a long moment of silence hung between them. Liz watched a muscle twitch in his lower jaw as if he was debating with himself on how to respond. When he finally spoke, he said "It appears to me you are not genuinely interested in resolving your issues with grief for your late colleague. If you actually have any grief for her." He opened a desk drawer and pulled out a business card. "Here is one of my colleagues. I suggest you consider meeting with her if you are sincere in your quest to understand your feelings of grief. For now, I must ask you to leave."

Liz took the card from him, put it in her purse without looking at it and fled back to the comfort of Sylvia. She knew she'd need to be better prepared the next time she tried to interview a suspect.

CHAPTER 35

As she started to back out of her parking space, Liz's phone beeped with the sound she'd set up for when one of the trackers in moving. She stopped Sylvia and pulled her phone out of her purse. KT's car was moving west on Route 9. Liz debated with her conscience for a few moments, but she told her conscience that she still had time left over from the 'counseling session' she hadn't finished. She headed west instead of toward LHS.

Liz set her phone in the holder she'd bought and stuck to her dashboard after she'd trailed Professor Ingraham to the casino. Juggling her phone and watching where a suspect went wasn't safe to do while driving; this way, she could just glance at her phone and be a lot less likely to rear-end the car in front of her. She stayed about a half-mile behind KT's car for almost a half hour, before she saw the tracker pull off the road and into the parking lot of Delaware Technical Community College, known as Del Tech to locals. *That doesn't seem right. I wonder why KT would be taking community college courses?* Liz pulled into the parking lot and circled until she spotted the car she and Ned had placed the tracker on. Her mood fell when she saw a young man climb out of the car and head toward the main entrance. While he definitely wasn't KT, he had a slight build like her and hair the same color as hers. *Darn. That looks like a younger brother. We picked the wrong car. And now I'll have to hustle to get back to work. I've lied to Diane for nothing.*

As Liz left LHS the following afternoon, she saw KT leaning against the bike rack, arms folded and scowling as Liz approached. *Uh oh. Better get this over with.* As she drew near, Liz began, "KT, I need to apologize..."

"Damn right you need to apologize. You were snooping in my front yard! Do you not remember I told you I didn't kill Meg?"

"KT, you're right. I shouldn't have been there. And, yes, I remember you telling me you hated Meg in high school but didn't kill her." She tried to appeal to KT's sympathy. "I didn't want to be there, and I believe you didn't do this, but I'm still trying to find out what happened." Liz hoped to see a little of KT's anger diminish, but KT's scowl remained. Liz continued, "I'm worried, since my friend Ned has been arrested for the murder. And I'm sure he didn't do it."

KT continued to scowl at her. "You're sure he didn't do it, but you're not sure if I did? I told you everything I know. I have helped you all I can. Now you need to leave me and my family alone." At last, KT's fury seemed to be subsiding. She looked into the distance for a moment and sighed. "Last night I told my father it was just an opossum that had set off the security lights in the yard. But if you come back, I will call the police and tell my father you are burglars." KT's eyes locked onto Liz's, "And you better hope the police get to you before he does." After another glare, KT stomped away.

Liz called after her, "There won't be a next time. And I really am sorry." As Liz watched, KT got into a nearby car and sped away. But KT's car was not the one Liz had placed the tracker on. That car was probably at Del Tech or wherever else her brother went. *Great, I've made KT mad for nothing, too. I'm zero for two this week.*

At last Liz was ready to do the actual quilting on Maria's quilt. She'd practiced free motion quilting and, while she wasn't happy with most of the designs she tried, she was confident in her stippling technique. One of her guild mates had suggested drinking a half glass of wine before doing free motion quilting on a 'real' project for the first time. Liz had initially laughed at that advice, but thinking of her college days and how she had danced more freely after a drink or two, decided to try it now.

Relaxed and as confident as she ever would be, Liz practiced stippling once more, then picked up Abner from where he lay on top of Maria's quilt. She held him and scritched behind his ears for a moment, then tipped him off her lap. Offended, he scowled at her and stalked out of the room. After a couple deep breaths, Liz stitched on one set of Flying Geese on Maria's quilt. Pulling the quilt out of the machine so that she could examine it, she found a couple spots where she'd made a sudden turn, resulting in a sharp point, but otherwise the quilting was smooth. And it highlighted the Flying Geese beautifully. She stippled the remaining sets of Flying Geese. These looked flawless to her. *Success! I'll have to remember to thank Pam for the advice about a glass of wine.*

Liz took a break before quilting the rest of Maria's gift. The peacock blue and coral stripes ran horizontally and vertically; it would echo the sixty-degree placement of the Flying Geese strips if she quilted over the stripes at a sixty-degree angle, too. She changed the settings on her machine from free motion quilting to walking foot quilting and tested on a small scrap of a stripe set. She used Jacquie Gehring's technique of placing painters' tape at intervals across the quilt to keep her quilting lines straight, then began to quilt. This was a familiar technique, and with her mind more free, Liz could mull over the case. But all that came to mind was how she'd blown it with KT and how much she hoped KT would eventually accept her apology and forgive her.

Liz felt restless after classes ended on Wednesday. Hoping to blow the cobwebs out of her mind and burn some energy, and with the weather at its autumnal best, she decided a bicycle ride on the Junction Breakwater Trail would be just the ticket. She rode hard all the way to Rehoboth Beach, turning around when she reached Rehoboth Avenue, the main drag of the adjacent town. After a pause to drink most of the water in her bottle, she turned back toward home.

Liz could feel her restlessness fading as her legs tired, and took it easier on her return trip. On the bridge over the glade, she glided to a stop, finished her water, and enjoyed the view along with the earthy, salty scent of the marsh. Tucking the empty bottle into the cage on her bike, she rode a bit further back into the wooded part of the trail. Here the sunshine flickered through the few leaves that still remained on the trees. She slowed when three deer bounded across the trail fifty yards in front of her. She knew many people hated the deer, but Liz still loved the muscular and athletic animals, with their sleek coats and big, sweet eyes. So what if she can't grow hostas or tulips? As she mused on the life a coastal deer, she heard the whine of an electric bike coming up behind her on her left. She sighed. She didn't really like them, but they'd become a fact of life on the trails. She slowed and moved right to let it pass.

Whomp. Liz shrieked as something hit her left side hard. She struggled to keep her balance, but the blow had knocked her too far off balance to correct. She knew she was going down and gave one last swerve to avoid a large oak tree, then landed hard on her right foot in the damp ditch by the path. She stretched to look for her assailant, or perhaps help, but the whine of the electric bike faded in the distance and the silence was complete. Even the birds and the breezes were still and quiet. How could the trail be so empty on a beautiful afternoon? She seen walkers and other bikers on the first part of her ride. But now she was completely alone.

Liz waited for a few minutes, hoping for a good Samaritan to come along, but also fearing her assailant would return. As she sat in the damp ditch, she recalled Rob's words that she should call him if anything happened to her. And she probably would. First, though, she needed to take stock of her situation.

Liz rolled to her hands and knees and started to stand, but her right ankle had another idea. She quickly returned to sitting, although on slightly drier ground. If her foot couldn't take her weight, she knew she wasn't going to walk out of here. Maybe she could ride slowly home, with her left leg doing all the work and while she babied her right leg. With that plan in mind, she took a closer look at her bicycle and saw her front rim was bent too much to be ridden. Her ankle throbbed and her ribs hurt with every breath she took. She sighed, pulled her phone out of the zippered pocket of her jacket, and called Rob.

"Hi, Rob. You know how you said I should call you if anything happened to me?"

"What's happened? Where are you?"

"I'm on the Junction Breakwater trail. I'm. . . Let me see exactly where I am . . ." Liz used a nearby tree to push herself up onto her left leg. "I'm just south of Wolfe Neck Road, near the trail spur that goes out to the Bike Fix-It Station."

"I'm on my way. How badly hurt are you?"

"Someone on an e-bike pushed me off the trail. Whoever it was hit my side hard, and I landed on my right leg. It hurts to breathe, and I can't put any weight on my ankle. And my bike is too banged up to ride. Can you come get me?"

"It sounds like you're hurt, but don't need an ambulance. I should be there in about . . . eight minutes according to my GPS. Don't hang up. If whoever did this comes back, I want to be able to hear you."

"Okay. I'm sitting back down now."

CHAPTER 36

Liz heard Rob's siren through both ears – one through the air and the other, slightly delayed, coming through her phone. She looked up to see his unmarked car driving slowly along the trail toward her. She'd never been so happy to see anyone. If she could move, she'd run and hug him. Instead, she watched as he stepped down into the ditch beside her.

"All right. Let me check you out a little bit."

"Okay, but I just want to go home."

"Let's see if that's the best place for you. Can you show me where you were hit?"

Liz pulled her jacket, pullover, and tee shirt up enough to let him see her ribs.

Rob pursed his lips and blew out a whistle. "You have a bruise already starting to form. I'm going to touch that to see if I can tell how badly hurt you are."

Rob gently touched the skin over her ribs and with just that light pressure, Liz thought she was going to pass out from the ensuing pain. "Aaaaah! Please stop! That really hurts."

"All right. I've stopped." He looked at her with a concerned and resolute expression. "Now let's see if your ankle can bear any weight. Let me help you up to a standing position, where you can hold onto both me and that tree." He lifted her up and she gradually put a little weight on her right leg.

"No, that's not working at all. I can't put any weight on my right leg."

"Okay, then. I'm going to pick you up and put you in my

car. Stand here for a second while I go get the car door open."
Rob returned and scooped Liz up as gently as possible. Even
so, Liz gasped in pain. "I'm sorry, I know it hurts. I'm going
to carry you a little farther away from the car, so I can go up an
easier slope onto the trail."

Once Liz was settled into the passenger seat of his car, she
sighed from relief and pain in equal proportions. "You aren't
taking me home, are you?"

"Nope. You need medical attention for both your ribs and
your ankle. Plus the scrape on your head."

Liz's hand flew to her head. "Where? Oh, ow. I found it."
She closed her eyes. "I'm in too much pain to argue with you."

Rob gazed at her for a long moment. "I hate seeing you in
pain." Liz turned to look at him, seeing worry and concern in
his dark eyes. "Now hang on for a moment while I go get your
bike."

The Beebe Hospital Emergency Room was quiet as Rob and
Liz entered. Rob had parked at the entrance and locked the car
while he went inside to get a nurse and a wheelchair for Liz.
With as much pain as Liz felt, she was glad she didn't have to
wait a long time for treatment. After some initial questions, she
was admitted and had an ID band placed around her wrist. As
she settled onto her bed, an imaging technician arrived with a
portable X-Ray machine for her ankle. He took X-Rays of her
ankle from several angles, and departed, leaving her alone with
Rob again. Liz thought she'd need to answer questions about
what had happened, but when she looked at Rob, she realized
he was aware she was still in too much pain for that. He smiled,
and Liz appreciated their companionable silence.

The quiet moment was soon interrupted when the same technician returned and announced he needed to move her to get an MRI of her ribs. As he helped her into a wheelchair, he turned to Rob and said, "Just wait for her here, sir. We'll be back in just a few minutes."

At that, Rob stood, and pulled his ID from his pocket. "I'm sorry, but Ms. Murphy is a crime victim, and I have reason to believe her assailant is likely to attempt to hurt her again. I'll need to stay with her while she is here. And if she needs to stay overnight, she'll need a private room and I'll station an LPD officer outside her room to prevent any unauthorized people entering."

The imaging technician raised his eyebrows and then nodded. "All right, then. Just follow along behind us, we won't be going very quickly."

Is a police guard an over-reaction? Wait — did someone just try to kill me? I'm in too much pain to think about this now. Giving in to the pain, Liz let her mind drift.

On their return to the ER, they passed a baby-faced young man in a white coat. As the doctor turned a megawatt smile at her, Liz remembered that Victoria had met her husband in this very emergency room. Victoria had fallen during a tennis match and broken her arm. And she'd fallen in love at first sight with Javier Benitez, the handsome resident who treated her that afternoon. It all seemed like a fairytale to thirteen-year-old Liz, although their parents had been concerned about the rapid romance between nineteen-year-old Victoria and a much older man. But Victoria was sure he was the man for her, and Javier insisted Victoria finish college before any serious commitment was made. They'd been married for eighteen happy years before his sudden death.

Moments later, that same baby-faced doctor opened the curtain and strode over to Liz. "Hello, I'm Dr. Kurtz." They shook hands, and after he confirmed her name and birthdate, he turned to Rob. "Detective . . . um . . . I know I've met you, but I'm afraid I've forgotten your last name."

"I'm Detective Jackson, with Lewes PD. I'm with Ms. Murphy to make sure the person who injured her doesn't have an opportunity to hurt her again."

In a quiet, pain-laced voice, Liz said, "I'm happy to have the detective here with me. Please feel free to discuss my situation with him here."

Dr. Kurtz nodded. "All right. I have mostly good news for you. Your ankle is sprained, but the X-rays do not indicate any fractures. I'd like for you to see an orthopedist in the next day or two to confirm that, though. You'll need to RICE your ankle – Rest, Ice, Compress, and Elevate. Rest means to keep your weight off your ankle until your orthopedist tells you otherwise. Ice is pretty obvious. It will reduce swelling and reduce pain. Twenty minutes on and twenty minutes off. Compress means to keep this brace on your ankle any time you're awake. Do not sleep with it on. Again, do this until your orthopedist tells you otherwise. Finally, elevate means to keep your ankle above the height of your heart. Elevate and ice are your best tools for swelling." He paused for a moment. "Any questions?"

Liz considered. "I have crutches at home. I'll use them."

She and the doctor said together, "Until the orthopedist tells me otherwise," and even Rob laughed.

"All right, then. Let's move to your ribs. You have one rib that's fractured, but no damage to any of the nearby organs."

"I'm not surprised one is fractured; I'm only surprised that it's just one. Every breath hurts. Are you going to tape it up?" asked Liz.

"No. We don't do that anymore. Tape and braces and the like make it even harder to breath, and that means some patients develop pneumonia. Which we don't want. Instead, the current protocol is to give you pain medicine that will make breathing easier and much less painful. It's strong, so read the directions and follow them carefully. If you have any questions, call the ER and ask.

"The other part of the protocol is breathing exercises. The admission nurse will give those to you as part of your release process, along with a few days' doses of pain medicine. And, again, if you have any questions about your breathing exercises, call us back here at the ER.

"Finally, you need to have someone with you when you take your pain medicine. It has the potential for serious side effects while making you groggy enough that you may not notice. Do you have friends or family at home?"

Liz shook her head. "I guess I could go stay with my sister, but she has teenagers, and her home isn't restful when they're home. I'm in too much pain to think clearly right now."

Rob jumped in. "I'll stay with her, Dr. Kurtz. I have to make sure her assailant doesn't get another shot at her. Especially with her on heavy pain meds."

Dr. Kurtz looked back to Liz. "Is that all right with you, Ms. Murphy? This needs to be your decision. If you want to stay with your sister, that's your choice."

Liz smiled. "I'm okay with the detective staying with me. My neighbors will notice, but I don't care. Disapproving neighbors are nothing compared to keeping bad guys away."

Liz dozed as soon as she and Rob were back in his car. She woke with a jolt when the car stopped. She looked around. "This isn't my house."

Jackson smiled at her. "I know. I'm getting some dinner for us. I hope you like Vietnamese food. I pre-ordered a large bowl of pho and a stir fry, figuring you could take your pick or we could split them."

Liz closed her eyes again. "That's very kind of you, but I'm really just not hungry."

"You'll need to eat a little, though. I read the instructions for your pain medicine, and you need to take it with some food." Liz sighed. "I'm going in now to pick it up, but I won't be gone long. I'm locking the car doors while I'm inside. I'm sure you know not to open or unlock your door." Liz sighed again and nodded.

As promised, Jackson returned in just a few minutes. Liz dozed and again jolted awake when the car stopped, this time in her driveway. "All right, let's get you inside safely. Do you want me to get your crutches for you or just carry you inside?"

Being carried sounded good to Liz – and it had when he'd picked her up at the trail – but she didn't want to sound too eager or too helpless. "Which do you think gets me inside faster and safer?" she asked, stalling.

Jackson grinned at her. "Carrying, definitely." With that, he scooped her up from the passenger seat and she wrapped her arms around his neck. "Have you got your keys handy? I probably should have asked that earlier."

Liz chuckled. Despite her pain, it felt great to be in his arms. "Just hit 4758 on the keypad for the garage door. The door into the house should be unlocked."

Jackson settled her into her favorite mid-century recliner

in the living room and began filling a bag with ice cubes from her refrigerator. "Here. Put this one on your ankle, and I'll get another one for your ribs." After her ice packs were in place, he continued. "You'll need a blanket, too." Liz waved her hand toward the hallway; Jackson strode to the linen closet and selected a pillow, sheets, and a blanket. "Relax a little bit and I'll get the food ready."

The next thing Liz knew, Jackson was gently shaking her shoulder and the house smelled wonderful. "Gosh, that smells good. Maybe I could eat a little bit after all." She raised her head and saw the table set for two.

"I've got your crutches here, so go ahead and try them out. Or I can fill your plate and bring it to you so you don't have to walk just yet."

"No time like the present, I guess. And you've already set the table so nicely." Liz carefully got out of the recliner and, with the crutches, maneuvered her way to the chair Jackson pulled out for her. "Could you bring the kitchen stool over here for me to put my foot on, please?"

Rob positioned the stool. "How's that?"

Liz nodded. "That's good."

"Now for your medicine. Here's tonight's dose and a glass of water."

After dinner, Liz felt sleepy like she'd never felt before. And, as advertised, her pain was gone. "I'm going to bed now," she announced, with the crutches again under her arms, thumped slowly into her bedroom.

"Sleep well. Don't forget to take off your ankle brace. I'll bring you an extra pillow to elevate your foot while you sleep. And then I'll keep the bad guys away." Jackson stood and followed her to the bedroom door.

"You can't be serious," Liz said, rolling her eyes.

"I'm totally serious about keeping the bad guys away. I'm not going to sleep here, at least not tonight. I'll rest, of course, but first I need to do is a security scan of the inside and outside of your house." He strode to the open window in the room. "An open window is a huge vulnerability." He closed the window and locked it, and then checked that all the other windows in the room were locked.

Liz balanced on her left foot and crutch and used her right hand to pull sweatpants and a tee shirt out of her dresser. "I sleep a lot better with the window open."

"If the window's open, I'll have to stay in the room with you. I can rest on the floor, but I will do a better job securing your house if I can move around during the night."

Liz sighed again. "Fine. I'm too tired to argue." But she wasn't too tired to have picked up on his comment about not sleeping here *tonight*. She knew Caroline would have a field day with his staying overnight here. But if she did spend the night with Rob some time, she'd want to be at her best, without either her body or her brain in the state they were now.

As Rob headed back toward the bedroom door, Liz climbed into bed and Abner stretched out next to her. "Please leave the door open a few inches, so Abner can go in and out if he wants to."

CHAPTER 37

J ackson had told Liz he planned to rest on her sofa, but his real plan was to stay awake all night. Her attacker would know she was injured; if he or she wanted to hurt her more – or worse – tonight would be the best opportunity. He was determined that wouldn't happen.

The first item on his list was to make a large pot of coffee to help him stay awake. While that brewed in Liz's old-school Mr. Coffee machine, he put the leftovers in her refrigerator and tidied up the kitchen. Next on his list was to finish checking all the doors and windows from the interior. He found another open window in the room filled with fabric and sewing equipment. He closed and locked the window and then paused for a moment to admire the bold quilt in progress. As he moved around the interior, Jackson was pleased to see the front door had a quality deadbolt on it and the rear slider had a sturdy metal bar locked in place. He turned on all exterior lights and was pleased to see both the front and back yards were lit up like daytime. No one could lurk there, but the side yards were both dark. Time to cruise the exterior.

Jackson started for the front door, then realized he needed to lock the door behind him while he was outside. And he'd forgotten to get Liz's keys from her before she fell asleep. He looked in a couple of kitchen drawers, hoping to find a spare, but only found neatly organized cooking tools. *Didn't everyone have a junk drawer with odds and ends and spare keys in it?* Apparently not Liz Murphy. Nothing to do but root through her purse. Before he did that, he tiptoed to her bedroom door, and heard soft regular breathing. As he peeked in, Abner raised his head and gave him a 'don't come any closer' look. He didn't want to wake her just to ask for a key, so with a sigh and a little trepidation, he unzipped the top of her purse. All her keys were in an interior pocket, so he pulled out the housekeys, and tested them in the front door to be sure he had the right one.

After locking the door behind himself, Jackson scanned the front yard again to verify that no one was around. He went to his car and removed his heavy-duty flashlight, closing the car door as quietly as he could. He moved around the end of the house next to the garage, looking into the darkness and listening for any sound that didn't occur naturally. Seeing and hearing nothing, he shone the flashlight on all around the side yard. Still nothing.

Jackson moved quietly to the opposite side of the house with all his senses on full alert. He heard tiny sounds that might be someone brushing against shrubs. Even the air smelled a little different on this side. His intuition told him that there was someone malevolent here. Standing motionless, he listened for almost a full minute but heard nothing else. When he shined the flashlight through the yard, he saw no one. Still, his senses told him someone was there.

Back in the house, Jackson replaced Liz's keys in her purse. He again tiptoed to Liz's door, and again heard gentle breathing. With Liz resting comfortably, he could review the case. He sat down at the kitchen table and pulled out his notebook to jot down his thoughts. First, was the murderer the same person who threatened and injured Liz? It seemed likely, but he was pretty sure York wouldn't have hurt Liz. Even if he did look pretty angry when they were at Agave. So, did he get it wrong when he arrested York? York had motive, opportunity, and means. He was the best suspect at the time of his arrest, but this attack on Liz changed things. Jackson didn't like the idea that he'd screwed up by arresting York, but today's events made it seem more likely that he had.

Why don't I think about it from the murderer's perspective? He (or she, but for now I'll just think he) wants to stop Liz from discovering his identity. He knows she's trying to clear York. And he's panicking. A smart murderer would just sit tight and wait for Ned's trial and hope for his conviction. *Is it possible the murderer doesn't know York was arrested for the murder?* Maybe, but not likely. York's arrest was on local news for a couple days, and it was the lead story in the *Cape Gazette* for both issues that week. Only a total hermit would have missed it.

Maybe I ought to take a closer look at Ingraham? He's a terrible husband, and in financial straits. It's possible he was involved with Meg, and if so, she could she have been blackmailing him. Over the affair or something else. The mortgages were public record even if he'd struck out when he tried to get a warrant for a closer look into Ingraham's financial records. Jackson spent a moment fuming about the judge's smug condescension to him; the judge didn't think it was anything other than a fishing trip into the finances of an upstanding member of the community. *Moving on.* Ingraham had easy access to the food in the lounge. Jackson recalled his smarmy speech at Meg's funeral. Ingraham seemed to be trying awfully hard to make it look like Meg had quit her graduate program, when Jackson knew she'd been canned. At least that's what Ned had told him after being arrested.

And thinking of Meg being sacked from Lewes College's math program, Jackson knew also Ned had been the one to sack her. Yet another issue between them. But wait, Ned was her advisor. He'd have been the one to deliver the bad news, even if he hadn't been the one to make the decision. *Who actually made that decision? Was it York? Or was it Ingraham, and York was just ordered to deliver the bad news?* Jackson jotted this in his notebook – he needed to ask both men more detailed questions about Meg's dismissal from the math department.

Jackson stood up, stretched, and went to the kitchen for a cup of coffee. He found cream in Liz's refrigerator, stirred some into his mug and returned to the kitchen table. Now, the caterer. He flipped through his notebook to find her name. Katya Tereshchenko. No wonder she goes by KT. Ms. Lucas had found out her history with Meg from high school. A long time to hold a grudge big enough to murder someone. KT had easy access to all the food in the lounge, and she would have been in there alone for long stretches when all the teachers were out doing their Math Bowl events. We didn't find any lithium or St. John's Wort when we searched her house. Of course, she's smart enough to have bought one bottle, used it to kill Meg, and gotten rid of it. If she killed Meg, the bottle will be at the bottom of Delaware Bay. Or in a dumpster in downtown Wilmington. Which brought his thoughts back to Ned. Ned was a smart guy. Surely he'd have dumped the St. John's Wort before they searched his house? Math professors are smart, but academics could be clueless about how the rest of the world works.

Thinking of clueless academics turned his thoughts to MacKenzie. Now there was a guy who lacked real-world smarts. MacKenzie had tried to hide the fact that he and Meg had lived together. As if even Ms. Lucas wouldn't see through that; Meg hadn't yet changed the address on her driver's license. The grad student had admitted he and Meg had been roommates, but added he thought he'd be a suspect if he admitted they had been living together. *As if misleading the police wouldn't make him a suspect.* Jackson flipped back to his notes from his interview with MacKenzie. MacKenzie had insisted that it hadn't really been a lie because Meg had moved out a few weeks before she was murdered. So they weren't technically roommates at the time of her murder. Had MacKenzie been scrupulously precise in answering his questions? Or had MacKenzie been misleading him on purpose? Not clear. He'd seen some of that elaborate precision in the answers he'd gotten from York and Ingraham, too, so maybe it was a mathematician sort of personality trait. He hadn't seen that with Liz.

Is there something the murderer thinks Liz knows that points to him or her? But what? And does Liz even know it's the key to the case? Whatever the situation is, Liz is clearly in danger. And I don't want her hurt again.

CHAPTER 38

When Liz awoke the next morning, sunshine was streaming into her bedroom. She blinked at the light and realized she had overslept and would be hours late for work. Homeroom had ended a long time ago. She started to jump out of bed, but her ribs and ankle reminded her she shouldn't move hastily. Her pain meds had definitely worn off. Struggling into her old fluffy bathrobe, she grabbed her crutches and hobbled into the kitchen to give Jackson a piece of her mind.

As she entered the kitchen, Rob looked up at her and smiled. "How are you feeling?"

Liz scowled at him, "Better than yesterday, but I won't be happy if I get fired. How could you let me sleep so late?"

Rob stood up and pulled a chair out for her. "Here, sit down. It's okay. I called your principal at seven o'clock this morning to tell her you'd been injured and treated at the ER yesterday, and that you wouldn't be in today. And probably not tomorrow. She sent her wishes for you to get better soon and said she'd arrange a substitute for you for both days. She seemed curious about what happened to you, but I didn't give her any details."

"Well. . . Okay then." Liz knew she was being rude and ungrateful but wasn't ready to lose her grumpy mood just yet. "It's hard not being in control of my own life."

"Are you hungry? I can make you some breakfast. I found eggs, bread for toast, berries, yogurt. Your fridge is pretty well stocked. I found Abner's food and fed him earlier, too."

"Oh, I don't know if I'm hungry just yet."

"You'll need to eat if you want to take your medicine. How about a couple of poached eggs on toast?"

Liz nodded and excused herself to go get dressed. Showering would be difficult, and not something she could ask Rob to help with, so she postponed it. Getting her teeth brushed and her face washed would be enough effort this morning.

When Liz returned to the kitchen, Rob was just placing a plate of eggs and toast in front of her chair. He headed to the refrigerator and returned with butter and raspberry jam. Liz tucked into her breakfast. "Yum. This is terrific. How did you know I love poached eggs?" she asked.

"That's always what I want when I don't feel good." He pushed her bottle of pills across the table. "You're only supposed to take one of these this morning, not two like last night. Only taking one should let you get a nap and then be awake for your appointment with the orthopedist at three o'clock."

Liz stared at him as she swallowed a bite of toast. "How do you know I have an appointment this afternoon?"

"I made the appointment for you when their office opened this morning. You might not remember, but the ER gave you the name of the orthopedist they recommended. As it turned out, they were expecting you to call this morning."

"Thank you. Seriously. And thank you for staying here last night. I don't remember anything after my head hit the pillow."

Rob poured two mugs of coffee, added cream to one and brought them both to the table. "I guessed you like cream in your coffee, since you have some in your fridge." He took a long sip of his before adding, "I have a confession to make, though."

Liz looked at him with wide eyes. "What?"

"I snooped through you purse. Twice, actually."

Liz frowned. "Why?"

"First, I needed a key to your front door when I went

outside last night. I wanted to check your yard, but I had to be sure no one could get in the house while I was outside. And then second, I needed your birthdate to make the orthopedist appointment for you."

Liz nodded. "Yes, they always need the birthdate now." As she looked at him, she noticed dark smudges under his eyes and a fresh set of wrinkles on his face. "Wait, you didn't sleep last night, did you? You stayed up all night, didn't you? Keeping me safe? Thank you so much. I'd have been a sitting duck last night without you here."

"Yeah, I fibbed about sleeping on your sofa. I drank a lot of your coffee and kept an eye on things instead." He took a few more sips of his coffee. "I also reviewed my case notes and tried to make sense of it. I figured out more questions to ask the Lewes College people. Different people are describing Meg's departure from the college differently."

"Meg talked about it to me when we first met. I wasn't interested enough at the time to remember her exact words, but I can tell you the gist. She said she'd mostly been doing well in her studies, but she'd had a poor semester. She said 'some old guy' had kept trying to get her to have an affair with him, but she kept saying 'no.' Then the last time he pushed her up against a wall and groped her. She pushed him away hard, and he stumbled and fell. He said she'd regret it. And a week later, her advisor told her she was being dropped from the program for not making good progress. Now that I think about it again, it sounds like the groper and her advisor were different people. So, I don't think Ned was the groper. She was unloading – she would have told me." After a pause, she added, "I probably should have told you that earlier."

Jackson wrote in his notebook for a full minute after Liz ended the story. He looked up and nodded. "I know witnesses forget things. But that's really interesting. It doesn't match what Ingraham said at her funeral, does it?"

"No. I wondered about that at the time. Whoever was harassing her, Ingraham wouldn't have wanted that to be the public story. He could have been covering for his own misbehavior or keeping his department from looking bad."

"But then she filed a harassment complaint against Ned York. The simplest explanation would be that York was the guy harassing her."

Liz sighed. "But it didn't quite match up with the way Meg herself told me what happened. And I asked Ned about that right after I met him. He denied it and said he'd never laid a hand on her. And pointed out that the investigation had cleared him. Officially at least, if not in the eyes of all of his colleagues."

Jackson stared at her. "Did you believe him then? And do you still believe him?"

"I mostly believed him, but still kept in mind it might have been him. You know, I have teenagers lie to me pretty often, so I'm pretty good at reading their tells. I didn't see any of those with Ned. If anything, he seemed perplexed by me telling him she really had been harassed."

Just then the doorbell rang. Rob sprang up to answer it. Liz could hear Victoria thanking him for calling her. "Hey, how's the patient?" she asked as she entered the kitchen.

"Better, especially with you here."

Victoria walked around the table and leaned down to give Liz a careful hug. "The detective gave me a scare when he called this morning." She pulled away and studied Liz. "You look pretty good, all things considered."

"My ribs still hurt, but my ankle is a lot better this morning. I've got a lot less swelling, although the bruises are going to be colorful."

Jackson stood up and put his notebook in his pocket. "Now that you're here, Victoria, I can get back to work. But some ground rules, first. Don't let anyone in the house. In fact, don't open the door for anyone. Not a delivery guy – if he really needs a signature, he can come back. If someone sends flowers, leave them on the porch. And definitely don't open the door to anyone connected to this case.

"When you get ready to go to the orthopedist appointment, get in Liz's car inside the garage, lock the car doors, then open the garage door. And don't forget to close it when you're outside. Drop Liz at the door of the medical building and wait until she's inside before you go park. And reverse all that when you come back. Just make sure she's never alone."

Standing in the entryway, he continued, "All right. Don't hesitate to call me if anything concerns you. Or 911 if you need to. I'll check back in with you this evening." With that he smiled and waved and headed out the front door, sticking his head back in to say, "And lock this door after me. Bye."

Liz and Victoria smiled at each other for a moment. "Wow, I've officially changed my mind about him. He's both hot and nice," Victoria said, as she headed to the front door to lock it. Just as she reached the door, it swung open and Jackson reappeared, his face a picture of barely contained fury.

"All four of my tires are slashed. I've got to call a tow truck and my office. It looks like my being here last night frustrated someone."

CHAPTER 39

The rest of Thursday passed without incident; at the orthopedist's office, the doctor confirmed that Liz hadn't broken any bones in her ankle, but she had fractured one rib. The sisters returned to Liz's house so that Liz could pick up essentials for spending the weekend at Victoria's. For Liz, essentials included everything she needed to finish Maria's quilt, if the RICE regimen permitted. By Friday morning, Liz was able to place some weight on her foot, but her pain medicine was still knocking her out for hours at a stretch.

Just as she woke from her nap Friday afternoon, Liz's phone rang. She smiled to see it was Rob calling her.

"Hi, Rob. Have you caught him yet?"

"No, I'm still working on it." Liz imagined Rob smiling as he spoke. "I just called to see how you're doing."

"I'm feeling a lot better, and I can put a little weight on my foot now. The pain medicine still knocks me out, so Victoria brought me over to stay her house for the rest of the weekend."

"That's a good place for you; it's safer. Does she have an active security system for her house?"

Liz laughed. "It's top-notch. Her husband wouldn't have had it any other way."

"Good. But still make sure she and her kids know not to answer the door and to keep all the windows locked. You know, I could come over and do a security check if you think she'd be okay with it."

"I appreciate your offer, but Victoria has been very security conscious since her husband died. I'll make sure Maria and Jamie know not to answer the door."

"I'm glad you're okay." Liz could hear him stifle a yawn through the phone. "I'm gonna have an early evening. Pulling an all-nighter is harder than it was in college."

"I'm sure you're tired. And speaking of tires, did you get yours replaced?"

Rob groaned. "Yep, that's one of the perks of the job. I'm back driving the city's car again."

"I'll let you go. And thanks again. For everything." Liz hoped her smile came through in her voice.

After her nap and conversation with Rob, Liz felt alert and well enough to do some quilting. With her sewing tote on her shoulder, but still wanting to baby her ankle, she took the elevator to the top level, where Victoria had an office-sewing room combination next to her bedroom. Unpacking Maria's quilt and all the fabric, thread, rulers, and other equipment needed to finish her project wasn't difficult in Victoria's spacious sewing room. Liz hadn't brought her sewing machine along; her sister had a top-of-the-line machine by the same manufacturer as Liz's sewing machine. More features and no learning curve!

As she was threading Victoria's machine, Maria and Ripper joined her. "I knew I heard the elevator. You're up! How are you feeling? Would you like a stool or ice pack for your ankle?" Maria asked as she kissed her aunt's cheek, careful not to bump her ribs.

"My ribs still hurt when the drugs wear off, but it's a lot better than yesterday or the day before. And my ankle is much better, I'm just being careful with it for awhile."

"Oooh, is that my quilt? I love it. It's gorgeous!" Maria exclaimed.

"I'm so glad you like it." Liz replied, smiling at Maria. "It's the colors and the pattern you picked."

"I love it. I can't wait for it to be done." Maria stopped and blushed. "I don't mean to hurry you. I feel like a little kid waiting for Santa to come."

Liz laughed. "I know. I feel that way about all my quilting projects – when I'm getting near the end, I can't wait to see the finished product."

"It looks like you're getting ready to put the binding on, is that right?"

"Almost. I want to make sure the corners are square and the sides straight, but after that, you're right, it's time to put the binding on."

As Maria watched from the spare chair, Ripper joined them in the sewing room. Liz paused to pet the cocker spaniel, and then used her large right-angle ruler to square the sides and corners of the quilt. To double-check her work, she measured both diagonals and was pleased that the two measurements were within a quarter inch of each other.

"I bought enough fabric to be able to bind it in any of the four colors. Or we could use a contrasting fabric to add some pizzazz."

Maria laughed. "I think we've got a lot of pizzazz in there already. What did we decide when we designed it? I think we agreed on the blue for the binding."

"I brought my design notes along, and at the time, we thought the fuchsia would be best. What do you think now, seeing the entire quilt put together?"

Maria mulled that over for a moment and put a scrap of each fabric against the quilt top. "Yes, I do. I think the fuchsia will work best. The fuchsia picks up the Flying Geese. The blue doesn't pull it all together the way the fuchsia does."

"So, fuchsia it is!"

Maria stood and headed toward to the door. "I'm going downstairs to see if Mom wants any help with dinner this evening. That way, you can work in peace, without any audience or distractions. And if you need anything, I'm only as far away as the intercom."

"Hey, Maria, before you go, I've got a few favors to ask. First, and most important, I want to make sure you know not to open the door unless you're absolutely sure who it is. The detective still hasn't caught the person who hurt me, and he thinks he might try again."

"I'll be careful. I feel awful that you were attacked, and I sure don't want to let anyone into our house to try again."

"And let Jamie know, too. I haven't seen him since I got here, so I haven't had a chance to warn him."

"I will."

"And last, can you go give Abner his dinner and some fresh water tonight?"

Maria smiled, "I'd be glad to. I guess he'll need breakfast and dinner every day you're staying here, too, won't he? I don't mind that at all. You know I love the big guy."

Maria stood, Ripper bounced beside her, and they both left the sewing room. Liz heard Maria's sturdy footsteps echo down the stairs to the main level and smiled, remembering Maria's first tiny steps as a toddler. She cut enough double wide strips of fuchsia to go around the perimeter of the quilt, with ten or twelve inches to spare, then then sewed the strips together and pressed them in half lengthwise. After starting to attach the binding, Liz remembered that she needed to attach a label to the back, plus a way to hang it, if Maria ever wanted it on a wall instead of on her bed.

Liz re-threaded Victoria's sewing machine with white thread and re-configured it to embroider her name, the year, and 'Quilt for Maria' on a square of fuchsia fabric. She then attached the square to the lower right corner of the quilt back. Finally, she cut two twelve-inch squares of the same fabric, folded each into a triangle and attached them to the top rear corners. These would allow Maria to hang her quilt by inserting a dowel into the triangles and placing the dowel on an ordinary picture hanger.

After those tasks were completed, Liz re-threaded the machine with fuchsia thread and returned to sewing the folded binding onto the quilt. As she sewed, her thoughts strayed to Rob. It'd been so kind of him to stay with her and make sure she wasn't harmed. Plus call her today to check on her. His slashed tires convinced her there was someone out there who was frustrated by his protection of her. And, she mused, Rob had never been anything other than kind to her. Well, except for that initial questioning and warning her not to leave Delaware. And then telling her to stay out of the investigation. Oh, and threatening to arrest her. But other than those, he'd been wonderful. *I've got a crush on the hot detective. And Ned, too. How did this happen to me? And, oh, I do NOT want to tell Ned about Rob spending the night. I'll put that off. Maybe forever.*

After pressing the binding and using clips to roll the folded side of the binding to the back of the quilt, she had one last design decision to make – should she hand-sew the binding to the back of the quilt or use her machine? Hand-sewing would be better if she wanted to enter this quilt in a local (or bigger!) quilt show. She was proud of both the design and her artisan-ship of this quilt, so it could easily be a quilt show entry. On the other hand, Maria wanted to use this on her college dorm bed every day. That meant frequent trips through commercial washers and dryers, so Liz settled on the more robust machine stitching. She made one more lap around the quilt, stitching in the 'ditch' of the binding seam and making sure the binding was secured on the back.

Liz stepped back to admire her finished quilt. *I love it! And it seems Maria likes it as much as I do. I hope she agrees to let me enter it in the next local quilt show, 'cause I might just have a winner with this one.*

CHAPTER 40

L iz looked at her watch for the hundredth time. It was 7:30 on Monday evening, and Ned was thirty minutes late. He had asked to have dinner with her to go over what she'd learned from interviewing both Ingraham and Westborough, and he'd been specific that he wanted it to be just the two of them, without Caroline. She'd agreed, wondering what he had in mind, and why he didn't want Caroline there. *Did he hear about I was attacked on the bike path? Did he hear about Rob staying at my house overnight? I hope not. I don't want to explain that.*

Fifteen minutes ago, Liz had texted him, but received no response. Ten minutes after that, she called him, but her call went straight to voicemail. Now that a half hour had passed, it was time to admit something wasn't right.

After signaling to the waiter for the check, Liz pulled out her credit card and paid for the appetizer she'd ordered, adding a generous tip. She then headed to Sylvia, grateful she no longer needed her crutches, but aware that exerting herself with a broken rib would be unpleasant. Sitting in her car, she considered what might have caused Ned to stand her up. None of the possibilities were good; her mind created terrible scenarios. He might be at the local hospital, either for himself or Ross; she knew cell phones weren't allowed to be used inside the hospital in case they interfered with sensitive medical equipment. Or he could have taken into custody again. *Could he?* Liz didn't really know enough about the justice system to know if that could happen while he's out on bail. If so, he might not have been able to

keep his phone with him in an interview room or a holding cell.
If he had been deeply involved in his current research project
and lost track of time, the ringing of his phone would have
pierced his concentration. *Wouldn't it?* Their relationship might
be up in the air, but this just wasn't like him. And there was no
way she would call Ross to ask why his dad was standing her up.

Liz drove to the Yorks' condo complex in Five Points. She
had never been inside Ned's condo, but after taking Ross home
to get Ned's keys last week, she knew in which complex he and
Ross lived. As Sylvia crept through the parking lots in front and
behind the buildings, Liz looked for his car. As she drove, she
wished she'd put a tracker on *his* car. His car was not anywhere
near the condo complex. Her next stop would be his office.

When Liz drove into the Stalnaker Hall parking lot, she
saw only two cars – Ned's and Brian MacKenzie's ancient black
truck. Even though they had all but dismissed Brian as a suspect, Liz was concerned. *Had they been wrong?* She backed into a
parking space right in front of the main entrance to the hall.
Thinking about what she might encounter, she decided to lock
three of her car's doors but leave the driver's door unlocked. If
she needed a quick escape, having Sylvia's door unlocked could
be a life saver. Even as she hoped for a reasonable explanation.

Liz entered the building. *I'm glad I could get in, but why was the door
unlocked at this time of night? That's another thing that isn't right.* Her heart
pounding, she used her phone's flashlight to scan the first-floor
corridor. It was deserted. For a moment she considered taking
the elevator but rejected the idea, recalling the loud chimes it
made at each floor. If things were ugly in Ned's office, she didn't
want anyone to know she was there. Instead, she tiptoed up the
stairs to the third floor. The black slacks, black coat, and flat
shoes she'd chosen for their not-a-date would blend into the
shadows, plus let her make a run for it if she needed to, at least

as far as her mostly healed ankle would let her run. *Please don't let me need to run tonight.*

Once on the third floor, she could see light coming through the glass panel in Ned's office door. As she crept down the hallway toward the light, she heard voices, but the words were muffled. She edged closer to the door until she could make out the words. For a moment, the words were replaced by the sound of skin slapping skin, followed by a low groan.

Brian chuckled, "That woke you up. How the mighty have fallen." Then, ominously, "We need to talk. Or, more precisely, I need to ask questions and you need to answer them."

Ned cleared his throat and croaked, "Can I have some water?"

"Sure, Professor, whatever you want. I'm here to do your every wish. Not." Brian laughed again. "No, you don't get anything until I get what I want. And I want answers. What did you tell him?"

"Who?"

"The detective, of course. What. Did. You. Tell. The. Detective?"

"Ummm, okay. Let me think. He already knew I'd told Meg she wasn't cutting it in the graduate program. He already knew Meg had filed a harassment claim against me. He asked me a bunch of times whether I was still angry at her."

"No. About me."

"You? He questioned me for hours, but never asked about you, and I didn't volunteer anything about you. I just wanted to be done with him as soon as I could." Ned's voice was fainter now.

"Did you tell him about me and Meg?"

"After he arrested me, I told him I'd heard you two lived together, but he already knew that."

"So, you did try to implicate me!"

Liz slipped across the hallway, so she could look into Ned's office with less chance of being seen. She stifled a shriek when she saw Ned duct-taped to his chair at his wrists and ankles, with a bloodstain on his shirt collar. How badly was he hurt? As she watched, she noticed the blood was running down the side of his head to his neck. Brian must have hit Ned in the head, knocked him out, and then taped him into the chair while he was unconscious.

"I'd come up with a genius plan. And it was working out great. See, after Ingraham groped her, and *you* told her she was out of the program, I got her to file the harassment complaint against you. That let Ingraham see just how badly his little world would be ruined if *he* got investigated the way you had been. And after that, he was happy to keep paying Meg to keep her from telling people what had *really* happened to her, and who had *really* harassed her."

Ned nodded slowly. "Yes, that was pretty clever. And it kept everyone in the department upset."

"I'm glad you can see it. Nothing against you, York. You were just collateral damage, as the army always says when they kill the wrong people." Brian laughed. "Of course, you won't be collateral damage tonight – killing you is the plan tonight."

"I don't get why you want to kill me. I've never done anything to you or to Meg."

Brian laughed again. Liz found his laughs unsettling. *No, deranged is more like it.*

"I've got enough money to get out of this horrible, nosy backwater, and I can't spend it here without people like you figuring everything out. And you *did* try to implicate me. Plus, I know you and your new sweetie were investigating. I saw some lady put something on my truck. When I found it, I knew someone was keeping track of where I was. Not good. So I left it in place, when I was going home or here, but took it off when I didn't want whoever was keeping tabs on me to know where I was. Or I just used my bicycle."

Ned nodded even more slowly this time, his eyes almost closed. "I knew you were smart, but you're even smarter than I realized."

"I rented an electric bike for my 'chance meeting' on the trail with your sweetie. And I *sure* didn't put the tracker on that. I wore gloves, so I didn't even leave fingerprints on the bike."

"Still doing the smart thing with that," Ned whispered. *That's good, Ned, keep him talking.*

"When the payoffs from Ingraham kept coming in, Meg had enough to go get some help for her mental problems. And wouldn't you know it, the shrink she saw couldn't keep his paws off her either." More laughter from Brian. "Of course, I understood. She was gorgeous. I couldn't keep my hands off her, either."

"You're right, Meg was beautiful."

"So we checked out the shrink and guess what? He'd been pawing a bunch of his patients and probably would have lost his license if Meg had complained. As it turned out, he was able to pay even more than Ingraham! Life was working out great. We had a nice nest egg. We were going to get out of this place and go to some lovely Ivy League university where I could get my doctorate and she could either teach or finish her degree. She could do whatever she wanted! We had enough money for years, and maybe even buy a house if I got a tenure position there. It was all gonna be amazing." Brian paused. "But she ruined it all."

"How did she ruin it?" Ned asked.

"As if you don't know. She left me. She told me she was

going back to you," Brian snarled.

"Oh, no, Meg and I were never a couple."

"Well, it doesn't matter now. I fixed her. If I can't have her, no one can. Just some herb – what's it called? Oh, yes, St. John's Wort – in her cream cheese and she's gone. I sliced open a bunch of the capsules and squeezed them into her food." Brian brushed his hands together. "And that was that."

As Brian leaned on the shelves behind him, Liz caught a glimpse of his face. His eyes and mouth twitched, and Liz realized he was unhinged. "And now you have to go, too."

With that, Brian pulled a handgun out of his backpack. He twirled it, dropped it, picked it up, and then gestured with it, looking increasingly unhinged. "Should I shoot you in the head? In the heart? What to do, what to do? Where to shoot, where to shoot?" He cackled and again waved the gun and then the gun went off. Ned screamed in pain and Liz clenched her jaw to keep herself from screaming in response. As she watched, fresh blood pooled on Ned's shoulder.

"Oh, shoot! I didn't mean for that to happen. Ha, ha, *shoot*, get it?" Brian peered at the gun. "I was just scaring you. I was sure I had the safety on." He poked at the gun, and Liz heard a click. "Okay, *now* the safety's on."

Liz knew she had no time left. She had to stop MacKenzie before he hurt Ned anymore. And fast, before Ned lost too much blood. With swift and silent steps, she tested each office door, hoping one would be unlocked and she could find something to use as a weapon. Two doors without luck. The third door opened at her touch; it had been locked, but not completely closed. She rushed into the office and looked for heavy textbooks. All the books she saw were slim. If she were in the English department, she could find a huge dictionary. Then she spotted the not-yet-awarded Math Bowl trophy, on its square marble base. It would have to do. She thought about calling 911 but knew Ned could be bleeding out as she fumbled with her phone.

Clutching the trophy, Liz slipped back to where she could see Ned. She was alarmed to see even more blood on his shirt. And now his head had dropped to his chest. Even though she was afraid MacKenzie might shoot her, too, she realized this was not the time to let her natural timidity keep her from helping Ned. She put her hand on the doorknob, still in the shadows.

"And now I'm going to light a little fire, so no one knows I was here. They'll find your remains after the firemen are done. So now I'm just going to gather up these test papers you won't have to grade now, toss a match on 'em, and be on my way. You know, this will give the coroner a little puzzle to figure out." MacKenzie changed his voice as if he were the perplexed coroner. "Did York die from his head wound? Or from the gunshot? From smoke inhalation? Or from his burns? Or was he crushed to death when the roof collapsed and a beam fell on him? So hard to figure out, for a dumb southern Delaware guy like me."

MacKenzie began to toss open notebooks at Ned's feet. And then he started crumpling papers from Ned's desk and throwing them at Ned's slumped body. It was slow going while holding the gun. With Ned apparently unconscious, Brian set the gun on Ned's desk, continuing to crumple paper. He knelt to brush the papers into a pile under Ned's chair.

Now! Liz charged into the room. She held the top of the trophy and swung the base. It gave a satisfying thump as it connected with the back of Brian's head. Brian crumpled on top of the papers. Liz shoved Brian's limp body away from Ned's feet and rushed check on Ned.

Ned's eyes snapped open. "I'm fine. Quick, tie him up with

the duct tape. He just nicked me, but it hurts a lot," whispered Ned. Liz grabbed the duct tape Brian had left on Ned's desk. She lashed it around his wrists, then taped his ankles to Ned's desk. *Got to slow down Ned's bleeding.* She reached for a jacket from the coat rack and pressed it onto Ned's shoulder. He moaned.

"I know it hurts, but I don't want you to lose any more blood. I'm calling for help now."

With her free hand, she pulled her phone out of her coat pocket. She called 911 to request police and ambulance. She gave the operator all the information needed to reach Ned's office. Even though the operator wanted her to stay on the line, she disconnected and called Detective Jackson. He answered on the first ring.

"I've got your killer here, Detective. It was Brian MacKenzie. I knocked him unconscious, and he's tied up with duct tape. I already called 911 to come to Ned's office – he's been shot."

"I'm on my way. Apply pressure to his wound until the EMTs arrive."

After she disconnected, Liz peeked under the jacket and squelched a gasp. There was way too much blood. Looking at his head wound, she thought he probably was concussed, too. She knew from her first aid training the bleeding was more dangerous than a concussion. And he was still bleeding. A lot.

CHAPTER 41

S irens sounded in the distance and grew closer. Within a few minutes, EMTs burst into the room and clustered around Ned. On their heels were Detective Jackson with two uniformed officers. The EMTs moved Ned onto a stretcher and rolled him to the elevator, saying MacKenzie could wait for the next team. Jackson told them he'd need to be handcuffed and under police custody. Liz moved to go with Ned, but Jackson caught her arm. "I need to ask you a few questions, and then I'll let you go over to the ER. Just tell me what you saw and heard."

Liz recounted what she'd heard Brian shout at Ned, including what he'd said about deliberately poisoning Meg with St. John's Wort in her cream cheese. She added that his ranting became less coherent as time went on. After she described hitting Brian with the Math Bowl trophy, Jackson congratulated her. "You did a number on him with that trophy."

"I hope I didn't kill him. I just wanted to get him away from Ned."

"No, he's not dead. We'll be taking him to the ER, too, though. And he'll be handcuffed to his hospital bed." Jackson studied Liz's face. "Are you ok to drive?"

"I'm fine for now. Adrenaline is keeping me going. I'll crash later." *Yes, he's Jackson when he's a cop, but now he's Rob and he cares about me. That feels good, but right now Ned is more important. And even if I'm really not fine, I'm good enough to get to the hospital, and I need to go now.*

The second EMT team arrived and began to treat MacKenzie, under the watchful eyes of Jackson and the uniformed officers,

allowing Liz to make her escape. Holding her side, ribs protect-
ed, she raced to Sylvia and sped toward Beebe's ER.

Ned was already being treated when she arrived. Liz ap-
proached the ER desk, asking "Has anyone contacted his son?"
Learning no one had, Liz called him. "Ross, it's going to be OK.
There's been an emergency. Can you get to Beebe Hospital?
Your dad is here, being treated in the ER. But listen – he's going
to be ok. Would you like me to come and get you?"

"No, I'll ask Maria to drive me. You stay with Dad."

I hope I haven't lied to him. Please let Ned be okay.

Liz, Ross, and Maria sat in the waiting room until Ned was
stabilized and able to be transferred upstairs. He was moved
to a hospital room around midnight, for continued care of his
gunshot wound, as well as observation for the concussion the
ER staff had confirmed. Ross accompanied him, waving to Liz
and Maria as he followed his dad's gurney.

After Maria yawned for the third time, Liz said, "Thank
you again for bringing Ross. It's late. I'll be leaving in a little
while – you don't need to stay here in the waiting room with me
any longer if you don't want to."

"If you're okay with that, I'll head home. I'm so glad
Professor York is going to be okay. And I'm glad Ross called me.
I was happy to drive him here. He's a great kid, but don't tell
him I called him a kid. He kinda feels like a second brother to
me." She yawned again, hugged Liz gently, avoiding the broken
rib, and waved as she left the hospital.

Liz waited twenty minutes to let Ned and Ross get settled
into his room. Stepping out of the elevator onto his floor, she
saw Jackson was there, too. The floor nurse stopped them from
entering his room.

"I need to understand your relationship to the patient before I can let you into his room."

Jackson showed the nurse his ID. "I need to ask him a few questions about what happened to him tonight."

"Oh, no way are you questioning my patient tonight. He's groggy from pain medicine, and likely to say anything with a concussion, if he remembers anything at all. You just come back tomorrow – or better yet, ask him your questions after he's back home." She turned to Liz. "Who are you and what do you want with my patient?"

Liz started to explain that she was his friend, but Jackson cut her off, "She rescued Professor York from the man who kidnapped him and shot him, at considerable risk to herself. Maybe she could visit him for just a few minutes?"

"Hmmmph. All right, you can go in. But just five minutes, no more. He's exhausted and needs rest."

Liz pasted a bright smile on her face and stepped into the room. Ned had large bandage on side of his head, and an IV attached to his hand. An even larger bandage on his shoulder was visible through his hospital gown. Liz's smile faltered. Ned opened his eyes and mumbled, "I would never stand you up."

Liz squeezed his free hand, whispering, "Everything is okay now." As she held his hand, Ned's effort to stay awake failed. Liz kissed his cheek and told him to feel better.

Turning to Ross, Liz whispered, "Would you like a ride home?"

Ross shook his head. "They told me I can stay here with Dad tonight, and that's what I want to do." Ross swallowed hard. "I heard the detective say you rescued Dad. You saved his life."

"He's going to be okay, Ross. Really. Call me if you need anything, any time of day." Ross hugged her briefly. As he turned away, Liz saw his eyes were moist. With a small good-bye wave, she tiptoed out the door.

Returning to the ER waiting room on her way out of the hospital, Liz was surprised to see Jackson at the entrance, still apparently in detective mode.

"How's the patient?" he asked.

"He fell asleep as soon as I got in his room."

"Can I ask you a question?"

Liz shrugged. "Sure, but haven't all the investigation questions been answered?"

"No, not yet, but that's not it. Can I walk with you out to your car?"

Liz chortled, "That's not much of a question, Rob, but sure. I feel pretty safe in Lewes, but it is late."

Jackson grinned at his own foolishness. When they reached Sylvia and he'd looked inside it, he said, "That wasn't my question." He cleared his throat. "I know you said you're just friends, but I want to ask again – are you and Professor York a couple?"

Liz wanted to laugh and throw her arms and face open to the sky to release some of the day's tension. Of course, at this point, her ribs would have protested, but her heart still skipped a beat. Instead, she kept her cool, grinned back at him, and shook her head, "Oh, no. We're really just friends." She shrugged and added, "because that's what he said he wants, no matter what conflicting signals he sends."

Detective Jackson gazed into her eyes. "Perhaps we could have a real date some time? Planned in advance and everything?"

Liz smiled. "I'd like that."

Jackson looked around the parking lot until Liz was in her car and driving away. She saw him wave as she turned onto the road. *Things are looking up.*

260

CHAPTER 42

"We're taking a short break, now don't go away, and we'll be back with more dance music in just a little while," said the bandleader. Ned held Liz for a few moments after the last note of music faded away. It had only been three weeks since the craziness in Ned's office, but Ned was well on his way to full recovery. Liz had been delighted to discover he was an excellent dancer. For the last half-hour, he'd cued her into turns and spins around the dance floor, despite having one arm in a sling. His skill made her look like an excellent dancer, too. Her ankle was completely healed, and her ribs felt fine. She was glad she'd chosen an evening gown with a full skirt for dancing. Her sapphire blue gown flattered both her complexion and figure, plus it made her eyes sparkle. Ned's eyes sparkled, too, when he looked at her.

"Let's step outside for a moment," Ned said as he slid his good arm around her waist and guided her toward the balcony overlooking the golf course. On the way, he snagged two glasses of champagne from a passing waiter. The evening was warm for November, but still a little chilly for Liz in a sleeveless, low-cut gown. Ned wrapped his tuxedo jacket over her shoulders and his free arm back around her waist. "I hope you're having half as nice a time as I am."

They sipped their champagne in companionable silence for a little while. Liz pointed out an airplane passing in the sky. "Look, a shooting star."

Ned laughed, "Yes, a special shooting star with blinking

lights." He turned to face her, and Liz thought he might be leaning in for a kiss. Just then, Maria and her date, a sophomore from the University of Delaware, came out onto the balcony. They entwined with youthful intensity, their hands and lips in constant motion. Maria's attention was completely focused on her date; Liz knew her niece was unaware that she and Ned were standing right next to her. Ned chuckled and tipped his head toward the door. They left Maria and her date alone and headed back inside to Victoria's table.

Javier, Victoria's late husband, had reserved a table at the annual Beebe Charity Ball for years and Victoria had decided to continue his tradition this year. She'd told Liz it would be good publicity for the shop and had invited all the Mariners' Compass employees to be her guests at her table. Aware of the unsettled situation between Liz and Ned, Victoria had told Liz she didn't believe Ned really meant this 'just friends' thing, and had pushed Liz to invite him. Liz had decided it might be a good 'occasional date' for them, recalling Ned's words. Despite the uncertainty between them, Liz was glad she had invited him. Ned was resplendent in his evening clothes, and obviously enjoying the evening with her. Still, every time she looked at him, her eyes went to the black sling on his arm and the not-yet-healed scar on the side of his head. Her breath caught every time she thought she might have lost him forever. Even if he sent mixed signals, she cared deeply about him.

As they approached her table, Victoria was beaming at a handsome man who looked vaguely familiar to Liz. Victoria was glamorous tonight in a magenta gown, sapphire jewelry, and her hair in a sophisticated updo. "Liz, I'd like you to meet Stan Pierce. This is my sister Liz Murphy and Ned York." Ned and Stan shook hands, and Stan kissed Liz's cheek. Victoria noticed Liz's confusion and helped her out, "Stan is the news anchor on one of Wilmington's television stations."

"Oh, of course. I knew you looked familiar, but I was pretty sure I'd never met you."

Just then the band returned from their break. "Would you like to dance?" Stan took Victoria's hand and they headed off to the dance floor.

Caroline appeared at Liz's side and gave her a gentle hug. Wearing a gorgeous gown and plenty of jewelry, she looked every bit the part of a successful real estate agent. "I've seen you two across the room all night, but I haven't had a chance to come over until now." She scanned the room and smiled, "I think I've sold a house to half the people here." She crooked a finger at a nearby waiter and selected a glass of champagne from his tray. Raising her glass and grinning at them, she said, "A toast. To our sleuthing." Liz and Ned laughed and rolled their eyes but toasted their sleuthing with her. "I'm still not clear on what you learned about KT, Westborough, and Ingraham."

Liz laughed. "We learned a lot of stuff about innocent people, or at least people who were innocent of Meg's murder. First, we know Ingraham is a gambler and sweet-talking ladies' man." Caroline hooted with laughter. "And that Meg actually *was* blackmailing him." She paused, then added, "But you might not know KT's family occasionally gets an opossum in their yard." More laughter from Ned and Caroline. "We learned Meg was blackmailing Westborough, too. And then there's the crucial information that KT's younger brother takes classes as Del Tech, because we put the tracker on the wrong car. I'm pretty sure we're not going to win any sleuthing awards."

Ned laughed, shook his head, and winced at the motion. "We learned a lot more about Ingraham than I wanted to know. I'd have been happier if the rumors about him and women half his age were just gossip. There's some stuff you really don't want to know about your boss."

Liz sipped her champagne, "We got the most important things done – we cleared both Ned and Maria. And KT – I really didn't want KT to be the murderer, and she wasn't. We didn't have any idea how much Brian MacKenzie was trying to control the people around him. He had the idea to have Meg claim Ned had harassed her and then blackmail both Ingraham and Westborough. He was totally in free motion."

Caroline shook her head. "We were so sure Brian and Meg couldn't have been anything other than roommates, we totally ignored the actual murderer. We didn't think Brian had any motive."

Ned turned serious, "Hey, I was so sure Brian was innocent that I turned my back on him and let him knock me out and tie me up." He turned to Liz, "I'm so glad you figured out where I was and took him out. You could have been mad at me for standing you up and just gone home." He shook his head and winced again. "I've got to stop doing that. It still hurts sometimes when I move my head. Anyway, he wasn't planning to let me walk away – he was building a bonfire under my chair!"

Liz added, "And I learned I'm not very good at interviewing suspects. I didn't learn much from any of them. But I sure did antagonize some of them pretty well."

"What happened to our devices?" Caroline asked, dropping her voice to a whisper. "We shouldn't leave them out and about where they might get into trouble. Or get *us* into trouble."

Ned laughed. "Always dramatic, aren't you, Caroline?" He continued, "I removed the device from Ingraham's car."

"And I removed the one from KT's van," Liz added.

Caroline mulled that over. "The tracker was on MacKenzie's truck when the police impounded it? I wonder if Detective Jackson will ask us about it."

Ned visibly bristled at the mention of the detective, but he didn't say anything about him. Instead, he commented, "One of the things MacKenzie told me when he had me tied up in my office was that he saw some lady put something on his truck, and he found it right away. He kept putting it on and off his truck, depending on where he was going – knowing someone was keeping track of his movements." He took another sip of his champagne. "So it might be on MacKenzie's truck and it might not be. Wherever it is, the police are likely to find it." Ned raised his glass, "Here's to hoping he put it in a drawer in his house, where they'll find it, but won't connect it to us."

Liz and Caroline raised their glasses, and echoed, "To hoping he put it in a drawer."

Caroline laughed and then turned serious, "What about the tracker on KT's brother's car? Should we try to get that back?"

"No!" exclaimed Ned and Liz together. After their laughter subsided, Liz replied to Caroline's puzzled expression. "KT caught us in her yard and threatened to call the police or sic her father on us if she ever saw us there again. I don't want to risk it. I think it'll just have to stay on his car."

Ned said, "But what we should do instead is delete the tracking apps from our phones and promise each other we won't do something like that again."

They sipped their champagne as the band began another set. Caroline broke the mood, saying, "Hey, let's get back out on the dance floor."

Liz and Ned danced until the band packed up their instruments and the waitstaff removed the remains of the dessert buffet. As they went downstairs to wait for their hired car to arrive, Liz wondered where their uncertain relationship was going. Wherever that might be, this was a romantic night, and the night wasn't over yet.

CPSIA information can be obtained
at www.ICGtesting.com
Printed in the USA
BVHW040342010623
665165BV00004B/10